T\

CW01631493

Fair Exchange

Richard Arthur

Published by: R A Walton

Email: publisher@rawalton.co.uk

The characters and events portrayed in this book are fictitious. Some individuals have been influenced by historical figures from Earth but as denizens of an alien planet their characteristics are entirely fictitious. Otherwise any similarity to real persons, living or dead, is coincidental and not intended by the author.

Published by R A Walton

Email: publisher@rawalton.co.uk

Cover design and illustration: Philip Bannister

ISBN: 978-1-9196529-1-7

To the women in my life,

Audrey, Jackie, Helen, Mary and Jackie

Table of Contents

Foreword

The first book in the series very much begged the question "What Next?" This direct sequel addresses the influence of the more advanced culture on its more primitive neighbour, and also the way that the connection with an alien planet affects the balance of international politics on a culture that somewhat mirrors our own.

I've wanted to see how the coming of email and instaneous communication might be employed in the traditional epistolary novel. Much of the story here is told through correspondence. Thus we learn of the changes as seen through the eyes of the main Duplosian protagonists as they become exposed to the more advanced ideas and technology from Geos.

This book requires illustration by maps of the entire planets, rather than just the one small corner shown in 'Twin Worlds - First Contact'. I have tried to improve the presentation within the limits of the small book format, but the result is still less good than ideal, and the ebook format is even more challenging. As before, I am supplementing the book with a free download available from my website. Don't forget to look at the site. I shall also update it from time to time with short blogs from some of the characters and news of further tales from Duplos and Geos.

www.richardarthur.uk

The third story, which may be a novella rather than a full-scale book, is in progress and will chart events on Isla from the time Arté left to the time of reconnection chronicled at the end of this book - i.e. covering the years 2606-2615 in the decimal Geosian Calendar. There is much scope for future exploration on Duplos since its indigenous humans know so little of their own planet.

I have included the appendices from the first book on duodecimal numbers and the weights and measures on the two planets. I have also added as Appendix 1, a list of characters and their relationships.

Lastly, please feel free to contact me at my email address.

author@richardarthur.uk.

I very much welcome your opinions and reactions. Finally if you've enjoyed this book please post a review/rating on Amazon. This is really important for independent authors such as myself as search engines rely on these ratings to prioritise their results.

Richard Arthur

Worcestershire, December 2021

Twin Worlds History

Geos and Duplos are Earth-like planets in orbit about each other in the Goldilocks zone of their sun, which they orbit in 360 of our Earth days. Thus their year is pretty much the same as ours. Their main time units are the period (12 days) in which they orbit each other and the watch (Geos - 6 per period) or phase (Duplos - 4 per period) of their respective rotations. They also use the selenth (one quarter of a year) which is close to the orbital period of a moon, Selenos, which orbits them both.

The people on Geos are at a level of development more-or-less equivalent to Earth today. They are at the threshold of space travel, and in the first book they prepare for the first landing on their sister-world, Duplos where they make first contact with the people there. The expedition is led by childhood friends and lovers Wild Cat Waters and Flying Eagle Forest.

Duplos is more primitive. Because of the extreme tides on its the oceans the inhabitants have not developed sea travel. We meet two isolated civilisations. The more advanced is approximately at the level of seventeenth century Europe while an isolated island is closer to Roman Britain. Both societies are strongly matriarchal, to the extent that on the island men are all slaves. In both societies men are treated principally as servants and sex objects. The story is very much that of an exceptionally gifted island man who is washed ashore on the continent. He, Arté, succeeds in gaining a continental education. He meets the much younger woman, Rastu, first as his study partner and then best friend. After his studies he is employed by leading astronomer Astra as her assistant and, later, business partner. Together they accumulate the evidence of mysterious activity from Geos and predict the arrival of the Geosian expedition.

During the course of all this Arté creates inventions that they exploit through forming a company 'Wheels within Wheels together with three others: Rastu, Astra's daughter, Zorro and the only female islander ever to have reached the continent, Créezy, who becomes close to both Zorro and Arté and happens to be a second cousin of Arté's former owner on the island.

The book ends on the threshold of a new beginning for both planets as contact between them is made, captured in a later famous photograph of Astra grasping the hands of Wild Cat and Flying Eagle.

Maps

The three maps that follow are all available in a free download from my website in A4 size. The first two maps show the full landmasses of Duplos and Geos respectively in Mercator projection, i.e. as latitudes increase from the equator the distances between longitude lines are exaggerated. The grid shows 30° intervals of longitude and 15° of latitude. The diameters of the planets are 10,403 and 14,550 km respectively. Thus a degree of latitude or of longitude at the equator is about 91 km on Duplos and 127 km on Geos. Which compares with 111 km on Earth.

Abbreviated country names in the maps are:

Map 1:	G.S.E. - Great Southern Empire
	S.U. - Shadowlands Union
	W.F. - Western Federation
Map 2:	E.S. - East Sylvania
	G.K. - Golden Kingdom
	GPRG - Grand People's Republic of Geos
	K.N.N. - Kingdom of Northern Nations
	W.S. - West Sylvania
Map 3:	W.F. - Western Federation

Map 1: Duplos (Mercator projection) West

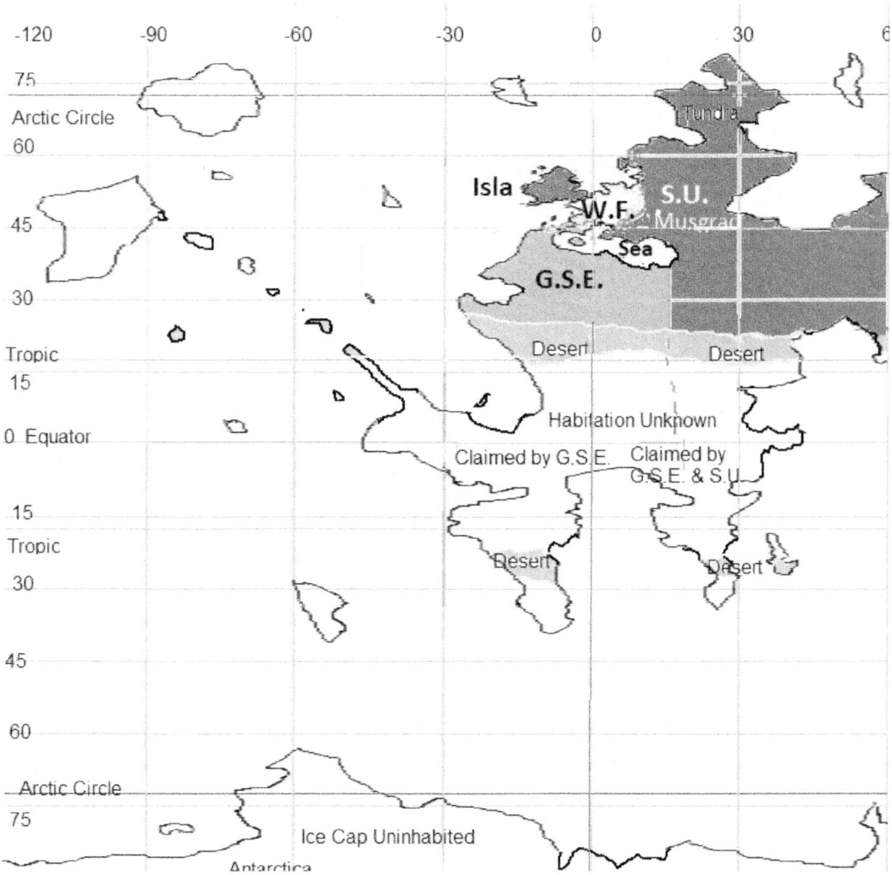

East

60
90
120
150
180
-150
Tundra
Tundra
Nomadic Tribes
Sea
All claimed by
S.U.
S. U.
Desert
Desert
Sea
Desert
Habitation
Unknown
Ape-men
Desert
Desert
Probably
Uninhabited
Southern Continent

Map 2: Geos (Mercator Projection) West

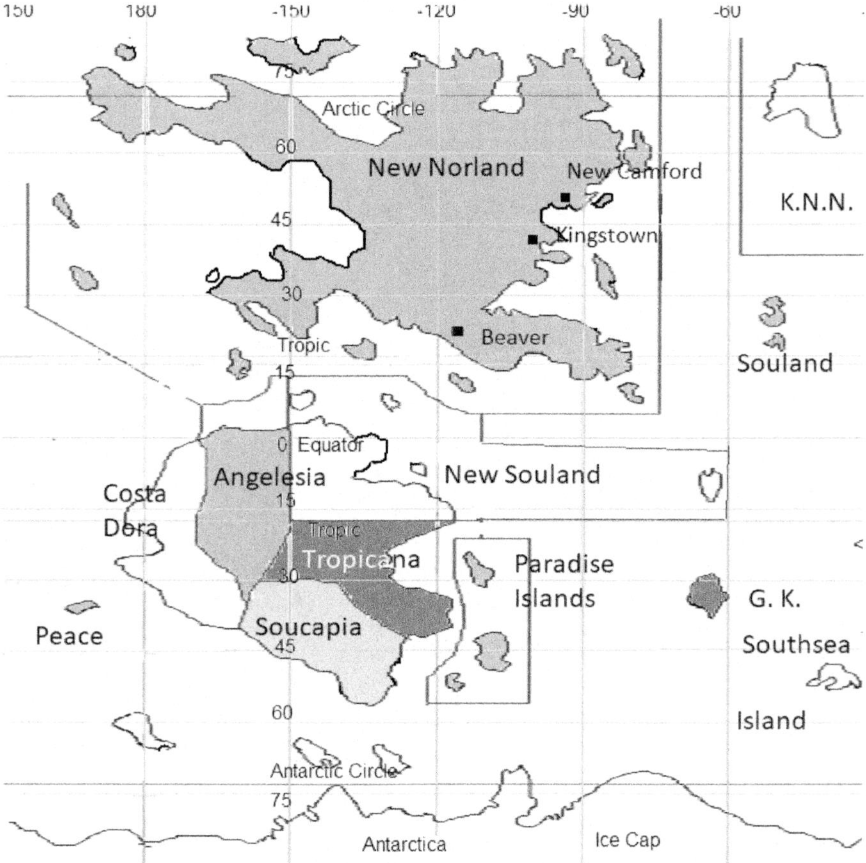

East

30
0
30
60
90
120
150
K.N.N.
Camford
Shopharbour
Eastern Empire
Midgeos
Gendalfo
Space Port
Souland
GPRG
Haven
W.S.
E.S.
Equatoria
Central Sylvanic Republic
New Hope
G. K.
South Sylvania
Frioland

Map 3a: Isla & West W.F.

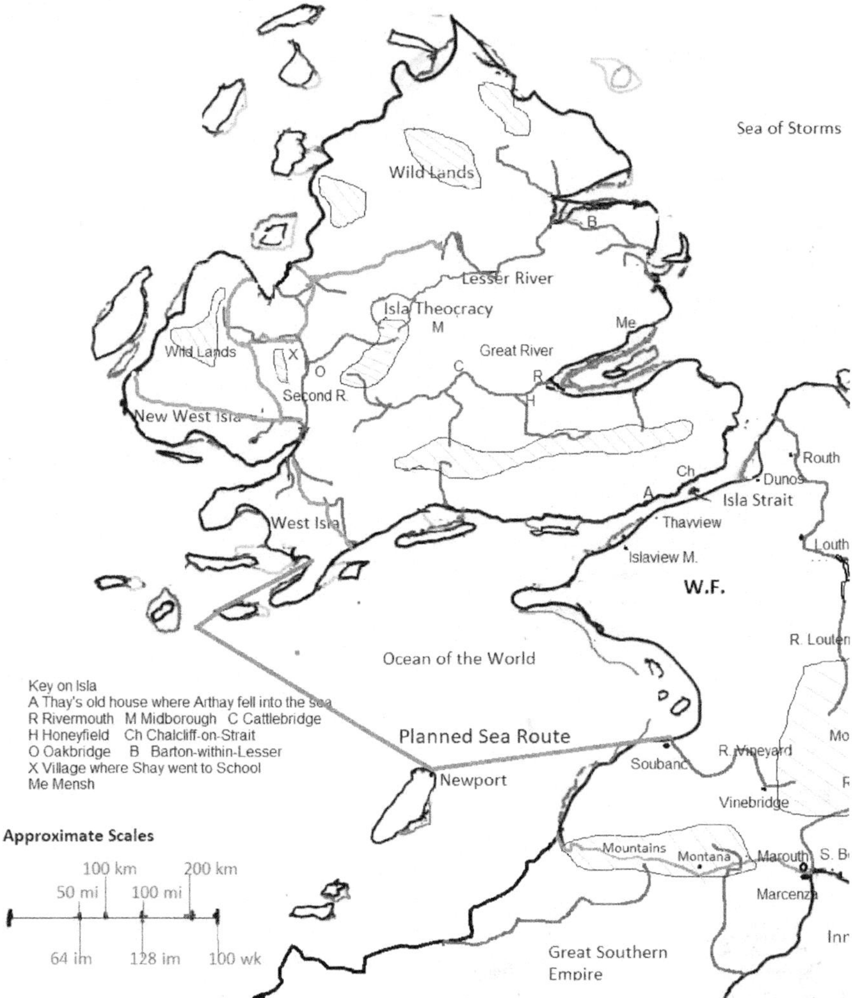

Map 3b: Western Federation and E. Isla

Twin Worlds II

Part 1: Exchange

1
Space

Space Station 5 Duplos Ph 2 Pd 9 (18/Spring) 261

Dear Arté

It's hard to believe that I am now actually in outer space. Looking down on our planet is just amazing - it's like a giant map. Through a telescope I can see large buildings but not individual people. There are so many wonders to tell you that I really don't know where to begin. Jezzie flew me up here in their aircraft and space shuttle. She has helped me to my bunk and introduced me to some of the people up here. It is quite cramped for people our size; and I'm quite small, at least compared with you and Astra! They have made maps of Duplos, both on flat paper as we're used to but also on a globe, which shows how it really is. They can use clever optics to make images of the planet, like with the pinhole camera you set up in the observatory, but using powerful lenses, and then being able to store the images and print them. It's all pretty magical. Anyway Jezzie is going to bring a globe and some maps down to you. She has a number of things to do back on Duplos before she and some of the others come back here and we travel on to Geos. Actually, that's not quite right. As you know the station is continually orbiting both planets and I shall be staying on board for two full periods before Jezzie gets back here.

When you see the globe and maps, you'll see just how big the world is and how little we know of it. The whole of the WF occupies just a tiny corner of the main continent. Between them the GSE and SU claim all the rest of the continent but they actually only occupy a small proportion of the land. There are probably zillions of people who live quite contentedly without knowing anything about these two territories of which they are formally citizens! There is even another whole continent in the South. This is a lot smaller than ours but is still pretty big and the Geosians think it is probably uninhabited by people. They can't be certain but there are no signs of habitation like towns or even buildings. What exciting times lie ahead of us all.

While I'm here I'm being studied by doctors. They are worried that I might carry diseases that are harmless to us but may harm them, or vice versa. A couple of phases before I left their base they gave me some 'shots'. This involves sticking a long thin needle right into my arm and injecting some liquid into my blood stream. It seemed quite fearsome but I didn't really feel much, just a very short sharp prick. I was warned that my body might react and make me feel unwell for a couple of phases, but that is apparently quite normal and nothing to worry about. All this is supposed to protect me from a variety of diseases that are common on Geos and they might have without even knowing it. My arm did feel a bit sore for a phase and I had a slight headache and developed a bit of a scab on the arm. But, as they predicted, it soon passed and the scab is nearly healed. Unsurprisingly, their medical knowledge is vastly superior to ours and they can cure almost anything. They don't live forever. Their lifespan is similar to ours. The difference is that most of them live their full span. All the horrible things that carry people off, especially as children, have been conquered. Their major problem is overpopulation. They have cities with more people in them than all of Duplos put together.

Talking of their advances reminds me to tell you about lightening conductors. The magical power source that they use so much of is called electricity and it is the same force that produces lightening. I plan to study it when I get to Geos. Anyway they have a simple trick that very much reduces the risk of tall buildings being destroyed by a lightening strike, and it is well within our capability to use. Essentially you attach a long iron rod to the top of the building and then join it by a copper wire to an iron stake that you bury in the ground. What happens is that if a lightening strike occurs to your building, the rod somehow attracts the lightening which then travels down the rod and wire into the ground where it dissipates. Anyway, you should talk to Flying Eagle about it and she should be able to help you to protect the towers at the observatory and Thayview. I don't know a lot more yet but this is what Jezzie told me when I asked if she could tell me about the power source for their aircraft.

Another piece of magic is how this letter is going to reach you. I was just going to scrawl a quick note that Jezzie could have taken back down with her; but apparently the note doesn't have to be sent physically with a courier but is sent using the same sort of magic as electricity. On this occasion I have written the letter on paper as usual and they will make a picture of it which they can then send automatically to be printed on paper at their island base and then take that copy to you. Jezzie says that later they'll be able to arrange it so that I don't even have to write the letter on paper in the first place. Even when we are a whole planet apart we'll be able to communicate as easily as between two cities in the WF.

Even though I'm going to have such an exciting and full time I'm still going to miss you very much and will always be thinking of you. Please also give my love to Astra and the others. I am writing separately to my mum. Jezzie says they'll give that letter to you so I'd be grateful if you can send it on to her.

All my love

Aimée

Observatory Island: Ph 4 Pd 9 20/Spring 2614

Dearest Aimée

Isn't it strange how we've adopted a dating system so quickly after meeting the Geosians. How did we manage to keep track of events before? Flying Eagle came by last phase with your letters and I have sent the one on to your mother via the fast courier. I would have liked to take it to her in person but unfortunately I am so tied up with events here that I can't get away. I promise you I shall visit her as soon as I can and give her the news of our changed lives face to face.

We have so much to learn from these people and our lives and society will be transformed. Astra is quite jealous of you being able to look down from space and can't wait to get her hands on a globe map. We have been kept extremely busy with the preparations for the Kongholm conference. Zorro and Créezy are in Kongholm where they have taken over the biggest hotel for the conference. Fermos has been appointed to lead the WF delegation and Astra will also be a member. Zorro is in charge of the organisation, working with the colonels. Would you believe it! Astra says it's almost as if she's grown up at last, and about time too, she adds! Créezy and I are to be accredited representatives to look after the interests of Isla. This is because they can't yet get anyone from the Theocracy. The high priestesses would go nuts at the thought of being represented by a man. To be honest, it seems a bit weird to me, and I thought my place should have been to wait on Créezy in the way I used to do with Thay. At least Créezy's family status on Isla is such that she can legitimately take on such a role. When I suggested I ought to just be her servant for the duration, she blew her top and said it was time to end that sort of discrimination. Fermos also made it clear that I should be accorded official status and faced down opposition from the more conservative members of the WF parliament.

In the meantime Astra and I are still at the observatory. We won't move to Kongholm until a period before the conference opens. Wise Owl is staying with us and she and Astra are currently ensconced in the tower poring over star maps and gazing into the heavens. Wise Owl brought a small telescope of her own that magnifies to an incredible amount. She is teaching Astra and me so much about Astronomy and what she calls Cosmology. (We have decided to use the female pronouns in Contish for all the Geosians regardless of their actual gender – which we don't actually know except for the two leaders and Jezzie). At the moment our studies are a bit hush-hush pending the outcome of the conference. Wise Owl says they are very concerned about the consequences for our culture and civilisation of the sudden contact with more advanced ideas that in the normal course of events would take several centuries to come about naturally. She reckons that we are about four hundred years behind Geos in natural philosophy and that although Isla sounds about a thousand years behind us, the pace of knowledge accelerates in a way that in practical terms that thousand year gap is much less than the four hundred separating us from Geos. Astra is really in her element and it is a joy for me to see her so happy.

6

Fair Exchange

My mind is such a whirl with all the new experiences that I forget just how much you know already. We had so little time together after your brief return from Base Island, and what we had we devoted mainly to our personal affairs and that family conference with the five of us.

After that first contact meeting when you went off with most of the Geosians to Base Island, Colonel Jacky and Zorro remained to help the militia sort out the oncoming Shadowlanders, while Wild Cat and Stripy Tiger came with us back to the observatory. Fortunately the Shadowland Colonel wasn't looking for a fight but wanted to find out what was going on and to ensure that Shadowland was included in discussions with the visitors. The basic idea for the conference sort of emerged from that meeting. Zorro says it was quite difficult not being able to speak properly with Jacky but her acting skills came to the fore and basically it was agreed that all the territories of Duplos should be involved in a meeting to be held in Kongholm. Since then, as you know, the Geosians have all made great efforts to acquire as much Contish as possible while some of us have also learned some Norse. Stripy Tiger is a language expert and it seems to me she is already almost fluent in Contish. The others struggle more but Jacky and Flying Eagle are pretty good. Wise Owl and Astra can communicate effectively in a sort of mixture of the two languages. Neither are natural linguists in the way of Stripy Tiger or Zorro – but they both speak 'astronomy'.

I spoke to Wise Owl about lightening conductors and she agrees that we really ought to have one on the observatory tower. She says that with the storms we get here it's a miracle that we haven't yet had a strike, seeing as how exposed the tower is. Anyway, she managed to explain to me what lightening is and how the conductor works. I have commissioned the village blacksmith to cast a 5 stride long rod of steel and also to draw out a long stretch of copper wire to about a tenth of a division diameter. When she's managed to do that we will be able to install it on the outside of the tower. It really is quite simple to accomplish and Wise Owl says it is just about the first application that arose on Geos when they first understood anything about electricity. Lightening is a perfectly natural phenomenon and has nothing to do with the anger of the Goddesses as I was taught on Isla. The way it works also explains easily why tall buildings seem to get struck most often, and is a much better explanation of why the Goddesses so often choose to destroy temples in this way! I shudder to think of the effect on Isla's theocracy when they learn that their religion is just a myth - as surely they will before too long.

On other matters, I have become more adventurous with my boatskin and it can be really exhilarating. Astra and Zorro won't go near one, but Créezy has had a go and thinks it could catch on for rivers and become a fun sport. She agrees that most women will be nervous about seafaring. She's game for it though and we are planning a few adventures. In the fullness of time we may add the boatskin to the product list for WwW. Don't worry, we will be careful, but it's good to know we are only battling nature and not the Goddess Nepa.

All of us are well and adjusting to our new family dynamics. Créezy and Zorro did have a rather wild night of debauchery together in Kongholm last period. Astra was rather sniffy about it. I know it's not the sort of thing you approve of; but I guess I'm relaxed about such needs. I'd been noticing for a while that Créezy is actually quite moderate and much of her public persona is a bit of an act. Apparently this escapade goes back to the night before the contact, when Zorro was feeling a bit randy and complaining that you had me in your tent without even wanting to take advantage. Créezy had already decided that I was really in love with you and Astra and sort of suggested that it wouldn't be long before changes had to be made. Zorro had no idea that I had feelings for Astra and felt guilty that she had stood in the way of her mother's happiness. Anyway, Créezy then agreed that they would go on a bender in Kongholm together and get their itches well and truly scratched. Fortunately they decided on two men between them so nobody got worn out. In fact, if my experience is anything to go by, the two men involved probably had an amazing time. Since then Créezy and Zorro have become quite close and Créezy has helped Zorro cope with the loss of my sexual services, all of which makes things much more comfortable for me.

I will stop now as Jezzie and Wild Cat have just arrived and I will give them this letter to transmit to you. These instant communications really are magic.

Astra sends her love also.

Lots of Love

Arté

Space Station 5 Geos W 3 Pd 11 (39/Spring) 2614

Dearest Arté

I've now been on board this cramped space station for a full cycle of 2 periods and if I wasn't kept so busy I'd be getting claustrophobic. By the way don't be too confused by the date above, I am having to adjust to the Geosian time and although the period is the same as on Duplos they divide it into six watches. The third watch of period eleven is the thirty-ninth of Spring. On Duplos you are now in the second phase of period 11, which is 26/Spring. In reality it is a bit more complicated for me: Geosians actually denote this date as ***3/B/161A*** or ***33***/Spring/***161A***. This is because they work their arithmetic with numbers base twelve instead of ten, so ***A*** is ten, ***B*** is eleven and ***10*** is twelve. Although in theory one base is as good as another, it is quite confusing when your brain automatically translates numbers as base ten. Anyway I'll stick to base ten in my letters but I'll use Geosian watches instead of Duplosian phases because that is how I'm having to adjust my sleeping cycles etcetera.

My time is divided between exercise and learning Norse, which is what they call their language and is spoken by all the people here. Actually they come from two different, but allied, territiories and speak their common language slightly differently.

I'm finding it quite difficult to get used to a totally different alphabet but at least the main concepts and phonemes are similar to Contish. Apparently there are some languages on Geos that are totally different in structure and don't use our sort of writing at all. At least I don't have to cope with that! What is more difficult is that, because they are so much more advanced than us, they have common words for things that we have no knowledge of. In fact when I'm able to write to you about that sort of stuff I'm going to have to use Norse terms. Nevertheless I'm beginning to appreciate your and Créezy's achievement in learning Contish when you were first marooned and had to cope with totally unfamiliar letters and concepts. It helps in some way that I am not totally monolingual because I am pretty fluent in

Pennish, which is the most common language spoken in the northern parts of the GSE; but that is fairly closely related to Contish and uses the same basic alphabet.

The exercise is designed to get my body used to Geosian weight, which is going to be a quarter as much again as on Duplos, so I will weigh nearly 72 dp instead of 54 dp when I get there, all without getting any fatter. On the space station everything weighs practically nothing which is weird and actually harder to deal with than you might think. The problem is that without weight you lose power in your muscles and it is very important to exercise them. They have a chamber where there is artificial weight which is where we do the exercising, but they have organised it to simulate Duplos weight because that is what they all are trying to get used to. They make me wear specially heavy jacket and trousers to exactly compensate for the extra that I will weigh on Geos. It is quite tiring. I will learn more about the philosophy of weight when I get to Geos but at the moment I just have to accept that is how it is.

I am at least beginning to get used to trousers which almost everyone in New Norland and the KNN wears, but I do miss the freedom of my usual loose tunics. The other thing is that I have to wear a sort of strap to contain my tits. This is because the Geosian weight will give me problems otherwise, and I find it quite uncomfortable. Geosian women have very small tits and are practically flat-chested so don't have to worry so much, but even they tend to wear a strap under their shirts. Although they are a bit funny about revealing their gender, close friends do in fact know because they are just as comfortable with nudity in appropriate social circumstances as we are. You will recall that Flying Eagle was prepared to show herself to Zorro. Well she and

Jezzie have done the same for me so I am familiar with Geosian anatomy. They are similar to us but smaller, obviously. Actually most of the height difference is in the length of legs and they are also much more thickset, stockier, than us and weigh more-or-less the same. It's a good thing Zorro is not Geosian, their men have no bump!

You may not know, but Wild Cat and Flying Eagle are an item. They have been best friends since they were eight years old. While I was on base island they had what they call a marriage ceremony, which is a sort of public declaration that they will stay together all their lives and not have any other sex partners. I don't know what they make of our arrangements on Duplos. Jezzie tells me that it is considered very bad to have more than one partner at the same time. Wild Cat and Flying Eagle lived together for a bit when they were younger but didn't marry because they both wanted to be free to follow their dream of coming to Duplos, and that meant working in cities a long way apart. In fact Jezzie had a brief relationship with Flying Eagle which suited them both at the time but was never intended to be permanent. Jezzie has become good friends with Wild Cat as well and there is no animosity or jealousy between the three of them, which is apparently quite unusual. Although Jezzie assures me that she no longer has any sexual connection with Flying Eagle. And when I asked, innocently, she was quite shocked at the idea of a threesome. I had to explain about how good friends often share a man on Duplos. It only goes to show that one cannot make assumptions when dealing with an alien race.

When the station got to the part of its orbit close to Geos I was able to get a good view of the planet. As we know, its diameter is about 1.4 times that of Duplos. This means the surface area is nearly twice as much as we have. New Norland takes up a complete continent and is huge. That's where I'll be going when eventually we land. We have to spend some time in quarantine in case we bring any nasty diseases from Duplos with us. Then, when we're released from that, I shall spend some time in New Norland before going to Jezzie's home in the KNN which stands for the Kingdom of Northern Nations.

When we got within shuttle reach of Geos we had an exchange of personnel and also took on board four passengers bound for Duplos. These four consist of a politician who is going to lead the Geosian contingent at the Kongholm conference and her secretary and two people who work something called television. This is another piece of magic. You can use it to watch events happening thousands of walks away. I don't understand it at all but one of these people interviewed me while the other used a bit of technology called a camera that enabled them to send pictures of us and the sound of what we were saying all the way back to Geos, where millions of people would be watching us on another bit of technology. In addition to my own studies I've also been roped in to teach these four a smattering of Contish.

Now that the station has arrived back near Duplos; Jezzie, Dr Great Whale and Col Mountain Lion have come back on board to return to Geos. The plan is that Wild Cat, Jacky and Bald Eagle will return after the conference and the plans for the others will depend on what is agreed.

Again I enclose a missive for Mum. As always, love to the rest of the family.

All my love

Aimée

2
Kongholm Conference

Kongholm: Ph 4 Pd 13 (6/Summer) 2614

Dearest Aimée

I thought I would delay this letter until after the Kongholm conference so I could give you the news about what was decided. Well, we have have finally finished and there is so much to tell you. Lord Rivers opened the proceedings and gave a short welcome to everyone, outlining the principles which will govern the Geosian relationship with Duplos. The key elements of this are the full recognition that Duplos belongs to us and that Geos does not wish to interfere in our internal affairs or to push us to do anything we don't want to. Lord Rivers said they made many mistakes in their history, that they now regret and they do not want to repeat those mistakes here. That said, they have knowledge and technology that could be very beneficial to Duplos and they do not wish to deny us the benefits. However, she also told us that there would be inevitable changes to our way of life that would make some people uncomfortable. It would be for us to decide the pace and level of Geosian involvement with us. The Geosians, too, will be uncomfortable with some of our ways and will have to exercise considerable self restraint on occasions. She cited the example of slavery to which New Norland and the KNN are fundamentally opposed on moral grounds. She understood that this was still the practice in parts of Duplos and they would not interfere, while hoping that over time we Duplosians would perceive its injustice and bring it to an end. Officially, now there is no slavery anywhere on Geos although there are some countries where people are not treated well by their rulers.

Throughout the proceedings, the Geosian cameraman has been busy filming. They are going to show it on television[1]. Some of this technology really is magic. It is clear to me that whatever else we do we must learn about electricity. Dancing Bear has given us all copies of a picture she made with a different sort of camera at the moment of first contact. She was standing on top of their aircraft and looking down on us. We can each be seen quite clearly with Astra taking Flying Eagle and Wild Cat's hands. Wow, that really is history.

After these general remarks she handed over to Stripy Tiger who was to be the lead negotiator for Geos, with Jacky as the spokesman for the KNN. The Duplosian opening remarks followed. First off, the Shadowlands spokesman gave what Fermos says is their usual spiel about how they were the most populous territory on Duplos and really should be granted higher status. She hoped the remarks about slavery were not aimed at their practice of serfdom which was not slavery as such, but a well established way of maintaining social order and ensuring the land is worked productively and avoiding unrestricted emigration to the towns. After them it was the GSE's turn. Their leader made only a very short speech welcoming the opportunity that the conference had brought and promising to work co-operatively to everyone's benefit. Astra whispered to me in an aside that she'd believe it when she saw it. Southerners are not to be trusted. Créezy then spoke for Isla. She explained the circumstances that

1 Obviously there are no Contish words for camera or filming or television. Arté is using a transliteration of the Norse words here, and elsewhere in this book where such words are needed that is what he and the other Duplosians will do.

made it difficult for her to truly represent the Theocracy. She acknowledged that Isla was indeed a territory that was guilty of slavery and expressed her hope that two of the outcomes of the engagement with Geos would be that with Geosian help we could end the isolation of Isla and that the ending of that isolation would indeed lead to the eventual abolition of slavery. Fermos then rounded up the opening addresses speaking for the WF and echoing the sentiments of Lord Rivers.

After these opening addresses we got down to serious negotiations and, much to Astra's surprise, both Shadowlands and the GSE approached them positively and in a spirit of co-operation. One of the first things that Stripy Tiger showed us all was the globe of Duplos. This was quite an eye-opener, especially for the GSE and Shadowlanders, who just hadn't appreciated the true extent of the land on Duplos and thus the absurdity of their historic claims. The existence of the southern continent and the more distant islands in particular caused a sensation.

Various agreements were made. Geos (New Norland really) is going to lease base island from both the WF and the SU paying annual rent to both territories, initially for twenty-four years and then re-negotiating for further twenty-four year periods. A Geosian Embassy will be established initially located in Goddess City; but the ambassador will work with all the Duplosian territories. Lord Rivers will head up the embassy for two selenths but then hand over to Stripy Tiger. The Geosian team will be dominated by New Norland but will also include a senior representative of the KNN and, in the fullness of time, other Geosian countries will be represented. Lord Rivers said that it is important that we treat on a whole planet basis so as to avoid either of us becoming involved in internal disputes on the other planet. Fermos and Astra very much saw the wisdom of this. Geos has no more delivered world peace than has Duplos and the last thing either planet needs is to export internal squabbles or fight proxy wars. The SU and GSE signed up. Astra thinks this is largely because they suspect that these Geosians would be likely to favour the WF here on Duplos, being closer to our way of thinking ideologically.

We then came on to cultural and educational exchanges. We agreed there would be opportunities for exchanges in both directions. You got a mention as a pioneer of such an exchange. A Duplosian embassy will be established in New Norland and a small number of Duplosians will be invited to follow in your footsteps to study advanced natural philosophy and engineering as part of a knowledge transfer programme. A committee is to be established to control this to ensure that we on Duplos are comfortable with what level of technology is to be transferred. All territories on Duplos will be represented by both academics and politicians. While Isla remains isolated I have been appointed to serve on the committee; much to the disgust of those that are finding it difficult to accept male participation. Zorro remarked that I should wear a gown and stuff a couple of balloons down the front, then people who thought brains lived in tits would accept me. I thought it quite funny, but Astra was not amused.

Some Geosians will come to Duplos both to study the planet and also to work within our universities. They will also help us reconnect with Isla and explore unknown parts of our planet. It is all very exciting. Of the initial landing party, Wise Owl and Jan will remain here working from the University of Louth. They will be studying what we know and then suggesting new things that we might like to learn from them. You know that Wise Owl is an astronomer (actually a bit more than just an astronomer) so Astra and I will both be learning from her. Jan's interests are in the composition of planets and also in animals. She calls these subjects Geology and Zoology and so will be pottering around all over the place to examine rocks and wild life. Dancing Bear and Red Robin will be primarily the medical team for the other Geosians but will also do some teaching at Goddess University as they will be based in Goddess City. Jacky and Flying Eagle will also be based in Goddess City at their embassy, but both are due to return to Geos after two selenths. Bald Eagle will be based on Base Island with other crew members from the space stations. Wild Cat will return to Geos next period but fully expects to return with Flying Eagle at a later date.

With some supervision from Wise Owl and Wild Cat I installed the lightening conductor on the observatory tower. I have had another made which I will install on my tower at Thayview. Zorro has written an article on them and how they work and is going to market them as a WwW product. I have agreed to adapt one of our SPC[2] models for the shorter Geosian legs and body and WwW will be making several for their use as it is impractical for them to use their flying machines everywhere. Wild Cat says it will be good exercise for them and is similar in concept to a machine they have on Geos they call a bicycle. Although their 'bikes' have only two wheels, one behind the other, and no actual cart. They sound interesting and we might try to produce something similar. Zorro thinks there could be a market for the smaller SPC for children. Some mothers over-indulge their daughters!

Talking of mothers, now that the conference is over and we are leaving Kongholm I shall make an early visit to your mother.

---

2 Self-propelled cart

I expect you are now safely on Geos, I'm really looking forward to hearing all about it.

Lots of love

Arté

3
New Norland, Geos

Q City, New Norland: W 6 Pd 13 (9/Summer) 2614

Dearest Arté

I've arrived safely on Geos and am staying in a bungalow in Q City, which is what the locals are calling the specially constructed town to accommodate new arrivals from Duplos. My bungalow was specially adapted for me while I was on the space station, basically by removing the upper floor from a two story house. Ceilings in regular Geosian domestic buildings are rather low at about 1.6 strides, and even though I am a bit shorter than average I still top 1.8 strides!

I'm going to be very busy. First thing each morning after breakfast I have to go to the gym and do exercises. Being so heavy puts quite a strain on my body and I have to build up my muscles. When I get back I'll be so strong I'll be able to toss you around. You'll have to be on your best behaviour with me 😊

That last symbol is called an emoticon or emoji or smiley and is meant to show that I'm teasing – I won't really beat you up!

After the gym I spend 36 tocks, which is just over 2 hora, studying the language, which is now really about learning about stuff that we don't have on Duplos. Then after some lunch I go into teacher mode to give some lessons on Duplos and our languages. That is I teach Contish and also tell the Geosians a bit about Pennish and even such Islish as I have learnt from you and Créezy. Then after a bit of recreation it's time for another meal and a mid-watch sleep. That's followed by a second breakfast and gym session. I then get to study some science and Geosian culture, or sometimes do a TV interview. Science is the Geosian term for Natural Philosophy.

Morrow-watch they want to give me a full medical examination. They are being awfully apologetic about it but they feel they need to understand a lot more about Duplosian anatomy and metabolism. All this is quite new to me but I quite understand the necessity and don't mind the intrusion at all. After all I had to expect that I would be both a novelty and an experimental subject.

I've been thinking about the gaps in my mathematical knowledge that Jezzie has mentioned. I'm going to have to wait to learn what this calculus is all about but I have been able to think about the idea of a number system with a square root of minus one. In this I'm grateful to you for the sort of formal thinking you did to construct the integer and fractional number systems from the counting numbers. I've been looking at the problem by considering ordered pairs of ordinary numbers and then defining the usual arithmetic rules. Thus I define

$$(a, b) + (c, d) = (a+b, c+d) \text{ and } (a,b)(c,d) = (ac-bd, ad+bc).$$

When you do this, the definitions of subtraction and division are obvious and you find that (0, 1) and (0, -1) are the two square roots of (-1, 0). It is easy to see that the pairs of the form (a, 0) make up a set of numbers that act just like ordinary numbers and so we have a number system with a square root of -1. Indeed in this system we can solve all quadratic equations. As for representing the numbers graphically we can easily do that on a plane, using the X axis for the first number in a pair and the Y axis for the second. I think there's lots of things we can do with this model. I'm going to talk to Jezzie about it.

Talking of Jezzie, she's having a bit of a bad time. Yesterday she had a long video call to the KNN with the person she was going to marry and they've called it off. It's all quite sad and Jezzie is somewhat distressed even though she says she was sort of expecting it, and agrees it is for the best. I had to give her a hug, which is quite difficult because she is heavier than me and I can't lift her up so had to bend almost double to reach her! She says she's going to buy a step-ladder so we can meet face to face.

It's bed time now and I'm quite tired so I'll stop and write again soon. Thinking of you has given me an itch - I must be getting as bad as Zorro. I'd better wear a pad in bed if I don't want a damp sheet!

Lots of love

Aimée

Q City, New Norland: W 1 Pd 14 (10/Summer) 2614

Dearest Arté

I know its only a watch since I last wrote, but I have such exciting news; I can't wait to tell you.

WE ARE GOING TO BE CO-PARENTS

(that's how they put it here on Geos).

Our farewell session worked just as I truly wanted. I know that back on Duplos this would still be too early for me to tell but here on Geos the magic of their medical and technical knowledge is hard for us to comprehend. As I said in my letter yesterwatch I was going to have a medical examination. Well they have technology that enables them to look inside a person and take pictures. Which they routinely do for diagnostic checks. However, this technology uses something they call X-rays which can be harmful to babies in a womb. All Geosians know this and anyone who thinks they might be pregnant avoids this technology unless it is a real emergency. In my case, Dr Great Whale was very embarrassed, but knowing I was female felt she had to ask. I answered that it was much too early to tell but that it was possible and indeed I hoped I was. Anyway she then said she wouldn't use the X-ray machine but did what she called an ultrasound scan. This takes 'pictures' using high frequency sound waves. It all involves lots of science that I'm going to have to learn. Apparently sound is just a pressure wave in the air and our hearing works by detecting the wave and converting it to electrical signals into our brain. Anyway the Geosians have a machine that generates these ultrasound waves and a specialist nurse called a radiographer rubbed my tummy with an instrument that emitted these waves and detected echoes which enabled them to build up a picture. The picture is a bit funny to look at, as you will see, because I have attached a copy to this letter, which the Geosians on Duplos can print out for you. You can see a tiny baby inside me and they could even see that he is going to be a boy. I'm so very happy. I must be the only Duplosian girl that wants a boy rather than a girl. Do you mind if I call him Mikos Artur? Please thank Astra for her help in making it happen. I'm not really that superstitious but there does seem to be some truth in the old adage:

Number one is just for fun
Number two is a son for you
But you know you really oughter
Go for a third to get a daughter

Well, although I didn't tell you at the time, that's why I stopped after the second and asked Astra to take the third go.

Twin Worlds II

Please tell my Mum when you see her, she will be delighted to be a grandmother. Also tell her not to worry about me because the medical expertise here is so advanced that I couldn't be in a better place to have the baby, even with the slight complication of the extra weight.

After Great Whale had done all her other tests on me and asked me all sorts of questions about my diet, she then went on to a long discussion on my pregnancy and general health. She is clearly a bit worried about the effects of the greater gravity on Geos on our baby's development. Gravity is what causes the extra weight. I'll learn more about it later, as I'm sure will you in your lessons with Wise Owl. Anyway she carefully weighed my tits and says I must have a specially tailored bra made to give them proper support. A bra is the name for the strap I have to wear around my tits here. She was especially interested to learn about our rhythm cycles on Duplos. Oh I forgot; you probably don't know much about them yourself, as it's not done to discuss such things with men. I expect if you ask her nicely Astra will tell you more. But I expect you know that we have to time things right to get pregnant and on Duplos the cycle takes about thirty phases or four times a year, which has led to the belief that it all depends on Selenos. The interesting bit is that Great Whale says that on Geos their cycle is about thirty watches, so rather than Selenos having anything to to with it, if there is an astronomical connection it is with the planet's rotation. That would interest Astra. Great Whale says she would like to know if a stay on the other planet would change things. Unfortunately for her, my pregnancy means that I won't be able to tell her. However, eventually, once regular exchanges between Duplos and Geos occur, she should be able to find out.

Obviously for us personally, that is the most exciting thing that has happened this watch. But it's not the only thing. Later on Jezzie and I were taken to a TV studio where we were filmed having a three way video conference call with none other than the President of New Norland and the King of the Northern Nations to welcome me to Geos. These are the most important men in their countries. It's an unbelievable honour to have such a call. Later, when I get out of quarantine, the President wants to meet me in person and then, when Jezzie takes me to the KNN, we will have an appointment at the palace to meet the King properly. Jezzie is terribly excited about that. She says her co-parents will be so proud of her. After that we had quite a long interview with the TV when I was asked about Duplos and about what I thought of Geos so far. It's been amazing. Apparently the TV programme is going to be watched by millions of people in New Norland and the KNN and also in other countries on Geos. Even the East Geosian Empire will show it on their state TV.

Give my love to all the others

lots of love

Aimée (and Artur)

P.S. You might need to get Flying Eagle or one of the others to explain some of the things I've been writing.

Thayview Farm: Ph 2 Pd 15 (12/Summer) 2614

Dearest Aimée

Two letters, almost together! And such wonderful news. I'd never expected to learn I had a son. I love you more than ever. I can't wait to hear of the birth, and of course to see you and baby

Mikos Artur when you come home again. You have chosen his names well and I am so honoured by your choice. I have just returned from visiting your Mum and she is excited at the prospect of being a grandmother. She also misses you very much; but loves the attention she is receiving as the mother of the first Duplosian to travel to Geos. You have put Montana on the map!

Astra came with me to Montana and she and Sturdon have become very close. They have agreed that Artur can be a grandson to both of them. Astra has given up on Zorro presenting her with a granddaughter but I think she is being premature and time will prove her to be mistaken.

Your quote of the old rhyme about sons and daughters reminds me that Jan has taken an interest in such matters and wonders if there is any scientific explanation for the anecdotal evidence for sex determination. She is launching a scientific study and needs men to volunteer to give her seed samples. Apparently sex determination is down to the man in Geosian life and almost certainly also for us. I expect Jezzie can tell you all about it so I won't try in this letter. Obviously I am going to volunteer myself and I expect Jan will be able to get enough others to conduct her experiments. More later!

Your observations on numbers with a square root of minus one are interesting. I spoke to Wise Owl about them. She calls them complex numbers and says she will get on to them sometime later in our seminars. We have regular sessions with Wise Owl leading us through new concepts in mathematics and natural philosophy. Astra and I attend as well as Fermos and several of the natural philosophers at Louth and Routh universities. We have made a start with calculus which follows on closely from work Fermos did some years ago and from the work

I've done on infinitesimals. We've got far enough that Wise Owl has been able to explain about weight and gravity to us. That is what really interests Astra. The force that causes weight is the same as that which drives the heavenly motions. It's actually very simple but at the same time deeply profound. What we've been learning is apparently just a working approximation, which is accurate enough for almost all circumstances. Wise Owl says the truth is even more astonishing but we have quite a long way to go before we can grasp it. However, she told Fermos that one of her questions got right to the heart of the philosophical problem with the approximation. This, said Wise Owl, concerned 'action at a distance'.

Fermos' question was this: "If there's a force between two bodies like the Sun and a planet, how is the force transmitted and is it instantaneous, implying an infinite transmission speed, or does it have to build up over time?"

Wise Owl's response was to say that the question was too hard for her to answer satisfactorily at the moment and that it had been over two hundred years after the laws of gravity were discovered before an answer was found.

On a totally different subject, as you see from the address, I'm currently at the farm. I've got Flying Eagle, Zorro and Créezy with me. We're going to be surveying the prospects for re-connecting with Isla. Yesterphase we visited Esau and while we were with him there was a knock on the door and we were confronted with a man who announced that he was Esau's son, also called Esau.

Esau was taken aback, he hadn't known he had a son but apparently had enjoyed a relationship with an archaeologist over a number of years; but lost touch when she returned to her home outside Goddess City many years ago. Although she had been in her forties she was pregnant at the time and the younger Esau was the result. She died last year and left her son as her heir. Until her last few months she hadn't told him anything about his father but in the end she did and urged him to go to Dunos to look him up.

Young Esau did this and thence the trail led to Islaview.

They were both overjoyed to meet but before we left them to catch up on each other's lives young Esau produced a copy of an inscription on an ancient clay tablet. His mother had found this while digging on the banks of the River of the Goddesses and had been trying to work out what it might be. It was certainly thousands of years old and she suspected was possibly from before the separation. She remembered something Esau had said about Islish writing and wondered if there was a relationship. Young Esau wanted his father to look and see if he could make sense of it.

As you know, Esau is illiterate in Islish and confessed he wouldn't have a clue but told his son that maybe Créezy and I could help.

As a result young Esau has spent the phase with us and we have been poring over the inscription. We haven't got very far yet but Créezy and I are agreed that there is a distinct similarity with the Islish alphabet and are hopeful that in time we might crack the system.

To give you an idea, I enclose a photograph of the inscription and also the Islish alphabet with transliteration to Contish.

However, the interesting bit to come from this is that while we were beavering away on the problem with Flying Eagle also making suggestions, Zorro and Esau entertained each other and got on like a house on fire. I think Zorro was quite surprised at herself because Esau isn't in her usual style. They have connected at a mental level and went for a long walk together. Knowing Zorro as we do, we can guess that one thing led to another, but she is being uncharacteristically coy.

I think she is smitten. I hope so, because I still feel guilty about her. She has been very good about it, and is evidently pleased for her mother; but Créezy tells me there are times when she gets needy. Créezy has become very close to Zorro and spends a lot of time giving her emotional support. That involves quite a lot of shared sex sessions and, while on the surface this makes Zorro as happy as ever, Créezy says that Zorro doesn't enjoy the men as much as she used to and has abandoned solo sex completely, insisting that Créezy is present every time. We've discussed it and concluded that Zorro is using Créezy as a sort of substitute for me. It's all been a bit worrying, so if Zorro really has connected with Esau that will be fantastic.

In her turn, Créezy has only had sex with Zorro present since our changed circumstances. But she says that isn't because of any problems of her own, but because Zorro's physical appetites haven't reduced and that has meant that Créezy is getting more than enough to scratch her own itches!

As for me, I feel so lucky that I have such a deep friendship with both Créezy and Zorro without any requirement for sex. I don't want sex at all now with anyone except you or Astra.

Thinking all this has made me want you more than ever. I'm going to need a cold bath. Astra is still staying with your mother.

Take care of yourself and that baby!

lots of love

Twin Worlds II

Arté

Montana: Ph 2 Pd 15 (12/Summer) 2614

Darling

What wonderful news. I'm longing to be a Grandmother. I'll be honest and say I would have preferred my first to be a girl but there's still time for that. It's really important that you look after yourself. I don't understand this bit about weight but dear Astra says she does and I trust her. She's going to talk to the Geosian doctor here and make sure that they learn how best to help you. I do worry that for all their advanced medicine they don't have any actual experience of a Duplosian birth and you really ought to have me with you.

Your news about speaking to the President and the King seems unbelievable. My little girl meeting the most important people in the whole solar system, and we are just such ordinary folk. Going to your graduation in Routh is the furthest from home I've ever been and now you are the most travelled girl in all of Duplos. I can't get my head round it at all.

Life here is much as normal except for a bit of attention from the pamphleteers on account of you becoming so famous. Astra is staying with me for a bit. She came down with Arté to give me your letters and this wonderful news. I'm so pleased that you have at last got together properly with Arté and hope it is for more than just getting yourself pregnant. He really is every woman's dream for her favourite daughter. And it really is OK for you to share him with Astra. She will look after you well. I've become really friendly with her. We have you in common and that to me is even closer than sharing a man, which I was never that bothered about, even with your Aunts.

I can't pretend to understand all your maths stuff but Astra and Arté both tell me how good your work is. I suppose I have to swallow the concerns I had about you being so bookish. Anyway anything can be forgiven to a darling girl who gives me a grandchild! Isn't it strange how our desire for children beats every other consideration. I suppose if it were not so, people would die out.

What times we live in, aliens from Geos, technology that is magic and a daughter who travels through space. And Arté is making plans to get the Geosians to help in establishing contact with Isla. I never thought I would live to see any of these wonders.

Look after yourself darling,

Your ever-loving Mum

4
Kingstown

Kingstown: W 4 Pd 16 (25/Summer) 2614

Dearest Arté

All the medical tests on me and the others have gone well and we have been released from quarantine. Before that happened Wild Cat arrived from Duplos and has been able to bring me up to date on a number of things. What a lot you have all achieved so far, and isn't it great that WwW are getting so much of the action. What will we do with all our money! I've seen how the lights work on bicycles here and they will have an incredible impact on our SPCs, and now bicycles! Jezzie has promised that by the time I get to the KNN, they will have built me a cycle that I will be able to ride. My legs are far too long for even the biggest models they have here. One of my problems is that I have to scrunch my knees up to my chin when sitting in any of the normal cars and even then keep my head bowed down. Fortunately for me some adaptations are being made to enable me to travel in greater comfort.

Wild Cat congratulated me on my pregnancy and told me that she and Flying Eagle were also expecting to become co-parents at about the same time. She told me that back when they were only sixteen, they were watching their President announcing the project to travel to Duplos and they had jokingly agreed that if they both managed to be in the landing party they would do their best to co-parent the first Geosian child to be conceived on Duplos. With Jezzie's help to ensure their privacy, they have succeeded in doing so. They are going to call her Snow Hare after the first animal they saw on base island. I hope Artur and Snow

Hare will be friends and come to symbolise the friendship between our two planets.

While on the subject of babies, everyone is being most solicitous of my welfare. The authorities in the KNN are going to find a doctor and midwife, that's a nurse who specialises in delivering babies, to look after me for the birth. They don't leave it to your mother and aunts or other female friends of the family like we do on Duplos. When they've chosen these two and I have had a chance to meet and approve them, they are going to be sent to Duplos to learn what we do and get some practical experience. They really are going to a lot of trouble just for me. I am so lucky.

Following release from quarantine, Jezzie has flown back to the KNN to spend their Midsummer holiday with her family. They make a big thing of midsummer in the KNN especially in the more northern part where it stays light for most of the watch. I shall be joining her in just over two periods time.

At the moment I am in Kingstown which is the capital of New Norland. I was greeted personally by the President and a banquet was held in the presidential palace in honour of myself and the members of the Duplos expedition. It was all very grand and I felt somewhat over-awed. I was seated next to the President, with Great Whale on my other side to help me feel more comfortable. Afterwards I had a conversation with the ambassador from the KNN. She gave me an invitation from the King to an investiture where the KNN members of the party were to be honoured. I would also be given honorary citizenship of the KNN and be made a Lieutenant of the most excellent order of the North (LN). Jezzie will also be made LN while Jan Martskind is to become a Scientist Companion of the same order, (SCN) and Jacky Jackson will be knighted as a Knight Commander of the order (KCN). This is a very distinguished honour. She is also to be promoted in the army to Brigadier. She will be known as Brigadier Zir Jacky Jackson which sounds very grand. You'll have to get one of the others, Jan is probably best, to explain just what this all means. Anyway I shall expect you and Astra and all the others to treat me with extra respect and salute me when I wear the medal that signifies the LN. (Visualise my tongue firmly in my cheek as you read this). Jacky is expected to be back in the KNN when the investiture happens but Jan will have her presentation when eventually she returns to Geos.

As well as seeing the sights here in Kingstown, like the parliament buildings, I am also being shown round some museums and art galleries so I can learn a bit about Geosian culture. However, rather than showing off their wonders, they are more keen that I should learn about the mistakes they have made over the centuries. They want me to understand what to avoid if we choose to adopt more advanced technology. They are ashamed of some of their history in dealing with more primitive people on their own planet and it seems extremely important to them that they don't repeat those mistakes when dealing with us. They also want us to be able to benefit from their hindsight when developing our own planet's resources. They say we have the opportunity to gain the benefits of their experience without having to suffer the ill-effects of their mistakes.

In this I am getting good insight into the potential pitfalls and can see how we might indeed benefit. A good example is is the production of electricity. At first the main means of production here on Geos came from using steam to drive turbines, great coils of copper wire wrapped round cylindrical forms, to rotate them between powerful magnets. The steam was produced at very high pressure by heating huge boilers full of water. The heat came from burning coal or other coal-like fuel. This released all sorts of particles and gases into the air that over the centuries have caused damage to the environment of the planet, as well as using up valuable resources that can only be renewed over thousands or even millions of years.

Nowadays they have found much cleaner ways of producing the electricity they need. These include the sort of technology they have used on base island to generate the electricity for their aircraft. Converting sunlight, wind and water energy directly to electricity, which is the way to go for us. It takes a lot of sophisticated manufacturing to be able to make the devices required for these generators and there is no way that we could do this ourselves from scratch. But they can supply the sophisticated components and we can quickly learn how to assemble them into the products we need and gradually build up our own capabilities.

There are real opportunities for WwW here. Tell Créezy to invest in copper and steel production. Also talk to Flying Eagle about electricity generation. Jezzie tells me she has some expertise on the subject.

One other material we need to get to grips with is called rubber. This comes in two forms, natural and synthetic. Natural rubber comes from the sap of certain trees that grow in equatorial climes of Geos, whereas the synthetic sort needs sophisticated chemical (like alchemy but with real science behind it) processing from oil. It's all very complicated but again, if you talk to Flying Eagle, she can tell you a lot about it and Jan could probably teach you something about the natural sort.

Unfortunately for us, the parts of the continent where such trees are likely to grow are all on land claimed by the GSE or the SU.

Love to you all, but most importantly, my love to you dear Arté

Your very own

Aimée

5
Progress on Duplos

Thayview Farm: Ph 1 Pd 18 (23/Summer) 2614

Dearest Aimée

What a lot of news in your last letter. We're looking forward to welcoming your doctor and midwife. Red Robin has been doing a lot of observing of birthing over here. She will be back on Geos by the time Artur is due to be born and will probably also try to get involved. She has been able to give our doctors lots of information about hygiene and general good practise that is already making an impact on mortality in childbirth, both of mother and child. She says that compared with Geos three hundred years ago, our mortality rates were not at all bad; but she was nevertheless able to make some recommendations for improvement. There are mothers and babies alive today who would not have been without her advice. Doctors and nurses in our top hospitals now wear white gowns and face masks that are laundered every day and they are forever washing their hands! All this reduces the spread of infections which we now know are caused by tiny 'animals' so small they can't be seen except through a microscope, which is rather like a telescope but for viewing small objects rather than distant ones.

We have all been ever so busy. Fermos has been employed as an elder statesman to try to cut through the political wrangling as the three territories try to appoint a diplomatic team to travel to Geos. Now you have been released from quarantine the Geosians have given the green light for the embassy. An architect spent a short time here to study our needs and has produced designs for buildings to accommodate us in Kingstown. The various territorial councils are hoping to establish the embassy there before Winter.

Astra and I have been keeping well out of it, politics is not our thing at all. Poor Stripy Tiger has been working all hours on these matters when she would much rather be pursuing her other interests. At the same time trade and exchange talks have also been proceeding. Zorro and Créezy have been heavily involved in these. Various food items from here have been identified as appealing to the Geosian tastes and Zorro has been brokering deals. She is actually in her element with such work and it looks like we will establish some valuable trade links.

They have been just as busy on behalf of WwW. With Flying Eagle's help they have added an assisting electric engine on to the SPC tricycle for the Geosians. Even with our lower gravity they find pedalling quite tiring because of their short legs and can't maintain anything like the speed or cover the distances that we can, especially uphill. The battery gets charged from the pedalling and downhill free-wheeling; then the engine can be called upon to assist when the going gets tough. You are right that we really could do with a source of rubber for tyres.

We'll be adding an engine to some of our other models for Duplosian use in due course. I am working on the design with some assistance from Flying Eagle. Zorro wants to have the first one! We have already taken delivery of some parts from Geos that enable us to add lights driven by dynamo to our vehicles. The demand is very high and there is a long waiting list. We are all now obscenely wealthy. Astra and I are starting a charitable foundation for improving education, especially for boys and for girls from poorer homes.

38

Fair Exchange

You'd hardly recognise Louth today. Roads everywhere are being dug up to bury copper cables anticipating the eventual arrival of electricity and at the same time the surfacing is being improved to accommodate our vehicles. There are yet more fortunes to be made in infrastructure development.

With all the time we have spent on learning our science, Astra and I have had almost no time to spend in South Beach this summer, but Astra is there at the moment having a short break while arranging to prepare the house there for electricity, and also start on the extension for when you and Artur return. We talk every day because we have acquired the only radio communications devices on the planet, apart from those used by the Geosians.

Créezy and I are also on a sort of holiday here at Thayview. Somewhat to my surprise, Zorro was right about the commercial potential of my boatskin. They are very popular with the more adventurous young women in their teens and twenties. Zorro's original thought was that a two person boatskin would be great for leisure activities on rivers, and indeed many people of all ages enjoy exploring the rivers up close in this way. What we hadn't foreseen was that young women in particular would get an enormous thrill from trying to boatskin on dangerous parts of rivers like the rapids you get on many mountain streams. This 'white-water skinning' has become the must-do sport for the thrill-seekers, or idiots as Astra calls them!

Well, Créezy and I are two such idiots. We decided to go one better and see what we could do at sea. Zorro quite enjoys a gentle river cruise, taking Esau for a picnic on a nice backwater, but she is terrified of anything too fast-flowing and won't go anywhere near white water. Anyway, we did take some sensible precautions, courtesy of Jan Martskind.

We set off in two boatskins from Islaview beach going down current. It was such an exciting thrill. We got soaked of course as we rolled the boatskin at regular intervals, but we had expected that so weren't encumbered by clothes. Eventually we passed North Cape beach and rounded the cape, eventually landing on the South Cape beach. We had kept within sight of land all the time and Jan and Zorro were following our progress with Zorro and Esau pedalling a SPC with Jan as passenger. Jan had one of their microlights and reckoned she could rescue us if we got into too much trouble.

We didn't go all the way to Soubanc but I think we could have done. When we landed on the beach we nearly collapsed with exhaustion but were both on an incredible high. Créezy said that if I'd been any other man I'd have been quite unsafe as her itch was almost beyond her control! However, she added she would die before breaking our family agreement. Jan and I went off to discuss various things about the strait and the others went for a walk along the beach. I think Zorro took pity on Créezy's state and I suspect she inveigled Esau into a quick threesome.

In case you're confused, this is the younger Esau. I suppose I ought to call him Esau II to avoid confusion. He is now a bit of a permanent fixture alongside Zorro and I won't be surprised if she plans to get a baby from him.

The sea in the strait is much too dangerous for most people to go skinning there, and it will never amount to anything other than an extreme sport for a very small minority of thrill-seekers. However, it is different in the bight between South Cape and Soubanc. Paddling there at slack tide is easy-going and the boatskins can enable you to reach high-tide islands. At other times skinning can be exhilarating in the waves and I can see a good prospect for a boatskin hire business. Jan agrees and has also described a sport they have on Geos called surfboarding, which she thinks would be possible here and also on the inner sea near South Beach. Yet more strings to the WwW bow!

While staying at Thayview, Jan and I have been discussing the options for reconnecting with Isla. Although it would be possible to take a microlight over the strait, the Geosians do not recommend it. In the first instance we are looking at making contact through communications. Having thought about it, I have decided that I will not return there myself as long as they continue to enslave men. Créezy agrees with this decision. She thinks that there's bound to be someone who'll try to get me punished as an escaped sacrifice. She doesn't trust the priestesses at all. She says she will go, however. She wants to see their faces when she returns from the dead to confute their whole religious nonsense. Créezy doesn't believe in Goddesses and thinks Isla is totally corrupt. I'm less sure about the Goddesses. Obviously the theological myths are just that, but I do think there is some importance to life in spiritual terms. The Geosians are generally secular but they do have various religions on Geos and Stripy Tiger tells me that many of them believe that there is a spiritual dimension to our existence beyond the mere physical.

Flying Eagle has requested that they send some drones from Geos to enable unmanned exploration. Actually they can fly their VTOL aircraft without anyone on board but that wouldn't answer. Imagine what a stir that could cause! I don't know if you know about drones or not. Flying Eagle tells me they are very small aircraft that they can use for reconnaissance without being observed from the ground. If they fly high enough the Islanders will just think they are birds. Indeed they can be made to look like birds even quite close up. Jan has prepared some stuffed birds for sending to Geos as models. She has been learning about migratory patterns here and we are planning something for next spring. Créezy and I will just have to be patient a little longer.

I spoke to Jan about the KNN honours system. They take it very seriously and she is thrilled to be so honoured. Jacky is due to leave here at the beginning of Autumn so I suppose your ceremony will be not long after that. Jan says that in New Norland they have a very different sort of system which involves them receiving quite large sums of money. She thinks that Flying Eagle and Wild Cat are each likely to pick up a hundred thousand pounds. That sounds like a lot to me. I expect you will have some idea how it might equate to our dollars.

I think I mentioned before that I had volunteered to be part of a study that Jan is conducting on our myths about sex determination in babies. Actually it's part of a much wider study. I have been doing my bit and she tells me that the work is proving very interesting. She says it's too early to be certain but she thinks there really could be something in the myths. So it appears you were right to allow yourself to follow the superstitions! Anyway it worked for you, and no man could ask for a better mother than you, so Artur will be born privileged. For myself, I am just delighted that I am going to know my own child, whether a son or a daughter. It's pure nonsense that men are not interested in their progeny. They just aren't given the opportunity to know. I suppose that's why I like to see my and Thay's daughter when I observe Isla through the binoculars. Although I won't travel to Isla myself, I hope Thay can be persuaded to let her visit me here. Funnily enough Créezy is sure that Shay will be amenable, assuming that she too has my daughter. Créezy knows both twins well and says she knows just which buttons to press to get them to do things. She's always been very careful about what she says to me because she knows how I feel about Thay, but as I've got to know her better, I realise that she was actually closer to Shay and took her part in childhood disputes. She has never disparaged Thay to me, but from something she once said when we were still having sexual relations I gather that Shay had been the one that helped her to lose her virginity. One of the complicated things in our relationship was how I made her feel the presence of Shay. In retrospect, I think that for her we always had threesomes and that Shay was the third person for her, as at first, Thay was for me. No wonder she wouldn't countenance Zorro joining in.

I hear a vehicle drawing up on the gravel, it's probably Flying Eagle. I'm expecting her, as we are going to be surveying the strait for a potential site for a power station. Apparently our strait is likely to offer the best opportunity for generating electricity from water power on the planet, and is better than anything they have on Geos. Flying Eagle thinks we could generate enough to power the whole of the WF, and still be below full capacity. I'd better stop writing now and let her in.

All my love

Arté

6
Kingdom of Northern Nations

Camford, KNN: W 4 Pd 19 (44/Summer) 2614

Dearest Arté

Here I am at last at Jezzie's house in the KNN. She lives in the ancient university city of Camford, not to be confused with the university city of New Camford where Wild Cat lives in New Norland. Jezzie has had a new extension built on her house to accommodate me. The old part of her house has two floors. Downstairs the ceilings are seven and a half lengths high and I can stand up without bashing my head, although you couldn't. Upstairs, where her bedrooms and bathroom are, the ceilings are a couple of divisions under seven lengths and even I have to stoop, which would be most uncomfortable if I were to sleep there. However the new extension is just single storey and has ten length high ceilings, which is very comfortable for us Duplosians. I have a good size bedroom, a sitting room and my own bathroom. I tell you, of all the magical luxuries here on Geos, indoor plumbing is the best. I don't know how I ever managed back home with outside privies and cold water from an outside well or pump. Before I come home you'll have to sort out the plumbing or I won't live with you!

Best of all, Jezzie has had a special bath installed for me that is two strides long. I can lie down in it completely. It is equipped with what they call a spa which circulates jets of water around me. It is the height of luxury. I've just got out after spending two hora in the bath. Being immersed in water reduces the effects of the greater gravity and I am totally refreshed.

Fair Exchange

The journey to KNN was quite stressful. They did their best for me but the seat was a bit cramped and the flight was not very comfortable. Also, crossing several time zones in a short time (about nine hora) plays havoc with your body clock and causes what the Geosians call jet lag. Anyway, I have now recovered after a good rest. Jezzie came to meet me at the airport, though I had to suffer the inevitable television interview and what they call a press conference where I had answer a load of inane questions from journalists. We soon got on our way to Camford which took about three hora with Jezzie driving one of their 'cars'. The traffic in their cities is horrendous, you just can't imagine how busy the roads are. New Norland has more space and it didn't seem quite so bad there, outside the urban centre of Kingstown.

Once we got to Camford, Jezzie was able to ensure I was left in peace until I had recovered.

A couple of watches ago the doctor and midwife came to meet me. They are very nice and looking forward to going to Duplos to learn how best to look after me. Their names and titles are Dr Anders Stevensen and Sr (sister) Les Mairdot. They'll see me every watch for the next period and then fly to New Norland to catch a shuttle to a space station and thence to Duplos. Many of the Doctors here specialise in just one aspect of medicine. Anders is an obstetrician and gynaecologist which means she specialises in women's sex bits and childbirth. It's a good thing that we Duplosians aren't shy about our sex organs, the way she was poking me about.

Otherwise, the departments of natural sciences and electrical engineering at Camford university have enrolled me as a postgraduate student. In actual fact a lot of the time I will be attending undergraduate science lectures and have both undergraduate and postgraduate tutorial partners. I am registered for an M. Eng degree (Master of Engineering) and will be enjoying an accelerated programme that is somewhat reminiscent of your experience at Routh. However, I won't live in college because I can easily walk in from Jezzie's house.

I'm not sure I approve of the risks you are taking with your boatskin. You must remember that you have responsibilities as a father now. I don't want to come home a widow because you and Créezy have pulled one stunt too many. It's good news about Zorro, though. I was worried that she would find it difficult to do without your sex sessions. While I don't mind for myself, I don't think I could cope with sharing you with both mother and daughter. Sharing you with just Astra is quite different. I love her too and feel warm and protected in her company.

You haven't said any more about that ancient inscription. Are you getting any where with deciphering it?

Oh, one more thing, I now have my own computer and email address: rastu@camford.ac.knn. Jezzie says that Flying Eagle is going to get you a computer too, once they have established the appropriate infrastructure, and then we will be able to email each other directly, and might even be able to arrange some form of voice communications, although there would be some time lag that might make that difficult.

The electronic communications that they use are waves that travel at a finite speed. The speed is incredibly fast, much faster than sound, but even so, over the vast distance between the two planets, the time taken is significant. Actually the speed is the same speed as light. Light is just another 'electromagnetic' wave. Jezzie says it's all very complicated because as well as being a wave, light also behaves like a particle, wave-particle duality she called it. The physics is horrendous and Jezzie says she doesn't think anyone really understands it, not even the so-called experts.

It's funny, you'd think that with all their knowledge of how the universe works that Geosians wouldn't have religious beliefs. However while many don't, and all but a few cranks recognise that their ancient myths are rubbish, there are respectable scientists who believe in Gods in some form or other. Reality really is weird, and while a lot is understood, an awful lot isn't and there is still room for a spiritual dimension.

On that philosophical note I will leave off. Jezzie has gone out to get a 'take-away' and she should be back any time now. We are going to settle down and watch some escapist fiction on television before turning in for a sleep. Life here may be hectic but it is ever so comfortable.

All my love

Aimée

South Beach: Ph 1 Pd 21 (5/Autumn) 2614

Dearest Aimée

I've stayed on here in South Beach for a bit to supervise some of the works. Astra went back to Louth on her usual schedule. Such a lot has happened since the arrival of the Geosians. Astra, Fermos and I have had quite an education in the appreciation of Geosian Science and Engineering. Based on this we have drawn up a curriculum for knowledge exchange. Fermos has presented this to the WF parliament in Goddess City and it has been approved. Stripy Tiger has passed the request back to New

Norland and they are going to advertise for suitable people to come here to teach courses at each of the universities of Routh, Louth, Marcenza and Goddess City. Some of the graduates of these courses will then be able to travel to Geos to follow in your footsteps to universities there.

Ironically one of the by-products is going to be an advance in the opportunities for men here in the WF. There is considerable concern about the sexual health of those going to Geos. The prospect of a year or more of celibacy is daunting in the extreme for most younger women. Even if they don't have the extreme libido of Zorro, very few feel they can cope with the levels of abstinence that you and Astra have been accustomed to. As a result there is a search for men who might also be able to benefit from an advanced education to be included in the exchange programme. In the other direction there doesn't seem to be a problem. Geosians are in general pretty moderate in their sexual appetites and those that don't have a permanent partner are mostly able to manage their single state without the health problems that affect us.

A propos the above, we are quite concerned about you. Créezy has become quite an artist and has inveigled me to pose for her. Her plan is to send you the result to help you. Astra is a bit dubious about whether it will really help but agrees it is worth a go. She also borrowed Flying Eagle's camera and got Astra to give me a nice relaxing massage before taking what Flying Eagle calls porno photographs of me. These are to be sent digitally to Jezzie for you so that only you two will be able to see them. The massage was nice, so I'm not complaining, but the same effect could have been achieved just by getting me to concentrate on thinking of you.

48

Fair Exchange

In my last letter I mentioned the survey that Flying Eagle was conducting at Thayview. She has produced an outline design for the power station on coastal land that I had acquired on behalf of WwW. A team of real experts are coming from Geos to do the detailed design and run the project. We have already engaged some local labour and some of the ground work has been started, both on the cliff-side itself and in laying cables and roadworks to connect both Routh and Louth.

However we don't have to wait for this long-term project to complete before enjoying some of the advantages of electric power. Several local projects have taken place all over the WF. In particular I now have electricity at Thayview, both on the farm and the tower. This is provided by a combination of solar panels and a wind generator, all with battery storage. Similar installations here at South Beach and a wind generator and tidal power generator at the observatory have meant that we have electricity on all three of our properties. We are less advanced in Louth but do have some solar panels there which enables us to have some electric lighting and the ability to power a computer. Astra and I have each been given laptops and are learning to use them. We can't do email yet but Flying Eagle hopes that we will be able to get the necessary infrastructure for a network connection sometime before the end of the Autumn selenth.

We had a bit of a farewell party for Colonel Jacky before she left to return to Geos and to welcome her successor as head of the KNN mission. Her name is Jero Dicks who is a career diplomat and has a lot of experience in overseeing educational exchange programmes to other nations on Geos. Her last posting was as ambassador to New Hope which apparently is a close ally of both the KNN and NN having also been founded as a KNN colony some two hundred and fifty years ago on the antipodal side of Geos from the KNN. At the party we were served some Geosian beer from the KNN. This was very good, reminding me of some of my favourites from Isla. While you're there you should try it. It's called WPA, standing for Western Pale Ale. It's a very light coloured beer but with bags of flavour characteristic of those normally of a deeper chestnut colour.

I'm off to bed now as I need to rise early for the journey to Louth. I shall be trying out our latest prototype SPC model with an electric engine. The battery is charging up at the moment and I'm hoping to set a new record time for the journey with both the engine and me pedalling. We'll then see whether to go ahead with production.

Lots of love

Arté

7
Jezzie's Project

Louth: Ph 2 Pd 21 (6/Autumn) 2614

Dear Jezzie

Flying Eagle explained your project to me and I thought I should write to you directly with the information. Zorro and I are also very concerned about Rastu. As you say, Duplosian women have a much stronger libido than Geosians (or indeed Duplosian men). It is true that we are by no means all the same and Rastu is on one extreme of the spectrum and compared to most of us is abstemious to a fault. Zorro or I would go nuts if we did without for more than a period or so, whereas Rastu was fully capable of managing a selenth of celibacy when engaged in her studies. However, even she needed to scratch her itch eventually to keep sane. It's true that Astra used to be almost totally celibate for a number of years but she had some unusual hang-ups and the desire does reduce as we get older. But Rastu is still in her twenties, pretty much at the peak level.

I've never been pregnant myself but I've consulted one or two friends and they say that in the later stages of pregnancy and after the birth they did experience a temporary lessening of desire, but not to the extent of total abstinence. My conclusion is that you are right to be worried, and in the absence of a man for her it is worth trying something else. We do have dildos here but they aren't very common because it's not usually difficult to get a real man to help you out. Zorro tells me she had recourse to them in the past when marooned on the observatory island during Astra's winter observation season. However, she said they were pretty unsatisfactory and didn't really help much.

Twin Worlds II

You've rightly gathered that our physiology differs from yours and I attach a more graphic description. Flying Eagle suggests this should be enciphered so as not to offend the sensibilities of anyone who might inadvertently see it. I've also included some illustrations, both in drawings and photographs, Flying Eagle describes these as pornographic and says they are also to be transmitted in enciphered form. She says you will have a program to decipher them. She has used your public key, so I suppose you know what to do.

For the female pictures I have used myself as the model. Rastu is slightly smaller than me if measurements are crucial. I had to use a bit of subterfuge to get Arté to pose for the male pictures. He thinks that Rastu has asked Astra to send them to help her. Actually I am quite pleased with the full size drawing of Arté and think Rastu will indeed like to have it.

If you are successful in your endeavours to apply your advanced technology please let me know. The market here could be massive and our company, Wheels-within-Wheels, would be keen to exploit it.

Yours in friendship

Créezy

Camford, KNN: W 6 Pd 21 (12/Autumn) 2614

Dear Créezy

Thanks for all the info you sent me, and the pictures. I think your drawing of Arté is fabulous and Rastu will love it when I give it to her. I found your information really interesting and I'm sure I'm going to come up with a suitable design. Yes, by our rather prudish standards, your photos would be considered pornographic, but actually they are very instructional for my purpose.

I'm taking Rastu on a break to one of the KNN continental capitals. The society there is avant-garde and they have a more open approach to sexuality than here on the islands, and especially compared with New Norland. I find it healthier, but then I am considered to be a bit way-out in my attitudes. They have a few of what are called sex-shops and I will be able to get the materials I need. I first noticed something was wrong when we were in Q city and Rastu was in the habit of having a cold bath after writing or receiving mail from Arté. Fortunately you Duplosians are much less inhibited talking about these things than we are and I was able to discuss it with her, and then wrote to Flying Eagle.

I've been working on my design for a while and have written the software to make it 'smart'. That is one of my specialities, AI software, which stands for artificial intelligence, but is really about arranging sensors to capture information about an environment and using that to govern the behaviour of a machine employing feedback loops for learning. Usually I do this for autopiloting aircraft but the principles apply more generally to any machines required to respond to their environment.

Anyway, thanks again for your assistance. Certainly if it works out I can see it could be quite important for other visitors over here from Duplos, and indeed if there's a ready market over there I don't see why you shouldn't be the ones to take advantage.

Yours, Jezzie.

Twin Worlds II

Camford, KNN: W 2 Pd 23 (22/Autumn) 2614

Dearest Arté

I'm afraid this may be shorter than usual as I have to write to Créezy with rather more details, which I don't want to bore you with - as it's all girl stuff. My brain is currently more concerned with sex than Maths.

Before that, I ought to tell you a bit about the investiture. Brigadier Zir Jacky Jackson, as she now is, Jezzie and I all went to the palace for a private audience with the King. It was all very grand. She gave us a tour of her art gallery and then we had the special investiture. Jacky was knighted, she received various insignia of office and was tapped on the shoulder with a sword as she knelt on one knee on a stool specially provided for the purpose. Then Jezzie was presented with a medal to make her a Lieutenant of the order of the North. Finally I was called forward and presented with honorary citizenship of the KNN and also a medal for LN. After that we all went to Zir Jacky's club (The Royal Military Club) which is just a short walk from the palace. There we had a slap up lunch. Jacky's partner and children were also there along with Jezzie's parents. They had all been at the palace to watch our investiture.

Afterwards we all returned to the palace except for the younger children. Jacky's oldest child is eighteen and allowed to come with us. We were invited to a garden party in the palace grounds. The King holds several such parties each year. It's quite an honour to be invited. There was quite a crowd there and we all had a very pleasant tea. The King came up to us briefly for a few words. Jezzie's parents were so thrilled and rightly proud of Jezzie. We were also a centre of attraction as I am very much a novelty and people wanted to be photographed with me. I've become a bit of what they call a celebrity, which can be somewhat tiring, but people mean well.

We also had to endure a press conference and TV interview. When I eventually got back home I had a good long bath and went early to bed until Artur woke me with a hard kick. It's becoming clear that he has ambitions to become a footballer. Football is a very popular game here in the KNN and the best players are very definitely celebrities.

Jezzie and I have also been on a short break to Shopharbour which is the capital of one of the continental kingdoms in the KNN. It was fascinating and very different from what I have seen here in Camford or in New Norland. We stayed in a spa hotel and had a wonderfully relaxing time. We also did lots of sightseeing and visited a number of museums. One maritime museum was devoted to ships and life at sea. It was fascinating. Their ancestors in ancient times were so brave to go out on the oceans in quite flimsy ships. They were also fierce warriors and must have been terrifying to the communities they raided and plundered. Fortunately all this was hundreds of years ago and today the people are really friendly.

While there, Jezzie got the material for a project she has been working on secretly because she has been worried about my lack of sex life. She has invented what she calls an intelligent vibrator. She has designed it specifically for the female Duplosian anatomy. And it is just wonderful. The 'intelligent' bit is actually also interesting from a scientific and engineering point of view. She used her specialist expertise on that. The vibrator picks up signals from my body and is able to respond to my physical needs, learning just what I like and when. It is uncanny.

It will never replace you, but is very much the next best thing. I won't need cold baths any more! I can scratch my own itch and dream of you.

As well as helping Jezzie with anatomical information, Créezy also produced a beautiful drawing of you, but I guess you know that. Anyway I have two life-size copies. One is framed and hanging in my bedroom. The other has been laminated, that is enclosed in a waterproof transparent coating, and I have attached it to the ceiling above my bath. I can attach the vibrator, lie in a warm bath and dream you are with me as I lie back and enjoy it, seeing you above me when I open my eyes.

I am longing to be back with you again, but Jezzie's gift makes it much easier for me and I'm sure also improves my temper.

I must now write to Créezy to thank her for her part.

All my love

Aimée

Camford, KNN: W 2 Pd 23 (22/Autumn) 2614

Dear Créezy

Thank-you for the lovely drawing of Arté and for your part in Jezzie's intelligent vibrator.

This is magic. I've asked Jezzie to make others for you and Zorro so you can see just how well they work and assess the potential. I understand you have already mentioned the possibility of commercial exploitation. Jezzie deserves to make a fortune from her invention.

It's difficult to know where to begin. This vibrator is about as similar to a dildo as as an ant is to a person. Firstly it has the functionality of both a penis and a bump, which is something that no dildo ever managed. Then the actual material feels lifelike. If you went by feel alone you would think you had a real man. Finally there is the 'intelligence'. The vibrator is self-lubricating, it receives signals from you body and adjusts its lubrication and its actions: speed, depth, pressure etcetera in response to its evaluation of your needs. This it does using a learning algorithm that over time tailors its responses to you. You can also make some interventions, speeding it up or slowing it down, but after a while it seems to know what you want before you know it yourself.

Of course it can't give you the emotional connection of a real person, which is as well. It would be awful if it came to replace actual live sex but it does provide a seriously good option when real sex is unavailable.

Another feature is that it can keep going as long as you want without incurring any hurt. If use of this device can replace the more extreme behaviour of girls like those who hurt Arté that time in Routh, or my brother all those years ago, it will provide a real service to society.

Being somewhat conservative in these matters, I'm not so convinced about the efficacy of some of the other possibilities of the technology. However, it is possible to deploy the vibrator between two women in a way that enables them to obtain the full physical pleasure of sex with a man, but without a man having to be present. I can see that this might be useful for those few women who really don't care for sex with a man. It could also help friends who want to share a session but don't have a suitable man available. As you know, I've never really been into shared sex. I really do need a very close relationship with someone first.

Thanks again for your part.

Love

Rastu

8

Further Developments on Duplos

Louth: Ph 3 Pd 23 (15/Autumn) 2614

Dearest Aimée

Your obstetrician and midwife have arrived on Duplos and came to see me and Astra yesterphase. They seem very nice and we're relieved that you will be in such good hands for the birth of baby Artur. They are going to be based in Louth while they are here and at first will just observe births. Before they leave they will give our doctors some advice based on their experience of advanced medicine and will also gain some practice in Duplosian births. They say their visit will be quite rushed because of the need to get back to you in time. They are observing their first two births tophase.

Flying Eagle called for the last time a couple of phases ago. She is now on the way back to join Wild Cat for their own birth. She says that our network in Louth will go live very soon. Astra and I each have two email addresses. I shall be arte@wheels.co.wf.dp and also, once the connection to Routh goes live about a period later will also have an address at our university, arte@routh.ac.wf.dp. Astra's addresses are astra@louth.ac.wf.dp and astra@wheels.co.wf.dp. Other addresses you might want are zorro@wheels.co.wf.dp, creezy@wheels.co.wf.dp and fermos@routh.ac.wf.dp. Zorro is also establishing a website for the company. Flying Eagle tells me you will be able to see it at www.wheels.co.wf.dp. How far we have come in such a short time since meeting our Geosian friends.

Twin Worlds II

Work has started on the power station but our plans for Isla are on hold for a while for political reasons. You may know more about this but I gather that there are some problems on Geos between different countries and the New Norland Geosians want to establish a 'protocol' between us before engaging on any explorations on Duplos. Créezy and I don't think our Isla project should get caught up in this, after all Isla is not unexplored territory. We were both born there and know it quite well. However, Stripy Tiger says that they are being super-cautious for internal Geos political reasons and we will have to wait before they can sanction drone flights over the strait, let alone an actual visit.

A conference is planned in Goddess City under Jero Dicks' chairmanship to come up with this draft protocol. Fermos and Créezy are both involved. Actually, from the WF point of view the proposals are uncontroversial. It's all about respecting the rights of indigenous populations in unexplored territories and agreements not to use certain advanced weapons and things like that. Indeed much of the protocol merely extends and formalises the agreements made at Kongholm. Here on Duplos the Shadowlanders could be awkward but I think they'll probably fall into line eventually. The GSE are largely content but there are some proposals regarding slavery that concern them and there will have to be some quite nuanced drafting to keep them on side.

To be honest we in the WF and the Geosians here present would like to see slavery abolished by all signatories of the protocol. That is not yet practical but we do want to ensure that there is no question of taking slaves from as yet unexplored territories, or by Geosians from anywhere on Duplos. Stripy Tiger says that although officially there is no slavery anywhere on Geos, there are countries whose practises are considered by New Norland and its allies to be tantamount to the same thing.

Créezy is also probably being realistic when she says that she cannot assume the authority to sign up Isla to an abolitionist agenda, but is prepared to impose a ban on them exporting their current practises. Thus just as with runaways from the GSE, any Islanders would become automatically free on arrival in the WF. She says it would serve them right if the price of their disgusting practise is that an Islander woman would have to choose between celibacy and emancipation if she wants to visit the WF!

It's funny how I, as a former slave, am much less vehement in my opposition than the privileged upper class Créezy.

Even though our Isla project has been put on hold, we are still going ahead with some of the work at this end. I have had a number of discussions with the Geosian Engineers and we have come up with what I think is an excellent solution for the short term. They agree that a bridge would be feasible but would probably take several years to build and would offer a number of technical challenges. Direct ferries across the strait have been ruled out, although a longer ferry service between Soubanc and West Isla does seem to be an option using Geosian maritime technology.

The preferred solution is what they call a cable car. The short crossing of the strait is to be bridged by a strong cable in a loop, akin to my railcart arrangement on observatory island. Cars will hang from the cable and with the aid of electricity the cable will circulate carrying the cars from the continent to Isla and back again. There are still some challenges, but the technology is well understood on Geos. WwW has started the construction project at our end. Créezy and I have agreed to accept the political risk that Thay (because it will be up to her) might refuse permission for the other end. Créezy says all we have to do is to persuade Shay to oppose the plan and then Thay will automatically assent. I regret to say she's probably right.

Astra has just come up with the suggestion that we should try out a cable car on observatory island. Now we've got electricity there we could rig something up between the bungalow, the tower and the other side of the causeway. It seems to me it's worth a go and I'll see what the Geosians say about it.

I feel bad that we are taking some of these decisions for WwW without involving you. However, once we have the email going it ought to be possible to have you joining in our board discussions and voting again.

One last piece of news. Fermos called in on her way to Goddess City. The university council at Routh have agreed that from next academic year they will admit men as full undergraduate or postgraduate students and allow then to be awarded degrees. They will be the first university on the planet to do so. Fermos kindly said that it was all credit to my achievements and that further it was agreed that I should be awarded the degrees of Master of Mathematics and Doctor of Philosophy at their new year graduation ceremony. So you'll have to call me Dr Arté now!

Until next time by email, all my love

Arté

9
Email finally arrives

W 3 Pd 24 (27/Autumn) 2014

From rastu@camford.ac.knn to arte@wheels.co.wf.dp

Dearest Arté

How fantastic, to be able to email you. I've got quite used to it over here, and am in regular contact with Wild Cat in New Norland as well as sending emails within the university here, and even to Jezzie despite living in the same house. Over here email is quite informal and we just send off brief notes to each other, omitting honorifics etc. But with you I want to continue to use 'Dearest' and 'love', and will continue to do so.

Wild Cat is really pleased to have Flying Eagle back at last. They are having a bit of a holiday to celebrate. Their baby is due in about a work's time (that's five periods). Artur should be arriving about a period later, I'm getting incredibly fat and my tits are really heavy. The extra gravity is taking its toll on my body. I do hope you'll still find me attractive. I promise I'll work really hard at exercise to get my shape back.

Politics over here are getting quite worrying. They have an organisation called the Forum of Nations where the various countries try to talk through their differences to avoid going to war. It's much more serious here than it would be on Duplos. They have invented the most fearsome weapons that can wipe out an entire city of millions of people at one go, leaving a poisonous hole in the ground where nobody can go safely for centuries. They've managed to avoid using them so far but they still have some disputes that end up with fighting and even their so-called conventional weapons can wreak devastation on a scale that is unimaginable to us.

There are twenty-three separate countries on Geos ranging from a small island with a population of about two million to the Eastern Empire and New Norland that are vast with populations to match. These two can agree on nothing, rather like us and the Shadowlands Union. I must say that I am with NN, the Empire sounds quite evil, though even they are not the worst. The Grand People's Republic manages to keep almost its entire population enslaved, in practical rather than 'official' terms.

The visit to Duplos has triggered a crisis with the Empire, who are livid that NN got there first. I have to say it's good for us that they did. Every sign is that the EE would have sought to exploit our planet's resources without giving anything in return and using us as cheap labour. The protocols you are working on offer the best protection for our planet. Politically for us, I think it is important to convince the SU that they should sign up too. A united Duplos with NN/KNN backing is the best chance we have to maintain our freedoms against any threat from the Geosian Eastern Empire.

Congratulations on your degrees. Probably I should have said that first. This is no more than you deserve and it makes me proud to be a graduate of Routh. Perhaps when I get back I can at last persuade my school to take boys as well as girls. We wouldn't have to mix them in dormitories like they do here. That wouldn't work with most teenage Duplosian girls. The poor boys would get worn out every night!

The cable car sounds like a good idea. I've seen one in New Norland at a ski resort. They do look a bit scary, and they usually get shut down in bad weather. High winds are the problem. The one I saw was relatively short, about a quarter of a walk, but Jezzie says there are some that cover a greater distance. Even so, crossing the strait could be quite a challenge.

Lots of love

Aimée

Ph 2 Pd 24 (18/Autumn)

From arte@wheels.co.wf.dp to rastu@camford.ac.knn

Dearest Aimée

Wow, how exciting to get an email from you and to able to reply in almost real time. You're right about the cable car. It will be a challenge, as we are finding with our mini-project of installing one at the observatory. I'm on the island at the moment where I've been discussing it with the builders. We are going ahead though. We've designed the cars, which will hold four people. The ones for the crossing to Isla will be a bit bigger. We are going to have one loop with three stations, at the observatory tower, the bungalow and on the continental shore. There will be four equally spaced cars such that when one is at the bungalow, another will be at the tower and the other two out of reach. That will be the normal 'rest' position. The cable can be moved in either direction and a car can be summoned to the shore station when needed. The cable is being manufactured at the moment and the installation of supports is going to start next period. We hope to have it running for the start of the winter observation season. As you suggest, the strait crossing will be much more challenging. Because we can't provide supports in the sea bed we will need a minimum of five walks for the central span. The engineers say that is more than they have ever done on Geos, but they think that in our lower gravity, it can be achieved. The cables will hang in a catenary (y = cosh x) shape from high towers on each cliff.

I've copied the political bit of your email to Fermos and Créezy. They are both working very hard on the protocol with Jero and Stripy Tiger. As I understand it, there is broad agreement between the Geosians and the WF and that the GSE will accept the main principles. The SU are still being difficult. It's not that they are against anything specific so much as they don't trust the WF and suspect we are trying to stitch them up in some way.

Take care of yourself

Love

Arté

Part 2: Politics

10
The Geos-Duplos Accords

Stripy Tiger stood up to greet xer guests. "It's good of you to come. Your email is very much to the point and I think it best that we take it forward face to face rather than by further email exchange. Please take a seat." Xe pointed them to a table around which were half a dozen chairs. "Jero Dicks will join us in about a quarter of a horum, but first I would like to give you my perspective on the issues you raise. Coffee?"

"Yes please, black for me and with a splash of cold milk for Créezy." Fermos sat down opposite Stripy and Créezy took the chair on her right. A secretary came in with the coffees and some biscuits.

"Rastu has it pretty well to rights. Back on Geos we are very concerned about the intentions of the Eastern Empire. Among the twenty-three countries on the planet, there is a wide variety of Government and developmental status. However, just two powers are of major concern to us. The Eastern Empire and the Grand People's Republic.

The GPRG is by far the nastier regime, its very small ruling class has a tight grip on the population which is held in abject poverty and complete ignorance of the rest of the world. The myth they are peddled is that the rest of the planet is ruled by warlords with no regard for the people. In contrast the dear leader and xer family have ensured that all the people in the GPRG are treated equally and enjoy the highest standard of living possible. The only truth in this is that the people are indeed treated equally, to equal misery. The only land border is with the EE who are content to seal it off and assist the GPRG to maintain its isolation.

We have some concerns about military developments in the GPRG but technologically they are quite primitive and a long way from developing any sort of space-going capability. Nor do they appear to have any ambitions in that direction.

On the other hand the EE do have capability and ambition. They are a more open society than the GPRG but nevertheless the majority of citizens have few political rights and are oppressed in a number of ways. The Government is theoretically democratic but in practice is a dictatorship with power held by a few individuals backed by the military and a strong police presence.

In the context of Duplos our concern is that the EE would like to exploit the resources of the planet while exporting its oppressive regime, keeping Duplos firmly under its control with little regard for the wishes or welfare of Duplosians.

Before we came here, the EE did all it could to whip up opposition to our plans in the hope of delaying us long enough for them to catch up technologically and get here first. They do have a space capability and indeed sent rockets into space in the fiftween-fiftwies before we did. They haven't advanced as fast as us, but, with the help of espionage, our experts consider they could launch a space station within the next two years and probably carry out an expedition to Duplos within five."

"Is there nothing you can do to stop them, or at least to delay?"

"Short of war, we don't think we can stop them. We could in theory blow a station out of space, but so could they. The last thing we need is to have us taking pot-shots at each other's space assets, or to export war to Duplos. The EE leaders are rational, and will avoid military action that might destroy themselves along with the rest of Geos, but they would not be so careful over here. We are certainly not prepared to risk war."

"No we wouldn't want that, Rastu tells us you have fearsome weapons that could destroy much of the planet."

"Rastu is right. We think our best bet is to tie things up here as best we can to enable us to protect you back on Geos. If we can get the majority of countries to sign up to an agreement on how we conduct relations, we will have the moral high ground in the Forum and make it much more difficult for the EE to interfere with your rights over your planet, or otherwise behave improperly towards you. The more agreement we can get between the territories here, the easier it will be to force compliance on Geos and prevent the EE from exploiting divisions between you."

"Right", said Fermos, "that's why it's important for us to get the SU on board, even though we are going to be uncomfortable with the concessions we might have to make. Does it mean we just have to cave in to them?"

"No, you don't have to do that. We genuinely need the protocols to meet your needs too, but it is going to be important to win the trust of the SU and the GSE that this is not about the WF gaining advantage at their expense. Nowhere is this likely to be more important than in exploration of Duplos beyond the boundaries of your existing territories."

"Like the second continent," Créezy chipped in, speaking for the first time.

"Indeed, or for that matter this continent south of the desert belt or the various unexplored islands."

"At least Isla isn't unexplored and there is already general agreement between the continental territories that it is the province of the WF."

"You're right as far as it goes, Créezy. But it's still best to be cautious. Wait until we get these accords signed off and I assure you we will then be able to make some progress there."

At that juncture, the secretary came in and announced that Jero had arrived.

"You've arrived right on cue, Jero, I've been explaining how these accords are important for managing the Geosian politics, following some insightful comments from Rastu."

"Yes, it might be helpful if we could get Rastu to address the Forum in support of the accords once we've got them agreed here. Let me lay out the process as I see it."

"Our first job is for the four of us to come up with a draft, to lay before the meeting here in Goddess City. We should incorporate as many of the suggestions made by the GSE and SU people as we can and then, after we've got that improved and polished, we need to gain ratification from the territories here as far as possible. The informal meetings we've all had so far suggest that we should get WF and GSE acceptance, and of course Isla," nodding to Créezy. "Our local difficulty is with the SU, but I think we ought to be able to get at least partial agreement from them, with perhaps reservations on just a few minor matters. To be blunt, the sort of thing we need to avoid is the possibility for the

EE to come here and bribe the SU with a promise of sovereignty over the second continent."

"At the cost of losing all sovereignty to the EE," opined Stripy Tiger.

"Indeed. Then once we've achieved our goal here, we will need to present it to the Forum on Geos. We can be certain of the votes from New Norland, KNN and New Hope. I have every reason to expect Midgeos and Souland to sign up as well as the minor nations".

"The minor nations?", queried Fermos.

"We have a few nation states with low populations, mainly small islands, rather like Isla here I suppose. Peace, Southsea Island, the Paradise Islands, and Frioland. I can't see why any of them would demur. Haven will vote opposite to the GPRG and thus undoubtedly be with us. That leaves the six countries in Sylvania and the five on the South-West continent. We can assume the GPRG will be against us on principle and that the EE might use its veto. In that worst case we need a total of fourtween nations on board. The above list gives us ten so we need to win over six of the others."

"We ought to be able to do that ", claimed Stripy Tiger, " especially with a strong showing from Duplos. Ideal would be vocal support from all three continental territories, but an official report from a senior Duplosian politician backed up by Rastu could swing it for us."

"There's also the possibility that, recognising its poor position, the EE would not use its veto but just abstain, in which case a simple majority of countries voting will suffice, and that will be in the bag. But we must plan on the basis of the worst case scenario."

"How do you suggest we proceed?" Said Fermos.

"I think we should produce a first draft paper, today. I propose doing so under four main headings: viz., Peoples Rights, Trade and Exchange, Interplanetary Travel and Exploration and Development."

Créezy interpolated, "I guess the anti-slavery clauses should come under the first heading."

"That's right. But here I think we will have to make some concessions to current Duplosian reality. I know the WF would like to use this opportunity to push the abolitionist agenda, and we certainly support that aim. But it is vital that we get the other territories on side, and the real focus in the context of these accords must be to protect Duplos from exploitation of their labour by unscrupulous elements from Geos."

"Yes we understand that, and indeed with my Isla hat on, I would be unable to deliver approval of abolition, but we could perhaps include some aspirational statements to encourage improvements. For example there has always been some discomfort about taking female slaves from raids in the wild lands. I think we could readily ban such slavery in private ownership and perhaps make moves towards ending female slavery altogether other than as a judicial penalty following a proper trial. Freeing men will be trickier but a start could be made by just allowing for the possibility of emancipation."

Fermos then added. "In the WF, slavery is limited to judicial penalty. I think the best way forward on that is for us to redefine what is meant by slavery to exclude properly imposed penal servitude. Although I am no longer in the Federation parliament, I am active with a group that is pushing in that direction. This group hopes to introduce a bill into the next session that will tighten up existing penalties. For example it will insist on time-limited sentences and restrict the type of servitude allowed. It will also exclude any requirement for sexual services and define some basic rights for the convicts. I would like to see this as a model for penal servitude throughout the planet."

"That's a welcome step, Fermos, I'm sure it can be included as a model for all to follow. What I'm more concerned about is how we word things so that the SU and GSE are prepared to sign up, while also ensuring at least there is no further spread of their practises. I'm thinking that we can exclude the SU's feudal system from the definition of slavery while preventing its export to new territory. The GSE is more difficult, we probably just have to acknowledge current custom while encouraging its demise. One thing we might get away with is to use a general ban on export of slaves between planets to also cover movement of slaves between territories, thereby giving interterritorial force to the current WF asylum laws for escaped slaves."

"I think we can live with that. I can see how these clauses should be written, let's move on, or do you have anything to add, Créezy?"

Créezy shook her head.

"OK, the other thing we want to cover under people's rights is the treatment of any inhabitants that we might find outside the current de facto territories here. From our point of view these are all land on the main continent south of the northern desert belt or north and east of the mountain ranges that delimit the current Shadowlands Union administration, the second continent and various islands in the ocean of the world. This will come up again in more detail when we discuss the fourth heading."

"That's probably said enough on peoples rights for the time being," said Stripy Tiger. "Let's move to trade and exchange. The goal here must surely be to prevent unfair exploitation by Geosian countries and to give Duplosian territories control over the pace of exchange so as not to overwhelm them or to destroy their economies. The thrust of the matter is that any country on Geos or territory on Duplos must sign up to these accords in order to benefit from knowledge exchange or trade. That is what should give teeth to the accords and thus give the best chance of guaranteeing Duplosian sovereignty over your own planet. We should then carry on with some more detail to control exports. For example we need to take great care in the export of military technology from Geos to Duplos, mutual protection of our planets' biodiversity and limitations on technologies that on Geos have proved harmful to the environment.

We have noticed that the territories here make some use of coal, for example in metallurgy and for some heating in the colder regions. This is something which needs to be managed carefully. With your tiny population of just a few million in the three continental territories, you are nowhere near to either exhausting supply or causing major environmental problems. However, on Geos with a population of over a twousand twillion (i.e. billions) we have done significant damage to the planet and our climate. We want you to learn from our mistakes, which is one reason we have gone ahead with the sustainable electrification projects we have started in the WF.

"More minor stuff that usually takes the effort in trade discussions are really too far down in the weeds for these accords. I mean things like tariffs. The main purpose of tariffs is to protect industries from unfair competition from cheap imports. The logistical issues and volume limitations of transport between the planets are such that these considerations are minor and we need do no more than acknowledge the right of territories and countries to impose such tariffs, but leave any negotiations for when they become necessary. Initially, New Norland and the KNN will work on a tariff-free basis."

Fermos responded, "I don't think the accords will be too contentious over here, as long as we keep it generic and leave the individual territories the right to some control as to what is imported. We are developing a process to control knowledge exchange and technology transfer for the WF. The GSE has been working with us to some extent. The SU are more wary about anything that they think might cause social upheaval or otherwise weaken the grip they have over their peasant population but I don't think the challenges are insurmountable. We should try to ensure that the next steps in knowledge transfer are more international over here. For example when we send academics to Geos next year it would be best if the WF didn't have a monopoly."

"That brings us neatly into the third heading. We don't want to see a free-for-all in population movement between the two planets. Nor do we want to see wealthy Geosians buying up your planet or swamping your resources with numbers of tourists or settlers. Your population is sufficiently small that Geos could cope with any likely influx but there will still be issues to address. We need to establish principles for local control of numbers and land tenure. For example, we advise that any land tenure on Duplos by Geosians should be subject to reversion to Duplosian ownership after a fixed time limit. We also need to lay down some basic rights and duties for visitors."

Stripy Tiger then added, "we also shouldn't forget rules about citizenship, you don't get a lot of movement between territories here on Duplos and for the most part your citizenship is determined by where you are born. On Geos there is much more interchange between countries and things get much more complicated. We need to have some mutual understanding about these matters. For example, if a Duplosian has a baby on Geos does it become Geosian and vice-versa."

"I'm afraid that the KNN has rather jumped the gun here by awarding Rastu honorary citizenship and announcing that her baby would also have KNN nationality. While it's a lovely gesture in the particular case I don't think it's a helpful precedent," commented Jero.

"I didn't know that," added Fermos, "and I agree with you about precedent. I think that we should make a general principle that everyone should have their primary citizenship on their ancestral planet. Here on Duplos that would be the citizenship of their mother. Thus baby Artur should have WF citizenship, regardless of his forthcoming birth in the KNN. If we then also allow for exceptional granting of citizenship by a Geosian country, that would be OK but secondary in some sense and there should be no requirement on a Geosian country to grant such citizenship to a Duplosian just because she or he happens to have been born there."

"Very helpful", responded Jero. "We should be able to express that idea in the accords. We would need to make it explicit because it is slightly different from the situation on Geos and would be an example where Geosians and Duplosians are treated differently. That is, in this aspect there would be discrimination on the grounds of ancestry, which is contrary to the general thrust of these accords."

"Absolutely," Stripy agreed, "but that really is the point of the accords. To lay down a general principle of equality of treatment and non-discrimination while also determining specific exceptions on practical grounds, without breaching the higher principles of mutual respect for individuals or for the other planet's culture."

A penny dropped for Créezy. "I'm beginning to really get the point of all this. It's more than just a way of managing current international politics on Geos or interterritorial rivalry on Duplos. All this work we are doing is going to set a template for generations to come. It's really of fundamental importance."

"Yes it is, which is why we Geosians on the ground are giving it our highest priority and delaying more practical stuff like helping you explore other parts of your planet until we've got agreement on these higher goals. I don't think our third heading will be contentious here. On Geos there will be some small disappointment at limits on tourism to Duplos and on commercial opportunities; but the reasoning will be understood and supported. The main contention will be the de facto control by New Norland. The Eastern Empire will certainly not accept that position and there will be moves for international control of our space stations and all sorts of bureaucratic nonsense will be inserted into the practical workings of interplanetary exchange. However, we are resigned to that and are prepared to manage it. Indeed it is such considerations that caused me to be asked to lead this working group rather than a New Norlander like Stripy.

If we now turn to the fourth heading. Although there is a dimension of Geosian interest here, the main impact is for

Duplos. From the Geosian point of view we want to avoid serious disputes between your three territories over the spoils of exploration and, despite our non-interference rules want to ensure you have proper regard for the ecologies of your unexplored lands. If you like, we intend to force our non-interference principles on you."

"I think Créezy and I both understand that. As things stand the WF doesn't really have territorial claims over the rest of the planet. We have an historic position regarding Isla, that will no longer be purely academic. But as Créezy has already pointed out, Isla is not completely unknown territory. We also have unspecified claims over islands in the Sea of Storms which are disputed by the Shadowlanders. More contentious will be the claims of Shadowlands and the GSE to the rest of the continent, let alone the second continent and other large islands that appear on your globe."

"What I want to propose is that we agree some primacy on the continent giving the leadership of exploratory expeditions to a Duplosian of the appropriate territory but with the parties all being constituted inter-territorially and with Geosian advisors within the expedition. The second continent is very much a special case and maybe initially a Geosian might lead an interterritorial expedition. Finally we could also divide the leadership of expeditions to distant islands between you all."

"Seems sound in principle, I can see that this is where there will be considerable room for horse-trading and squabbling." Fermos smiled and shook her head as she spoke."

Jero was pleased with the progress so far, but it had been a long and quite tiring session. Xe suggested a horum's break for some lunch after which they should break out and go into drafting session.

There was much to-ing and fro-ing between them all as they individually wrote straw-men clauses and then debated and polished them in pairs or all together. Finally after several hora, Jero pronounced that xe thought they had got as far as they were going to and they should sleep on it and return next phase to look with fresh eyes.

So it was, and after a shortish review the quartet agreed that the draft was ready to expose to the wider group, which included the representatives of the GSE and Shadowlands as well as Astra and other involved parties from the WF and Geos.

11
Ratification on Duplos

General Petrova was bemused. She hadn't expected the Feds to be so reasonable. Obviously the Geosians had put some pressure on them, but the accords were much more favourable than she had anticipated. She had hardly had to fight to get the Shadowland serfdom excluded from the definition of slavery despite the strong views she knew to be held both by the Geosians and the Feds. Fermos, in particular, had an interterritorial reputation as a liberal on all social matters. Also, while that ex-islander, Créezy, had to make some concessions to the practices on Isla; it was clear that at a personal level she was totally opposed to all aspects of slavery. It was almost as though they had agreed concessions before Jero even presented her draft.

Otherwise she would have liked to see less interterritorial involvement in decisions on trade and exchange but perfectly understood why it had to be this way. At a personal level she even accepted the more contentious results of the haggling over exploration and development of new lands on Duplos. All-in-all she felt she could recommend that the SU sign up to the accords. On the other hand she also recognised that getting that recommendation accepted would be challenging and she was not at all confident of success.

She mused on how events over the past two selenths had catapulted her into the centre of world politics. She had been just an obscure colonel in charge of a small military border force in the remote north-western corner of the union. Then she got orders right from the heart of government to cross the border in force to discover what was going on around Kongholm and ensure that Shadowlands was included in whatever was going on.

In the event she acknowledged to herself, it had been easy. The Geosians were keen to deal with the whole planet. Of course back in the centre, her bosses didn't know that and she received an overnight promotion to Major General, was awarded an HSU[3] and put in charge of the mission to the aliens with directions as to the union's political priorities.

Billini of the GSE was also pleased with the accords, but less surprised. She had had to fight hard, she thought, on the slavery issue. The only concession she had had to make was acceptance of the WF's position on slaves in their territory. The GSE had always disputed the WF's law that granted freedom to any slave arriving in their territory. However, they knew that in reality there was nothing they could do about it, and being forced to acknowledge the position was no more than accepting the status quo. Elsewhere, she was pleased with the outcome of the negotiations over the new lands, which were as accommodating to GSE interests as she could have reasonably expected. After all there was no way that the second continent would have been handed to the GSE. She could not only recommend acceptance to her government but was confident that the recommendation would be accepted.

Indeed ratification by both the WF and the GSE was almost immediate. Similarly Créezy signed on behalf of Isla but with the reservation that she didn't really have the locus to do so.

Petrova had a harder time. Her successes were acknowledged but there was unease about the trade agreements which her

3 Heroine of the Shadowlands Union

government thought were too favourable to the WF; and they didn't like agreements being regulated at planetary level. They wanted the ability to strike individual deals with specific Geosian countries without international sanction. They were also dissatisfied with the 'new lands'. They thought the compromise on the continent was too much in favour of the GSE and they wanted the second continent to be divided between the three powers. They had in mind that the division should be proportional to the size of the territories on the main continent. Petrova realised her bosses were living in cloud cuckoo land and worked hard to try to convince them that obduracy on these points would only be to their disadvantage in practical terms.

Unfortunately she was only partly successful. Shadowlands agreed to only a partial ratification. They accepted the provisions under the peoples' rights and travel headings but entered reservations under trade and exploration.

Back in Goddess City the Geosians were disappointed with the partial acceptance from the SU but were not entirely surprised, and realised it could have been a lot worse. On 1/Winter 2614. The accords were remitted to Geos for debate in the Forum of Nations.

12
Progress on Geos

W 2 Pd 28 (5/Winter) 2014

From RASTU to ARTE

cc fermos@routh.ac.wf.dp; astra@louth.ac.wf.dp; creezy@wheels.co.wf.dp

Dearest Arté

I thought I should update you all on what is happening here with the accords. As you know Gavos has arrived over here as the WF ambassador. She flew over to the KNN to meet me and then we went together to speak to a meeting of the Forum of Nations in support of the accords. It was good to see someone from home and to speak Contish again. (Actually Jezzie and I do converse in Contish occasionally but that is really to help Jezzie with the language). Gavos has a couple of men in her party and she kindly offered to ask one of them to 'give me some home comfort'. She then looked at my enormous belly and chuckled. Thus I was able to refuse her offer with good grace. Anyway we had a serious discussion on the accords and agreed the lines we would each take. Obviously it is for Gavos to do all the political stuff but she feels I can add the human touch; and that actually my protruding belly could be helpful.

Dr Anders was dubious of letting me go to Midgeos only two periods before Artur is due, but she pronounced me healthy enough and she and Les accompanied us in a special ambulance plane where I was able to lie down for the flight. Even without the extra room and comfort it was much easier than the flight from New Norland. It only took a couple of hora and Artur must have slept through it as he didn't have a single kick during the flight.

Our presentation to the Forum seemed to go well, and we have been told that it made a difference with at least two countries deciding to vote for the accords on the strength of it. The arithmetic of the voting was deemed to be tight. The EE was expected to exercise its veto which means that over two thirds of the countries would have to vote in favour for it to be passed. That is we needed sixteen votes.

In the event the only country to speak against us was the EE. The Grand Peoples' Republic were conspicuous by their absence. I understand that within their country they haven't even released the news of the landing or of the existence of life on Duplos. They think it would undermine their myth that they are the most advanced country of Geos, with the highest standard of living. All the other twenty-two countries were represented, however.

The accords were presented by the KNN since Jero Dicks was the lead author. Lord Rivers made a brief speech in support, in which she pointed out how it encompassed the principles which underpinned their whole approach, while preserving the rights of Duplosians and the opportunities for Geos. A banquet was provided on the opening day which featured a number of dishes of our food that have appealed to Geosian tastes. After Lord Rivers, the representative for New Hope gave a much fuller speech in support, wooing other smaller countries with the opportunities for them. She stated that without the generosity of New Norland, none of the smaller countries would be able to afford space travel and signing up to these accords would bring them opportunities that would otherwise be denied them.

There were other statements in support and some more neutral, expressing some reservations to particular aspects, but these were more about practical issues than the overall thrust of the accords.

After all the others had had their say the EE representative rose to make her statement. Essentially her opposition was to New Norland and its KNN lackeys. She attacked those aspects of the accord designed to protect Duplos and Duplosians, saying that this placed too heavy limitations on the rights of Geos to benefit from their natural superiority. Finally she said that it was quite unnecessary for smaller countries to have to kowtow to the Northlander capitalists in order to gain a few crumbs from their table. She announced that the EE is working on their own space programme and that they would be launching a space station of their own within a year. After that there would be but a short interval before they could offer others the opportunities to visit Duplos without the constraints being imposed by New Norland.

This last is very worrying to me as I'm sure that any EE led mission would be bad for Duplos.

When it came to the vote the EE offer didn't seem to swing opinion in its favour. Indeed it actually moved the two smallest countries, Peace and Southsea Island from mild opposition to support. In the end the twenty-three countries split seventeen in favour, three against with three abstentions (counting the absent GPRG). This was enough to pass. The accords are now official Geos policy. It is still up to each individual country, regardless of their vote in the Forum, to ratify them in order to participate in travel or trade with us or be open to visitors from Duplos. Naturally, New Norland, the KNN and New Hope ratified immediately. Others are awaiting internal debates but we know that a number will ratify soon. Midgeos is debating the matter this period whereas most others plan to do so after the new year holidays. New Hope have already appointed a head of mission and she will be joining the team in Goddess City early in the New Year.

Aside from the political purpose of my visit to Midgeos it was interesting to see another Geosian country and to hear different languages spoken. At the Forum our presentations were given in Norse but some of the other representatives spoke in their own languages. They had a system of simultaneous translation whereby you could hear the speeches through headphones translated into the language of your choice with only the slightest of delay as the very talented translators worked in real time. It was most impressive.

love to you all

Rastu

From RASTU to ARTE

Dearest Arté

Having got the political stuff out of the way, I can update you on other things. I have to say I am getting very bored with being pregnant. I think Artur is equally bored and impatient with it. He has developed a really vicious kick. If ever I meet Valray I shall ask her if you were as bad! Geosian women tend to be very shy of their pregnancy and most seem to go into hiding if their bulge gets too large, but in actuality they can disguise it for quite a while. No disguise could hide Artur. I'm convinced he's going to be the biggest baby ever and I will never get my nice slim body back. I blame you, why did I have to fall for a giant? I now know the evolutionary basis for our size dimorphism. Obviously, if a father out-sizes a mother the chances of a successful pregnancy is diminished. We need our babies to be small, and a smaller father will have a genetic advantage. What is less obvious is why our anatomy is such that we prefer a big bump, which we know correlates with a bigger man. Perhaps it acts as a counterbalance to prevent too great a divergence in size between the sexes. Perhaps you could see if Jan can shed light on the subject once she's finished testing you for potency.

I didn't have a lot of spare time for sightseeing but did get to see a little of the city of Gendalfo and some of the tourist sights there. The city is set by a lake surrounded by spectacular mountain scenery, some of which reminded me of home. Jezzie and Dr Anders accompanied me on my trips including a ride on a cable car, which interested me on account of your plans for linking to Isla. Artur clearly enjoyed the rocking motion of the ride and must have slept through it. When we stopped he woke up with a jolt and gave me a hard kick. I can't wait for him to get it over with and be born.

Although Gendalfo is in Midgeos, it is untypical as it sits at the boundary between two historic language regions. Thus both languages are in common usage, rather like Marouth/Marcenza. Dr Anders speaks one of them quite fluently and has a reasonable knowledge of the other. Jezzie has just a smattering of both. Also like at home, this is very much wine country, although Anders wouldn't let me have more than one glass. The KNN is more into beer and cider. I think you would like the KNN beer, Arté. It makes me think of you whenever Jezzie has a double cup (about one and a half scoops).

Jezzie had an email from Flying Eagle yesterwatch. Snow Hare was born the watch before. She weighed in at seven point five weights, that's four dupounds by our measure and is a healthy size for both Geosian and Duplosian babies. I think they are lucky. I'm convinced that Artur will weigh at least a rock (six point three nine dp). He certainly feels like a large rock in my tummy.

Jezzie has produced two more of her intelligent vibrators. I am going to send them to Zorro and Créezy and will be emailing them to let them know.

After that I'm going to go to bed and hope Artur stays quiescent long enough to let me get to sleep.

All my love

Aimée

From RASTU to CREEZY; zorro@wheels.co.wf.dp

Hi Créezy and Zorro

Earlier this watch I dispatched parcels to each of you. These contain one of Jezzie's intelligent vibrators. They really are magical and I'm sure you will each enjoy them when you are caught with an itch and no man in prospect. Perhaps they'll give you some recompense for your generosity in letting Astra and me steal Arté from you!

I've also included all the details you need to arrange manufacture as I'm sure that they'll be another money-spinner for WwW.

Take care and enjoy yourselves

love

Rastu

Fair Exchange

W ***1*** Pd ***25*** (***A***/Winter) ***161A***

From jezzie.peteschild@nordicaero.co.knn to arte@wheels.co.wf.dp

Hi Arté

Please forgive me for writing in Norse, but we've had a very long watch. The exciting news is that Aimée was safely delivered of Mikos Artur a few tocks ago. Both mother and baby are doing well but poor Aimée is quite exhausted. The extra gravity of Geos has not made the last **work** of pregnancy easy for xim and the birth was quite long and arduous. Artur is a fine big bouncy child weighing in at ***nine point five*** weights. However Dr Anders is very pleased with the way things have gone and Aimée has a beatific smile on xer face as Artur guzzles loudly on xer breast. So you are a co-parent at last.

As well as the injections that xe was given to reduce the pain, Sister Les advised a 'water' birth and Aimée lay in xer enormous bath while Les and I both stripped off to join xim in the water. I was with xim throughout the labour and held xer hand during the most difficult bits. Compared to babies here Artur's legs seem enormous, no wonder Aimée complained so much about xer kick!

When Artur has finished feeding we are going to put xim in xer cot to sleep and let Aimée get xer much needed rest. I'm sure xe will write to you when xe has woken up and feels more ximself.

Best wishes and congratulations 'Dad'

Jezzie

13
Space International

While Rastu was kept busy giving birth and looking after the newborn Artur, the worlds did not stand still and rapid progress was made on implementing the accords. New Norland took the decision to inter-nationalise the space-station constellation by offering other nations the opportunity to purchase their own stations to fill in more slots in the orbit. The KNN and New Hope were quick to take advantage and between them ordered four stations which would be evenly spaced within the existing constellation. The first two of these would be launched in the spring of ***161B***, just one year after the initial landing.

The new stations were also designed to accommodate Duplosians more comfortably than had been the case for Rastu and the members of the new Duplosian embassy. The other main innovation was in parts of the station under artificial gravity. Whereas the original dozen stations operated under simulated Duplosian gravity, these later ones would employ a variable pseudo-gravitational field that started at the Geos level and gradually reduced over the first part of the orbit down to the Duplos level and then after departing from Duplos gradually increased again. This new technology was also to be retrofitted to the older stations.

The eventual plan was to double the constellation from twelve to twentwy stations. All twentwy would work together but ownership would confer proportionate rights to berths and cargo space on the stations. The actual details are quite complex but suffice it to say that the result was to give participating nations a genuine stake in the trans-world exchange.

Fair Exchange

Once their countries had ratified the accords Midgeos subscribed to two stations while Souland and South Sylvania subscribed to one each.

When Gavos heard about these plans she wondered if the WF might also be able to get involved. She came to the KNN to confer with Rastu and then then engaged in some lengthy exchanges with her superiors on Duplos in which Astra and Fermos both took part.

The difficulty is that, frankly, these space stations are expensive and, even on Geos, are beyond the budget of the smaller nations. There is no way that any Duplosian territory can realistically meet the expense. However New Norland proved prepared to fudge the issue. Politically, they were attracted to the idea that Duplos should be partners in the enterprise and a suitable cut-price formula was negotiated. Two of the new stations were to be 'owned' by a consortium of the Western Federation, the Great Southern Empire and Wheels-within-Wheels, who put up much of the money. This made good business sense to Créezy who foresaw a lucrative near-monopoly on imports of Geosian technology. New Norland also insisted on a clause that would allow for Shadowlands' inclusion following their full acceptance of the accords.

That accounts for ten of the twelve slots. New Norland hoped that the remaining countries in the free world would manage to club together for the remaining two but was quite ready to fill the slots in any event.

Apart from the two stations that were ready to launch in ***161B*** the others would require a multi-year programme. The bottlenecks are the building of the stations themselves and the launch facilities. Production could be ramped up to provide for four new stations per year and with the up-grading of existing launch facilities in the KNN, Midgeos and New Hope, the new stations would be completed by the end of ***1622*** with two launched in ***1620*** and four in each of the two years following.

Upgrades to the existing stations to retrofit the variable gravity and improve the accommodation for Duplosians was scheduled to run in parallel over a six year programme from ***1620*** to ***1625***.

Improvements and upgrades were in no way limited to the space stations. The VTOL and Shuttle craft employed in the original landing on Duplos were very much a compromise development. Meadowcraft Aerospace had originally proposed a single vehicle to accomplish both roles and the two vehicle solution was designed by Flying Eagle Forest in order to meet the programme time scales. It was always intended by both Flying Eagle and Gnawing Beaver Meadows that the original proposal should be developed as the more satisfactory aerospacecraft. Since xer return from Duplos, Flying Eagle had continued to work with Gnawing Beaver on this project and over the next few years their designs would come to fruition simplifying both the space-ground and inter-station transport. Indeed while the bulk of transport of both people and goods between the planets would be accomplished though the orbits of the space stations, the improved vehicles would enable much faster travel between the planets where that was seen as essential.

Once they had returned to work from their co-parenting leave, Wild Cat Waters and Flying Eagle Forest were appointed to significant roles in the Geos-Duplos programme. At first they were both mainly planet-bound with Flying Eagle leading the technical development programme for the aerospacecraft and Wild Cat in charge of the training for space station staff. Then when the constellation was finally complete xe was to take overall command of the constellation while Flying Eagle was to be responsible for the entire aerospacecraft fleet. This would ensure that both spent a lot of time in space as well as on both planets. As for Snow Hare, xer earliest years would at least be with xer co-parents on Geos; but after that xe would be leading quite a peripatetic life which they planned to include boarding schools on both planets and time living with grandparents. Both Roaring Deer Waters and Basking Shark Forest were only too happy to have xim with them but their respective spouses were a bit concerned at how tired they might get.

South Beach Ph 3 Pd 29 (9/Winter) 2614

From ARTE to RASTU

Dearest Aimée

Congratulations. Do thank Jezzie for her email. We are all very excited at your news and Astra and your mother are putting together a parcel of baby clothes for Artur as we guess you will have difficulty getting suitable outfits for him on Geos.

I do hope you are making a good recovery from the ordeal of the birth but it does sound like you've been well looked-after by Jezzie and your medical team. Fancy giving birth under water! Sturdon is quite shocked at the thought but I'm sure that there was no danger of Artur drowning; and I can see how it would be much more comfortable for you under the extra gravity on Geos. I'm longing for you to come home so I can see and hold the baby.

We're all at South Beach at the moment. We came here after the end of term in order to get started on some of the building work. We are extending the house quite substantially to give

Artur his own bedroom and playroom. We are also installing an indoor bathroom with all the modern Geosian plumbing that you have become used to. Jan Martskind is with us and has been helping with the design. Her studies of our sexual mechanisms are nearing completion and she hopes to come to a definite conclusion soon. She has expanded the study to include some aspects of female fertility and says the results will be very interesting.

Astra and I will be going up north once the works start while Zorro looks after things in South Beach. Esau II is going to join her at New Year, I think she is going to try for a daughter.

In addition to the experimental cable car, we are going to improve the bungalow on the island to include modern plumbing and also to add central heating in both the bungalow and the tower. Wise Owl tells us that the technology we are going to use is very modern, even on Geos. It involves what they call a ground source heat pump and seems to break the laws of physics that we have just been learning. Namely the second law of thermodynamics as it somehow seems to heat up air and water using an underground source that is actually cooler than the temperature we are trying to reach. However the laws aren't actually broken because the conversion is done using electricity which prevents it breaking the conservation of energy principles. We will have plenty of electricity on the island from both wind and wave/tidal sources and apparently the ground source heat pump is very efficient. Eventually we may install something similar at South Beach and Thayview, but not this year. The apartment in Louth is more difficult to modernise.

While we're in the north, Wise Owl has promised us a tour of their base. I know you've already been there, but it is very exciting for us. Apart from those like you who have travelled to Geos we will be the first Duplosians to visit. If the weather is right we are going to fly there by microlight which is even more exciting. We're planning to stay north until mid-Spring when Astra will return to Louth and Créezy and I will divide our time between Louth and Thayview, where we will be planning for the expedition to Isla. However we'll all be at South Beach to welcome you home in the Summer.

Love from us all, but especially from me.

Arté

W 1 Pd 30 (16/Winter) 2614

From RASTU to ARTE

Dearest Arté

I'm snatching the opportunity to write while Artur is asleep. I'm just so busy what with him, studying and 'diplomatic' duties. Your son is so greedy! If he goes on like this he will grow even bigger than you. He's also a noisy feeder and he snores! Not quite as loud as you do sometimes but give him time!

Jezzie and Jo Jensen just love to watch me feed him. Mothers here are very private about these things and only let the closest of their families see them while feeding. Jezzie says she's never before seen a mother actually feed a baby from her tits and she is totally fascinated. Well, my tits have grown huge and after Artur's given them a good suck the nipples look enormous, so I can see why Jezzie and Jo go a bit goggle-eyed. It is the most wonderful feeling and I can't understand why Geosian mothers are so secretive and shy. I just love showing off my baby in this way and sharing the experience.

Jo is a lecturer in Zoology at the university and is tutoring me on genetics and evolution. She is a very close friend of Jan, I think she hopes to marry her sometime. She certainly loves her a lot and can't wait for her to come back from Duplos. I'm not sure whether Jan knows how strong Jo's feelings are, so you'd better be careful when talking to her.

Anyway, back to evolution, it really is interesting and so much more believable than Goddess myths. You must get Jan to explain it to you. One thing is obvious and that is that there must be animals of Duplos that we know nothing about. Over here it is clear that men evolved from more primitive animals known as apes. Jezzie took me to a Zoo a few periods ago and I saw some of these apes as well as other fascinating creatures. The apes look almost like people and are very intelligent but don't talk. In the wild they live in trees in tropical forests and can move about through the trees at great speed, swinging by long arms and being able to grip with their feet just like hands. Apparently they had a common ancestor with men about four million years ago, when the lines diverged.

Many of the animals, like dogs for instance, are similar to ones we have on Duplos, although like people they tend to have shorter limbs and a stockier frame. However there is one whole family of animals that are common here called felines that are most impressive. They have beautiful fur coats and while some feline species are large and very ferocious and dangerous, there is a smaller species called cats that make the most adorable pets. Wild Cat is called after a slightly bigger form of the domesticated cat. Although cats are friendly to people they are also quite vicious hunters of small rodents and birds. They are just what farmers need to keep the rats and mice populations under control. Much more efficient than dogs.

Anyway the big mystery about evolution appears to be just how people evolved their large brains and ability to talk. Apparently, the biological cost of such development appears to be too great for the initial small gains that would power evolution and nobody has yet come up with a satisfactory explanation. I've been reading a book about an idea that evolution doesn't only happen with genes (ask Jan) but also could be powered by other entities with similar reproductive properties. This book suggests that 'memes' could provide a suitable mechanism. Memes are in a sense 'ideas' and can propagate through a similar positive feedback loop to genes and these might in turn cause the necessary development of brains and speech. It all sounds very plausible but is, I think, ultimately unsatisfactory; and I can't see how the propagation of memes can have a strong enough linkage to animal reproduction and hence evolution. In my 'spare' time I'm trying to think about these problems. Perhaps you might also find them interesting.

On the 'diplomatic' side, I've had a visit from Gavos who, after she'd congratulated me on Artur and cooed over him enough to be polite, wanted to consult me in my capacity as a director of WwW. New Norland has announced its intention to double the number of space stations, and also to improve them to make them more suitable for us Duplosians. They have already built two of the new stations and plan to launch them in 2615. My eventual return is likely to be on one of these.

Other nations on Geos are being offered the opportunity to buy into the larger constellation and the KNN and New Hope together have agreed to buy four of them, to include the two already mentioned. It is expected that others will follow. Gavos would like for Duplos (at least the WF) to also take part and wanted to know if WwW would be interested in assisting the purchase. The big advantage is that with ownership comes rights for passengers, crew and cargo space. For WwW this would mean improved priority for imports from Geos and thus could be a sound investment. Actually Jezzie tells me that space stations are horrendously expensive and surely beyond anything we could afford from Duplos. However, after some initial soundings, Gavos says that New Norland is very attracted by the prospect of Duplosian participation and thinks she could cut a deal. I said I would put it to the board. I suggest you talk it over, consulting Wise Owl and Stripy Tiger. Gavos' email address is gavos@geosembassy.gov.wf.dp.

The other exciting thing to happen here in Camford is the trial of 'self-driving cars'. As you know the Geosians are very reluctant to transfer the technology of the internal combustion engine to us. This type of engine burns petrol, a highly volatile hydrocarbon mixture, resulting in the production of some quite noxious gases that contribute to changing the planet's climate for the worse. Until recently all road transport was dependent on this sort of engine. Additionally, a high proportion of electricity generation also depends on burning fuels that produce such gases. The Geosians, at least in the civilised countries, very much regret this dependence and are working to replace these fuels with electricity generated from sustainable sources like sun, wind and water power. As you know they are keen that we don't make the same mistakes, especially since with our much smaller population we can easily be self sufficient with these clean energy sources.

Fair Exchange

Amongst the improvements is a drive to replace petrol driven cars with electric ones; and from New Year 2615 Camford will be one of three cities in the KNN that will impose an outright ban on petrol cars. At the same time, the all-electric car is very suitable to use the sort of artificial intelligence technology that Jezzie developed for their aircraft. In fact, before she joined Nordic Aerospace Jezzie worked for a company that was developing smart cars that could drive themselves without the need for a person to do the driving. She says that it is not too difficult just to accomplish the self-driving. The real challenge is when the traffic on the road is a mixture of self-driving and man-driven vehicles, especially if some still use the old petrol technology.

Camford are not only banning petrol-driven cars, they are also requiring that all cars are fitted with technology allowing direct communications with the vehicle itself. Which is not too much of an add-on for electric cars. This means that some of the most challenging problems with mixed traffic can be solved. And as an experiment from 1/Spring 2615 self-drive vehicles will be allowed in Camford. Obviously Jezzie is especially excited about this and she has been getting some lucrative consultancy work as well as being lent a self-drive car for herself. She took delivery of this car towatch and we are going for a spin in it later. Of course she can't yet let it drive itself on public roads but from the first day of Spring she'll be able to let it loose in the city.

I can't drive myself because my legs are far too long for Geosian controls, but I will be able to be a passenger in Jezzie's car with no driver. Actually I expect I'll still stick to my tricycle, which is similar to our SPC with an electric motor to assist the pedalling. Jezzie is going to fit it with the necessary communications and other software to allow me to use it safely in Camford after 1 Spring. I also have a baby seat for Artur.

The other thing, apart from feeding and sleeping, that Artur really loves is his bath. If we're in a hurry I bath him in Jezzie's smaller bath, but what is best is to use my huge bath when Jezzie and I can both get in with him. There's plenty of room for us to sit at opposite ends with Artur between us. He just loves splashing about. I wonder what he makes of the two of us being such different sizes. Perhaps he thinks Jezzie is his big sister.

One other bit of exciting news that Jezzie has just told me even as I am writing this. Wild Cat and Flying Eagle are going to visit in the New Year. The date is not yet finalised, but they are going to give some lectures at the university on their experiences on the Duplos programme. They'll also be giving some TV interviews. They've asked Jezzie to look for a house near us for them to rent during their stay. They'll be bringing Snow Hare of course and Wild Cat's seed parent is coming with them to look after Snow Hare while they're working. She and Artur will be able to play together.

After they return to New Norland it is planned for them to return to work full time but will initially be planet-bound here. Wild Cat has been appointed as head of a training school for space personnel. The students will include people from the other countries buying into the programme and destined for jobs on the stations or on the ground on Duplos. There will also be places for Duplosians in the event that Gavos is successful in negotiating Duplosian participation. It is definitely envisaged that some of the jobs on the 'Duplosian' stations will be held by us. You might discretely advertise the fact around the universities to alert them to the opportunities.

Fair Exchange

Flying Eagle is going back to work on the next generation of their space shuttles. The plan is to come up with a single craft that can fly both on the planet and in space, combining the roles of their VTOL aircraft and the space shuttle. Eventually she will be in charge of the whole programme for upgrading the fleet to the new craft. Jezzie will take on some consultancy work for her.

Jezzie has resigned her position with Nordic to establish her own independent consultancy company. This enables her to work on technical projects following her own interests. At least to start with she is in much demand, not only with her former employer and Meadowcraft in NN; but also on the self-drive car projects. She is a bit worried about the long-term financial risk but, for the short term, she says she'll be raking it in and, she claims, single-handedly supporting the Government through her enormous taxes. Over here people have to pay a percentage of their income to the government. It seems iniquitous to me and the rates appear staggeringly high. Jezzie has to pay a marginal rate of fiftwy pertwent which is over forty-one percent. Colossal!

I hear gurgling. Artur is waking up and will soon be screaming to be fed so I'd better stop now and get my tits out.

Lots of love

Aimée

14
Greetings

Observatory Island Ph 1 Pd 1 (15/Winter) 2615

From ARTE to RASTU

HAPPY NEW YEAR

Dearest Aimée

Greetings from all of us here. That is me, Astra and Wise Owl. We've been having a good observation season, with Wise Owl helping us to locate the various bodies in the solar system that have hitherto eluded us. Wise Owl loves just looking at our night sky. She says that on Geos there is so much light pollution that the full glory of the stars is no longer visible from the more heavily populated parts of the planet.

The various works are proceeding well. The bungalow is more comfortable with both central heating and a bathroom. We have a large bath big enough for me and Astra to share, (I'm sure we could also squeeze you in!) and also a shower. You are surely familiar with showers from Geos. Our one has two shower heads, one at a height for us and the other at a suitable height for Geosians. The lower one points a jet right at my tummy button which is very pleasant. The bath also has spa jets which Wise Owl says is considered to be very luxurious. We have a suitable seat in the bath tub for a Geosian visitor like her.

There's really only a little finishing off required in the bungalow, and then work is to start on the tower. The heating there is going to be using a deep bore hole. This involves some specialised drilling equipment which we don't have here.

Fortunately the Geosians have recently undertaken a similar project on Base island and they are going to lend us the equipment. The plan is that we are all going over to the base next period using the microlights. We'll then be given a tour and return using the VTOL, bringing the drilling equipment and personnel back with us. The actual drilling will take less than a phase and then the heat pump can be installed and the equipment returned.

Construction of the cable car has also started and we plan for completion early in Spring. We hope it will be in time before Wise Owl and Astra have to go back to Louth; but if not, I shall stay here until the work is completed.

You can tell Jezzie that she won't need to worry about money if she moves to Duplos. I don't know all the details but I gather from Zorro that orders for the intelligent vibrator are booming. Jezzie's share will be quite a fortune. Of course I don't know how income tax will affect her over here. It sounds like just the sort of bad idea that our Governments will copy. Fermos and Astra are both lobbying hard in support of Gavos' proposal to participate in the space station constellation. WwW have agreed to partner with the WF government, and there has also been some interest from the GSE.

At the moment there are only rumours; but apparently there's a lot of turmoil in the Shadowlands Union. You'll remember Colonel Petrova who was the rather sensible commander of the Shadowland force that we met on the phase of first contact. As Major General Petrova she led the SU team at the Goddess City conference on the accords. She has been a strong advocate for SU acceptance of the accords and is apparently still agitating for them and for political reform within the union. She has gained quite a following and there is a fear in the WF that the SU Government might begin a repressive crack-down.

We are planning a big celebration for the anniversary of first contact. Zorro is using it as an excuse for a big marketing push and WwW is in the forefront of moves to make it a public holiday. All employees of WwW are being given the phase off and we are encouraging our contractors and associated businesses to do the same. Zorro is planning a range of special offers on selected products for orders placed in the period following.

Love to you and Artur

Arté

South Beach Ph 1 Pd 1 (15/Winter) 2615

From zorro@wheels.co.wf.dp to rastu@camford.ac.knn

Hi Rastu

Happy New Year from Créezy and me. We are down at South Beach for the holiday. We celebrated with a midnight dip in our new heated pool. Just the three of us, we also have Esau here. Afterwards we had a pleasant threesome, although Créezy doesn't have quite as much enthusiasm for sex as she used to. She won't admit it but I think she misses Arté. I am really grateful to you for the vibrator on her behalf even more than my own. I'm very happy with Esau. He may not have the physical attributes of Arté but we have ever so many interests in common and I can relate to him in a way that I have never before experienced with a man. I do try hard to include Créezy whenever she's willing because I find that I love her very much as a dear friend and feel a bit guilty that I have found happiness with a good man while she has not.

The improvements here are almost complete and when you return I hope you will be pleased with them. How did we ever cope without indoor plumbing? I'm not looking forward to the more spartan conditions in Louth and refuse to move back there until midway through Spring when it should be warm enough not to want central heating. We do have some plans to improve the apartment. The next door apartment has become vacant and we are hoping to buy it. Then we will be able to knock the two together and include a bathroom. To do this we'll be upgrading the whole block to also improve the lives of our neighbours. What a good thing that WwW has made us all so much money that we can afford to do this without having to ask them to contribute to the cost. With the two apartments together there'll be room for us all. You, Mummy, Arté and Artur in Mummy's old rooms and me and Esau in what was the next door apartment. Who knows, we may also have our own baby. My next fertile period is due in about three periods time and I hope to persuade Esau to give me a daughter. Isn't that modern of me, consulting a man on such a matter, Mummy should be proud of me!

In your last mail to Arté you mentioned Jezzie's concerns for the financial success of her new business. Well, you can tell her that over here she is fast becoming very rich. We are actually having some difficulty keeping up with the supply to meet the orders for her intelligent vibrator. Indeed one of the motives for buying into the expanded constellation of space stations is to help with capacity for the import of batteries and electronic components that we can't source here on Duplos.

Twin Worlds II

Below is a copy of the advertisement that is now appearing in all the main magazines in the WF. If, as I would prefer, the figure was as Créezy had originally drawn it you would easily see that I am the model. As it is, the others outvoted me on the board, and the more interesting bits have been covered up by some quite inappropriate garments. I would never wear anything that tight over my tits let alone lower down. I like the air to circulate around my nether regions. The thought of having cloth tightly bound round my waist and thighs like in the picture is quite abhorrent. After all, they're my tits and fanny and if I don't mind displaying them why should anyone else?

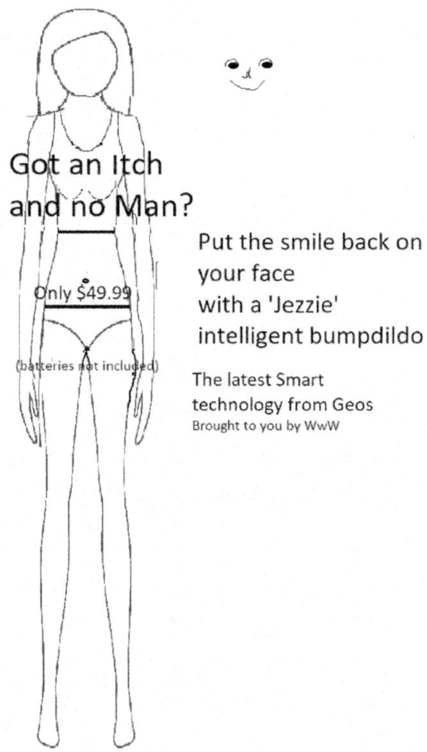

What do you think? You might be a bit shocked at the price we are charging but it seems that the main market is not youngsters, as you might think, but actually is women in their forties and fifties. These women are both willing and able to fork out a lot more for their pleasure.

I know this from the considerable amount of market research that I conducted and also from studies at the Universities of Marouth and Marcenza. I know you don't know much about the seamier side of Marouth life, but I have had quite of bit of experience in my younger days. Although most students and younger women in the vicinity do try out visiting brothels in Marcenza, most only go a very few times and, like myself, soon tire of the unsatisfactory nature of the experience. Apparently the mainstay of the trade are older women who still want regular sex but have abandoned the constant search for partners, either because they are just too busy or because they are tired of the whole dating process. Lots of such women visit brothels either alone or with close friends to get their itches scratched without having to go through the rigmarole of persuading a man to co-operate. With our vibrators we address the same market without having to resort to the morally dubious practise of prostitution. While Astra doesn't quite approve of our product, she does acknowledge that it may have some benefits in alleviating some of what she sees as the oppression of men.

My next marketing push, once we have improved the supply situation, is to the GSE. Unsurprisingly there has been opposition from the sex industry there, but I am hopeful of being able to turn it to our advantage. I have actually been on a tour of some of the top brothels in Marcenza. Not as a customer, but to talk to the Madams to persuade them of the value of the vibrators to their business. In this I have had some success and we are going for a low-key supply to a select few to see how they get on integrating the vibrators into their offerings. Although the Madams are generally sceptical I am confident that the pilot schemes will be successful and we shall all prosper together.

Love

Zorro

Montana Ph 1 Pd 1 (15/Winter) 2615

From sturdon@wheels.co.wf.dp to rastu@camford.ac.knn

Happy New Year my darling Aimée and my beautiful Grandson.

At last we have entered the year when I'm going to get you back home and I will see my lovely Mikos Artur in the flesh. Thank-you for the pictures of him that you sent me. I have been boring all my friends with them. I do miss you so very much.

Your friends have all been very kind to me and I was invited both to South Beach and to the Observatory to celebrate. However, I preferred to stay at home. I celebrated with my sisters and invited your father to stay the night in my bed. We had a nice cuddle but were very late in bed after a bit more booze than either of us is used to, so a cuddle was all we wanted.

Stay safe and come home soon

Love

Mum

Fair Exchange

Camford, KNN W 1 Pd 1 (15/Winter) 2615

From RASTU to ARTE; ASTRA; ZORRO; CREEZY; MUM

Dear All

Thank-you for your New Year greetings and we (Artur, Jezzie and me) send ours in return. Please forgive me for not writing to you all separately. We had a quiet celebration here. After Artur had eventually gone to sleep, Jezzie and I ran a hot bath and got in with a cold bottle of a very high quality sparkling wine. I think it is the best wine I've ever tasted. We finished the bottle between the two of us and became quite squiffy and giggly. You know Arté, now I've got over thinking of you as a brother, Jezzie really is that sibling I've longed for. She is indeed my dear soul-sister. If she were Duplosian I would definitely want a threesome with her. That would shock her to the core!

We all woke rather late this morning and I think all three with a bit of a hangover. I had woken Artur for a feed before going to bed myself. He must have also been enjoying the booze second-hand through my milk. At least it made him sleep in! We just have a two watch holiday here for New Year and we are spending it lazing about, which is why I've left it so late to mail you all.

We woke this morning to a white landscape. While we were sinking the booze, snow was falling outside. We've got a carpet of about 5 divisions deep in the garden. After lunch we went out in it and built a snowman and Jezzie and I had a friendly snowball fight. I think I won due to the significant advantage of my height. Artur tried to eat the snow and made a horrible face when he discovered how cold it is. It was quite funny. The cold weather is expected to last for about a period with more snow predicted in the next watch. However the longer term weather forecast suggests that it will all melt in the second period of the year and we'll be in for some very wet weather with a lot of rain.

Weather forecasting here is pretty impressive and based on a lot of scientific knowledge about the behaviour of the atmosphere. The mathematics behind it all is quite horrendous involving very sophisticated modelling to set up differential equations that cannot be solved analytically, but require sophisticated numerical techniques to produce approximate solutions under specific conditions. I don't pretend to understand it fully, as indeed very few people do. There is so much mathematics here that nobody can possibly get to grips with it all and individual mathematicians are experts in just a small portion of the whole. It is much easier with the more limited knowledge that we have on Duplos. However I expect that you, Arté, and Fermos would be fascinated to see the wide variety of accomplishments that are down to mathematics. Did you follow up on Complex Numbers? It is amazing that something as theoretical as the square root of minus one can be so useful in the solution of so many practical problems. Isn't the identity $e^{i\pi}$ = -1 just amazing? And as for the Zeta function - so that there is a sense in which

$$1+2+3+4+... = -1/12 ,$$

which seems quite mad. (Sorry Mum and Zorro - sometimes I get carried away with Maths. Just think of it as something incomprehensible between me and Arté. Astra, perhaps Arté can explain some of this to you).

I've told Jezzie about her fortune. She thinks that she will only have to pay KNN taxes on any money she brings back to Geos and that what she keeps on Duplos will be subject only to Duplosian tax law. She says she'll need to check that is the case. It's possible that she might want to return to Duplos on a more permanent basis. She's still a bit up in the air about her future plans because of her elderly parents. Her seed-parent is not expected to live much longer, being ill with lung cancer, which she blames on a disgusting habit called smoking, which has almost died out now, but which, when her parents were younger, was quite common and even fashionable. Her birth-parent is in reasonable general health but suffers from a condition called osteoporosis which means her bones are not very strong and she has to be careful not to fall. Jezzie thinks that the lower gravity on Duplos might be just what her birth-parent needs.

She is a bit dubious about the vibrator being given her name. I've tried to put her mind at rest by explaining that on Duplos it wouldn't give her a bad reputation at all but actually enhance her credibility. However, she definitely shares the general opinion that the depiction of Zorro should be decently covered. Jezzie is the least prudish Geosian imaginable; but although they are content with nudity in general; they do have some hang-ups, which include some objections to the depiction of nudes in photographs or advertisements. That is why in all the pictures I have sent you of us in the bath with Artur I only ever show Jezzie's back view.

Arté, did you get to talk to Jan about evolution and memes, and how we got our brains? We've got Jo Jensen coming to dinner in a couple of watches and that has called to mind my earlier thoughts on the matter.

Have you made any progress on Esau's inscription? It's been a while since you mentioned it and I'm intrigued as to how you've got on. I'm looking forward to meeting Esau, as I'm sure I will, since he seems to be a permanent fixture with you, Zorro. And,

Zorro, I'm really pleased for you. I did feel a bit guilty about taking Arté from you, although I recognise that it is on account of Astra that you had to give him up.

I share your concerns about Créezy and, honestly, I won't make a fuss or feel in any way let down if she has the occasional romp with Arté. They do have an important connection and I'm sure Astra would also understand. We're not like Geosians in this regard and there is room enough to spread the love among us.

Finally, Mum, I will be home soon, I promise, but it may be a couple of periods later than you anticipated. I am going to wait for the two new stations to become operational. They are due to launch in the next couple of selenths and will be much more comfortable for me, and more importantly, for Artur. The artificial gravity on the existing stations is set to simulate that on Duplos. On the new stations the gravity will change gradually in a sinusoidal wave to first bring it down from that on Geos to the level of Duplos as we arrive there and then for the journey from Duplos to Geos it will gradually increase again. This is much more suited to normal passengers in both directions as we gradually acclimatise to the conditions at our destination. Eventually the old stations will also be upgraded. Wild Cat is going to be in charge of the programme; but she says that while they should start in about a year or so, it will be several years before all the stations meet the new standards.

Artur woke up just as I started the last paragraph and he is now bouncing on my lap and grabbing at my shirt, as well as making a screeching noise. He doesn't like me typing and not paying him attention. As usual he's also hungry so I suppose I'd better feed him. Phew, and change him, the beast. He's leaked on to my trousers which were clean on. I'll go and find Jezzie to help.

Love to you all

Aimée

PS Zorro and Créezy, it really is time for me to get on private name terms with you both.

South Beach Ph 2 Pd 1 (16/Winter) 2615

From CREEZY to RASTU

Hi Aimée

I'm honoured to address you by your private name. We are indeed close enough to do so. You and the others are my real family. Even though I now expect to meet my mother and sister again I was never as close to either of them as to you all. Funnily enough the only person on Isla to whom I ever felt this close is Shay. Of course as an Islander I don't have a private name for you to use. My actual islander name was Crayza but that is just another version of Créezy and not really a different name at all.

You are very generous in your offer to let Arté help me out and I am truly appreciative. However, we all decided on the current arrangement and I believe it to be right. This is not only for your benefit but initially was also to give some solidarity with Zorro and to force me and Arté to move on with our lives. Consideration for Zorro is no longer relevant, but the other remains important. It's true that I have found it more difficult than I anticipated but that's no reason for me to go backwards. I think of it that you and I have sort of swapped relationships. It is so right that you and Arté are at last proper partners while to me he is like a brother, which was always more appropriate given both our connections to Thay and Shay.

However your gift of Jezzie's vibrator, which we sell as a 'bumpdildo' has been helpful. It deals satisfactorily with the physical need and thereby allows me the space to come to terms with my emotions without having to resort to more sordid mechanisms. I know you always had a more mature attitude to sex, and never needed to go overboard in the way that most of us do when young, so maybe you won't completely understand me when I say that I now find I don't have the desire to scratch my itches in the way I once did. I do still get frequent itches but just any hunk is no longer enough. I want a sex-object to be just that, an object, and not another person. I want a meaningful connection to a person in my bed and I don't want to have to kiss a lot of frogs before finding a prince. It seems I am not alone in feeling like this and the market for 'Jezzies' is really taking off for women like me.

So darling Aimée, we will not be sex-mates but we will be sisters and I intend to be a good Auntie to Artur.

Love

Créezy

South Beach Ph 2 Pd 1 (16/Winter) 2615

From ZORRO to RASTU

Hi Aimée

I had wondered if I would ever address you thus. Have you considered Mummy? She is terribly jealous of her special relationship with you. Deep down she thinks of you as the daughter she always wanted as opposed to the one she's got. She just might be a bit miffed at me for muscling in on her privileged position!

I know I'm being a bit of an amateur psychologist here, but I think that when the three of you were together for Artur's conception, Mummy got her real pleasure from seeing you enjoy the experience. Much more than the relief from her own celibacy. Even now I think that for her, possibly for both of them, you are present whenever she and Arté have sex. It's as if she sees her role as keeping him warm for you. They're always talking about you and including what they think you would want when making even the most every-day decisions. During the renovations in South Beach, Créezy and I got banished to a tent while they totally refurbished the place and tried to outdo each other in providing for your comfort.

Don't make the mistake of thinking I'm jealous. I'm not. I'm delighted to see Mummy so happy and anyway I love you too and am also longing to have you home.

I do have a private name for official record purposes but I never use it, nor have I ever done so as I think it's quite ugly and it has no emotional meaning. Mummy was so cross with her sister and mother at the time of my birth that she just told the registrar the first random non-name that came into her head. So I'm afraid you're going to have to just go on calling me Zorro.

Come home soon, love

Zorro

15
A Diplomatic Incident

Observatory Island Ph 2 Pd 3 (24/Winter) 2615

From ARTE to RASTU

Dearest Aimée

You may be amused by this. Last period we finally had our tour of Base Island. Travelling by microlight we accomplished the journey via five hops. The first two and the fourth were to uninhabited islands in the cold sea. Although these are all officially part of Shadowlands' territory there was nobody there to make a fuss. However, the third hop touched on a peninsular on the mainland and we were seen by a couple of hunters. I think we might have disturbed their game which is why they got shirty. The rental agreement that the Geosians have over Base Island allows them to stop on Shadowlands territory in this way, and when challenged by one of the hunters, Wise Owl was able to point to this agreement. Disappointed by this response, the hunters decided that the presence of Astra and me fell outside any such agreement and got quite abusive. We ignored them and thought no more about it when we continued on our way. However, the hunters reported the incident and, as a result, the Shadowlands Ambassador to the WF lodged a formal complaint under the terms of our border treaty.

Although this is a storm in a teacup and even the Shadowlanders didn't expect to make too much of it, I understand it is spiralling into something more serious. In a speech that has been widely reported in the WF, General Petrova has taken our (or rather the Geosians') side! She announced that as she was the one who negotiated the Base island agreement, she should know what the intent was. As far as she was concerned, anyone travelling in the company of Geosians and at their invitation is subject to that agreement and that therefore there was no treaty infringement. In this way our insignificant incident is becoming a casus belli between the reformist and traditionalist parties in the SU. Obviously, pundits in the WF are all backing Petrova and hailing her as the much needed breath of fresh air; but it also seems that she is gaining a lot of momentum in the SU and poses a serious challenge to their conservative leadership. It could get interesting.

We very much enjoyed our tour of the base and I also got to speak to a mathematician on the team there, Painted Jaguar. We had a very interesting conversation about complex numbers and the things you wrote in your new year mail. I asked her whether there were even further generalisations of number systems beyond complex. She said that there wasn't anything that was especially useful but that there were two such generalisations of academic interest. She called these quaternions and octonions. She says she's not an expert on them and really just knew about them as curiosities. Quaternions have some uses in physics but there are alternative ways of addressing the same problems. In quaternion arithmetic there are three independent square roots of -1 and multiplication is no longer commutative. Maths students tend to come across them as a simple example of a non-commutative number system. Octonions are a further generalisation but apparently there are no further extensions beyond that.

I hadn't heard of the zeta function. Painted Jaguar again said she was not very knowledgeable about it but was able to define it for me and told me about the 'Zeta Hypothesis' which she said is the single most important unsolved problem in pure mathematics. However it involves some very technical stuff in Number Theory, and Painted Jaguar's expertise is really in applied mathematics, her PhD is in Fluid Mechanics. She hadn't heard about the 1+2+3+4+.. .= -1/12 equation but guessed that -1/12 must be the value of ζ(-1).

We returned from Base island with the drilling equipment and heat pump. We drilled the hole yesterphase and will shortly be installing the pump. After that the tower will actually be warm. We'll be getting soft.

Our cable-car track is nearly complete. The four cars have been built and are now on the island. The propulsion cable is in place and it has been tested to ensure it moves freely. The two support cables are being put in place this period and then it will just be a question of attaching the cars and making some finishing touches to the stations. The cars are being transported up the volcano on my railway, which is itself actually a primitive cable car system. It now has an electric motor drive so I don't have to employ pedal-power. At the tower, the cable car station is at ground level so attaching the cars is fairly straightforward. It's all quite exciting and I'm really looking forward to it becoming operational.

Astra has decided to delay her departure for a period so she can try out the cable car and will return to Louth the phase after. I shall follow on a bit later.

You asked about Esau's inscription. To be honest we haven't got much further. Créezy and I are pretty well convinced by our transliteration of the script. The result certainly seems to be some sort of language but it isn't Contish or Islish. We do recognise 'Lana' appearing twice and we think it might be some sort of prayer. Later in the Spring we are due to go to some obscure college about twenty walks south of Goddess City, quite near where the tablet was found, to give a seminar on the topic. There will be a number of philologists in the audience and we hope they may be able to shed some light on the subject.

Once I get back to civilisation I shall get the chance to ask Jan about evolution and then I'll be able to think about your 'meme' question. I'm also expecting her to have the results of her 'sex' study.

Lot's of love

Arté

16
Contact Day

Camford: W. 4 Pd 6 (10/Spring) 2615

From rastu@camford.ac.knn to arte@wheels.co.wf.dp

Dearest Arté

Happy Contact Day. How much our lives have changed in the past year! I can scarcely credit it. Although we are now nearly in the third period of Spring it's still pretty wintry here in Camford. I suppose it's a bit warmer than the observatory but a lot colder than Louth at this time of year. The snow's gone but it seems to rain all the time and it's pretty miserable and damp. Artur and I have both been unwell with a cold. It's an endemic problem here but slightly different from the one we're used to on Duplos. Jezzie's had it too but shook it off in a couple of watches. She suspects that Geosians on Duplos are likely to be suffering from our version of a cold in the same was as Artur and I am here. The doctors think we'll be OK in another couple of watches but it is pretty miserable and my nose is sore and red and I look terribly ugly. Poor Artur doesn't understand why his nose is constantly streaming and he tosses and turns in his cot and then passes his misery on to me.

The colds and weather are dampening our enthusiasm for our visitors. Wild Cat and family arrived yesterphase and are settling in to the house that Jezzie found them just a tock's walk away. It's a nice house on three floors with good accommodation for the four of them. Most importantly it has two bathrooms. Most houses in the KNN have only one, whereas in New Norland, where there is a lot more space, houses are bigger and people are used to more bathrooms. Jezzie says the when she was over here working on the aircraft, Flying Eagle complained about only having one bathroom whenever Jezzie stayed over. She wouldn't let Jezzie move in with her because of this lack. Apparently in their houses in New Camford and Beaver they have four bathrooms. One for each of them and one for guests, so even Snow Hare gets her own. Over here Wild Cat and Flying Eagle are having to share while Snow Hare and Roaring Deer share the guest bathroom. By their standards this is slumming it. Jezzie just shakes her head and says New Norlanders are over-pampered.

You mentioned your incident with the Shadowlands. Well, over here we have a veritable storm brewing with the Eastern Empire. Apparently they've had spies in the New Norland space programme and Wild Cat has been involved in the investigations. They've unmasked someone on her space station team who has been leaking secret technical details to the Empire. This has allowed the Empire to advance their plans by several years and it is believed that they are going to launch their own station later this year. So you may need to brace yourselves for a less friendly visit from Geos. Anyway, as Fermos undoubtedly knows, the New Norland government has promised that all the Duplosian territories will be kept fully informed about what they know of the Evil Empire's intentions through the embassy in Goddess City. The trial of the spy opens in Kingstown next period and it is expected that she will be found guilty and sentenced to a very long time in prison, possibly even for life. Wild Cat will probably have to return to New Norland to give evidence at the trial. Jezzie says that prison in New Norland is pretty harsh. Not as bad as in the Empire but conditions are much less comfortable than in the KNN and sentences are longer. Given the option I think I would prefer our sort of penal servitude to the incarceration in prison that they go in for on Geos. I'll just have to be extra good and not break any laws while I'm over here! The only real danger is speeding and they don't jail you for that. I also get away with it because the police (Geosian for watch) don't believe I can go so fast on my tricycle. They think their equipment is not working properly. The speed limit in the city is sixtwy twilomen per **meal** which is just over four walks and is faster than Geosians ride a bicycle, but with my longer legs and bigger wheels I can go much faster as we know from our SPCs. The speed limit is really about cars which can go at tremendous speeds, and the limit is there for safety reasons in busy streets. Jezzie got fined sixtwy pounds just before New Year for doing sixtwy-six tpm[4] on her way to her office. The fine being twelve pounds for every tpm over the limit.

We're planning a party to welcome Wild Cat and Flying Eagle to the KNN and Zir Jacky will also be coming. We see her from time to time, but she is very busy now she is a Brigadier and is getting ready to be military attaché to the KNN embassy in Midgeos. That is a two year appointment starting on 1/Summer and afterwards she is likely to be promoted to Major General and take up an even more important appointment. Jezzie says she is clearly being groomed for great things.

When he's not sniffling, Artur is beginning to crawl and we are having to start child-proofing the house. Apparently our babies develop a bit faster than Geosians and it will be a while before Snow Hare gets so mobile. She is a sweetie, and looks so tiny after Artur. The Doctors here say I should try to prevent him from walking too soon because the extra gravity could be too strong for his legs. Geosian babies don't begin to walk until they are at

4 Twilomen per meal, see the appendix 3, ***60*** (72) tpm is just below 30 mph and is the default speed limit in built up areas in both the KNN and New Norland.

least a year old and the Doctors were quite concerned when I told them that two selenths is quite normal on Duplos. Let's hope Artur inherits your strength and manages to cope without breaking his legs. It's the leg difference that really marks us out. I guess that our legs account for around 53% of our height whereas as for Geosians it's about 43%. If their legs were proportionately as long as ours they wouldn't be all that much shorter at 81% of an average Duplosian woman instead of just 66%.

I've asked people at the university about quaternions and octonions. Quaternions are pretty well known and quaternion algebra can be used to describe rotations of a physical body and has some applications in particle physics but is not important for mainstream mathematics, while octonions are really just a curiosity that non-mathematicians haven't even heard of.

This is in total contrast to complex numbers, which are central to an awful lot of stuff in a way that is quite surprising. Apart from their use in electronics, where they save what would otherwise be a lot of very tedious trigonometric calculations, there are two really important properties. The first is the fundamental theorem of algebra, which tells us that every polynomial equation in n unknowns has exactly n solutions (if you count multiplicities) in the complex numbers. The second is the fact that if a function of a complex variable is differentiable then all its higher derivatives also exist and this leads to the concept of analytic functions and unique analytic continuation of a function, which seems to be a very strong property indeed, and not at all obvious. There, that's a lot of homework for you as you need quite a lot of difficult maths to get to where you can understand what I'm talking about here.

Twin Worlds II

Oh, talking of difficult maths, you may recall from our time in Routh various discussions about whether the sum of two nth powers of integers can ever also be an nth power for n greater than two. There were genuine arguments proving that it is impossible for third or fourth powers and nobody has ever been able to come up with any example for higher powers, whereas several people have claimed to prove it's always impossible; but there's always been at least one respectable mathematician who has remained unconvinced by these proofs.

Well, on Geos the same problem had haunted mathematicians for centuries and a tremendous amount of useful mathematics has been discovered or invented in attempts to solve the problem. Fairly recently there was finally a proof that has convinced the experts. However, it is way beyond the capability of the mathematics we knew on Duplos and involves some incredibly sophisticated constructions and arguments. There is no way we could have settled the question by what we knew at Routh. If I actually wrote down the theorem that was proved, you wouldn't understand a word of it or how it possibly related to the problem at hand, but nevertheless it is now a Theorem. It's just that if we want to understand the proof we're first going to have to go back to school and spend several years studying.

17
The Empire Strikes I

Musgrad Shadowlands Union, Ph 3 Pd 7 (11/Spring) 2615

Major General Petrova sat at the vast desk in the octagonal office belonging to the territory's leader, trying to come to terms with the events of the phase. She hadn't been sure how to react when the soldiers came to arrest her. She knew it was bound to come sooner or later. She had become too loud and too popular for the reactionary junta that ruled the union to tolerate. The crowd of supporters outside her house disturbed her. She wasn't ready to lead a revolt and she feared that being premature could lead to failure. She was about to go out to give herself up to the soldiers when the noise of the clash of arms and screams of the injured rang out.

She turned and went upstairs and out on to her balcony. Grabbing a megaphone she shouted above the din to call for calm. The two sides separated. There were a few that appeared to be dead, perhaps eight or so civilians and two soldiers, and several injured. Both the crowd and the soldiers waited expectantly.

"These soldiers are only carrying out their orders as they should do. I shall accompany them to the palace and then we can confront the Junta directly. Major," addressing the commanding officer, "you will march beside me and the rest of your escort can follow. "Then to the crowd, is there a doctor here?"

Three women raised their hands. "Good, please see to the injured and make arrangements to get the dead to the mortuary.

It appears I have urgent business at the palace." She then went back through the house to the front door.

The Major met her at the gate and saluted. "General, I'm sorry to have to do this but I have orders for your arrest."

"That's alright Major Mikhaila, I'm sure we can clear this up at the palace. Come walk next to me and it can easily be seen that you are doing your duty. You won't need those chains. I am offering you no resistance."

Major Mikhaila decided that it would be much easier to go along with the General's plan. She didn't like the look of the mob and realised that trying to lay hands on Petrova would result in a bloodbath with no guarantee of success. She was sure that some of the mob would be armed and she already had two dead soldiers, and maybe two more seriously injured. Besides, she also supported Petrova in her policy of accession to the Geosian accords. She came from humble stock. Her grandmother was a serf and her mother had escaped that condition through joining the army and rising to Sergeant. She herself had followed in her mother's footsteps and even won a commission, eventually reaching her present exalted rank.

Thus the procession marched to the centre of government. Petrova and the Mikhaila in step in the lead, the twenty or so soldiers in ranks of four behind them and the mob following a short distance behind. As they marched, the ranks of the mob swelled, as many on the citizenry came out of their houses to join them. There were even a few men in the crowd.

After they reached the palace and Petrova and the soldiers were let in, the mob followed and soon overwhelmed the guards trying to bar their entry. Petrova led the party into the council chamber where the junta were in session.

The mob then moved. They swarmed into the chamber, surrounded and dragged down the members of the Junta. One enterprising citizen leaped on to the table, drew a sword and proclaimed Petrova as Dictator. The mob yelled their approval and Petrova found herself lifted up and carried to the throne.

She stood, banged the hilt of her sword on the table and called for silence. She then proclaimed.

"Dear people of the Shadowlands, I am honoured to accept your nomination as Dictator of the Union for the period of one year, or until such time as we are in a position to install a fresh and reformed Government. Before doing so, however, I must resign my commission in the army as I will not live under a military dictatorship. Take these former rulers to the cells where they will await trial for their crimes. Now, we all have work to do to spread the news and reality of our revolution throughout the union."

The crowd cheered, the real revolution then began.

The junta had not been popular and there was little real resistance. But as she knew it would be, there was an awful lot that had to be done.

News travelled fast in the city and she received a stream of officials and army officers offering their support and assistance. Nevertheless, she knew she was nowhere near being properly prepared.

She should have been exhausted but her body was pumped full of adrenaline as she sat at that desk after the last official, from the foreign office, had left. This latter had undertaken to inform the embassies to the WF and GSE of the change of Government. She had opined that the WF ambassador would be supportive, and much relieved, because she had already incurred the displeasure of the Junta for her views on the Geosian accords, and was likely to have faced recall had the arrest of Petrova gone to plan.

The ambassador to the GSE would be more problematic. She was the sister of one of the members of the Junta and her appointment had been political. However, the Deputy Head of Mission was a career diplomat and likely to toe the new line. Petrova agreed a plan to recall the ambassador and inform the DHM of the new regime. Petrova also authorised the ambassador to the WF to announce the acceptance of the accords in full, but to explain there would be delay before formal acceptance because of the urgency of other priorities during the early stages of the regime.

The task of reforming the union and dragging it into the modern era was immense, and Petrova knew it. She couldn't believe she now actually had the opportunity to accomplish what she had for so long dreamed.

Louth Ph 1 Pd 8 (13/Spring) 2615

From ARTE to RASTU

Dearest Aimée

We had a fantastic party to celebrate the anniversary of first contact. The Geosians brought the most incredible fireworks and held displays in parks in the centre of both Goddess City and Louth. It's impossible for me to describe them but I suppose you may have seen similar displays on Geos. I can't even begin to understand how they arrange the chemistry to produce the effects they do, but then nor can any of the Geosians I've spoken to. In some sense their technology is as magical to them as it is to us. Lord Rivers had arrived to represent Geos and we had speeches from her and Jero that were relayed from Goddess City and shown on a big screen. Stripy Tiger was here in Louth and also made a speech, then Astra responded on behalf of Duplos and the WF. These speeches were relayed to Goddess City where the final formality came from the GSE ambassador. Major General Petrova was also invited but was unable to attend, more on that later. We seemed to party for hora and when we eventually went to bed we were all tired out. Esau tells me that, much to his relief, Zorro was too tired for sex - which must be a first! Astra and I slept for sixteen solid hora until our bladders forced us to get up.

The big political news is from the SU, which is why Petrova was unable to come to Goddess City. She had been causing such a fuss in the SU and gaining so much popular support that their ruling junta decided to arrest her and put her on trial for plotting to overthrow the government. When the soldiers turned up at her house they found a crowd waiting for them and several people were killed and many more injured before Petrova was able to calm the situation down. She then agreed to go with the soldiers to the Government Palace, but marched in triumph rather than in the chains brought to take her away. The crowd went with them and apparently it looked more like Petrova arresting the soldiers than the other way round. The long and the short of it is that the arrest attempt has backfired with the populus rising against their rulers in disgust, both at the arrest of their heroine and the brutality of the attack on the crowd outside her house. Petrova has been acclaimed as dictator pro tem while the old guard is languishing in the cells.

Consequently the SU is in turmoil while Petrova's supporters consolidate their position throughout the union. The revolution appears to be going well, however. The ambassador to the WF has come out in support and has announced that on Petrova's orders the SU will sign up to the accords. We all look forward to a more peaceful world with much overdue political and social reforms in the SU.

I haven't managed to speak to Jan about her research yet. She is in Marouth where she is going to be based for the rest of the spring and summer. I will see her when we go to South Beach. I'm going to spend two more periods here studying maths and science with the Geosians and then I'm taking a circuitous route to South Beach via Thayview, Soubanc and Montana.

While at Thayview Créezy and I shall look over our end of the cable car link to Isla. Then in Soubanc, we shall check on our boatskin business and also start preparing for a maritime venture that the Geosians think could be practical. We've come to a sensible political arrangement over the islands off the coast that the Geosians found and we are looking to establish a port on the northern shore of the largest one to see if we can establish a sea route from Soubanc via this island to West Isla. It will be tricky but the Geosians say they have the appropriate ship-building technology and we intend to establish a suitable shipyard in the mouth of the Vineyard River. I'll then visit your mother for a couple of phases on my way to South Bank. Créezy will stay in Soubanc to progress matters there.

love to you both from me and Astra

Arté

Fair Exchange

Camford Ph 1 Pd 9 (25/Spring) 2615

From RASTU to ARTE

Dearest Arté

You are seeing exciting times with the revolution in the SU. I recall Petrova when we met her as a colonel on contact phase. She seemed very sensible and quite unusual for a Shadowland officer. I really do credit her with avoiding an armed confrontation on that phase. If she is successful, there must really be an opportunity for a safer world on Duplos. Perhaps we might even get to visit the SU. I would like to see Musgrad. Pictures I've seen do look terribly exotic.

At least the prospects for peace on Duplos are better than here. There is great consternation right now. The Eastern Empire has announced that it has launched its first space station in a lower orbit than the New Norland constellation. This orbit is a lemniscate-like one, much of it being inside the planetary orbits. Wild Cat is appalled from a technical point of view. She says that she studied such orbits extensively but says they are incredibly unstable and she doesn't believe that the Easterners will have solved the problems. There are all sorts of comments being made on TV programmes and social media and it is very confusing.

Jezzie and Wild Cat have tried to explain all the politics to me but I'm not at all sure that I understand it. It is clear that both New Norland and the KNN consider it to be a hostile act and fear that the Eastern Empire are planning to undermine the relationship between them and Duplos. The exact intentions of the Easterners are unclear but rumours here don't sound promising. They range from making alliance with the Shadowlands Union against the rest of us to a plan to colonise the second continent and using it as a military base to conquer us. In any event, the President has been in secret talks with Gavos and promised all sorts of help in the event of hostile EE activity on Duplos.

New Norland has started an action in the Forum of Nations in an attempt to force the EE to guarantee that all actions on Duplos will be compliant with the accords. As I understand it, accession to the accords by the SU will be extremely helpful in the Forum.

Enough interplanetary and international politics! On the domestic front, Jezzie's seedparent died yesterwatch. Obviously, Jezzie is very upset even though it has been expected for the last selenth or so. The funeral is going to be next period and naturally I shall attend to support Jezzie. Wild Cat will look after Artur for me while we are away. Jezzie is concerned about her birthparent and is going to try to persuade her to move to Duplos to give her relief from her problems with osteoporosis.

This has long been Jezzie's plan and I've been able to give her the information she needed to decide on the most suitable location, which is somewhere on the inner sea coast. That means that South Beach would be ideal. Do you think you can find a suitable piece of land for her. Jezzie will come back with me when I return and will then arrange for a suitable house to be built.

Artur is progressing well and is into everything. Jezzie has had to move a number of objects out of his reach. He's developed a way of locomotion by shuffling on his bottom and can move at quite a rate, much faster than crawling. He has tried to stand but his legs aren't up to it. He finds it most frustrating. He looks so funny when he sits there waving his arms up and down, trying to get someone to pick him up. I do feel guilty that you are missing his babyhood but I have made a short video of him which is attached to this email. I want to go to Isla to meet Valray and ask her if you were just like him.

They've adjourned the trial of the SpaceDevCo spy in Kingstown while they consider the implications of the Eastern space station. This means Wild Cat hasn't had to go back to give her evidence. She and Flying Eagle visit us most watches with Snow Hare, who is now also crawling, and she and Artur play together quite happily most of the time.

My studies seem to be going well and my tutors tell me that I have reached a good standard of general scientific and mathematical knowledge to put me on a par with a well-educated Geosian. I've been thinking about the problems of electrification of the WF and it seems to me that the approach you have been following for our own properties is the sensible way forward. The infrastructure required for the sort of National Grid that they have here in the KNN seems much too difficult for our situation and, in any case, the huge central power stations are so damaging to the environment. I think we should mainly base our generation on small local schemes that can bring power at a community level with contributions from a variety of renewable resources from sun, wind and water and even from mechanical generation such as exercise bikes. Over here they have bicycles that don't actually transport you anywhere but are fixed and people ride them just for the exercise. Indeed, I've been using one myself to help get my figure back after Artur ruined it. I exercise this way for two hora per watch since I found that following Artur's birth I don't do anything like as much riding about town on my tricycle.

I think WwW could market such a model that also hooks up to an electrical generator which could feed into the local energy bank whenever it is used. I've calculated that two or three hora of such exercise per phase could provide a significant amount of domestic electricity, and be worthwhile as a supplement to solar and wind power, as well as being generally beneficial to health. I'm planning to connect an experimental generator to my exercise bike to compare practical experience with my calculations. It seems to me that we should do what we can to minimise or even avoid burning fuels to generate electricity, and I think we are a long way from being able to invest in nuclear power stations.

Love

Aimée

Thayview Ph 3 Pd 10 (23/Spring) 2615

From ARTE to RASTU

Dearest Aimée

At last I'm on my way to South Beach, but slightly behind my original schedule. Esau, Zorro and I had to go to a rather obscure college on the Banks of the River of Goddesses about twenty walks upstream of Goddess City to give a seminar on the ancient tablet. Esau talked about how his mother had found it not far from where the college now stands. I then described the Islish alphabet and how it bears similarities to the one used in the tablet. The writing on the tablet, like Islish, follows a boustrophedonic pattern. That is its lines alternate between left to right and right to left. One difficulty is that unlike modern Islish there is no word spacing, which makes interpretation more difficult. Anyway, Créezy and I had made a reasonable attempt at a transliteration into the Contish alphabet, but none of us had made any real headway with the language apart from seeing the name LANA appear a couple of times and then some guesses at more common words.

One of the academics in the audience looked at our attempts and said that she thought there was a resemblance to some words in an archaic form of Hidutish which is a dialect of one of the more obscure languages that is spoken in remote parts of the central south-east of the WF.

After that, in an extended session, we managed to come up with what I believe is a good translation that also corrects one or two of the guesses we had made about the alphabet and the word boundaries.

The inscription is indeed a prayer to Lana and was deliberately buried in the bank of 'her' river. It is further interesting in that it shows the ancient origin of some of our modern myths and practises. The prayer was a supplication to Lana to give the writer a grand-daughter. She explained, somewhat crudely, the steps she had taken to follow the rituals laid down by the Goddess. She had bought her daughter a man for her sixteenth birthday, the son of a good friend, for whom she had paid four groats. She had then personally supervised the conception, announcing that her daughter had been good and enjoyed the occasion and also mentioning three times. This was then followed by a cleansing ritual in the river after which she buried her tablet.

The purchase of a man for a daughter at coming-of-age is quite common on Isla, especially among the wealthier classes. Admittedly, the age is now twenty-four, but as most girls experience their first sex at fifteen or sixteen, it is easy to see how the onset of official adulthood came earlier in ages past. As you know, I myself was bought as a coming of age present for Thay. The practice of the mother being so closely involved in the conception is much rarer but not unheard of either on Isla or here in the WF. It is certainly part of the mythology. Finally the belief in three goes to ensure a daughter is still very much part of the common folklore throughout Duplos and is one of the questions that Jan Martskind is investigating in her study. You yourself subscribed to this belief, at least subconsciously, when you insisted Astra take over for the third time because of your unusual desire for a son. Furthermore it worked!

One of the reasons I believe I may have fathered a girl with one of Thay's closest friends is the way that Thay was most insistent that I 'cheered the friend up' and then ensured that she was in the receipt of the second time while her friend had the privilege of the third.

I've been inspecting the various works here on the strait coast. The buildings for this end of the cable car are now complete and the cable has been manufactured. We only have to await the opportunity to travel to Isla and undertake their part of the works. I have decided that I will not travel to Isla personally as long as there is even the slightest risk that I might be considered an escaped sacrifice, or that either Thay or Shay will claim ownership rights. Créezy approves of my decision and says she has plans for how to deal with the twins and bring about a suitable political settlement for Isla as a whole. She won't let me in on the details and I fear she will not be gentle as she is also determined to stamp out the sacrifices to Nepa and also some of the more disgusting rituals and practises. She gave me an example that has truly shocked me. The sacrifice to Nepa is the worst punishment they would inflict on a man but that is humane in the extreme compared to the fate of a woman deemed guilty of serious treachery, amounting to high treason. I'm not prepared to commit the details to paper (or electrons) but I cannot imagine a worse or more painful way of torturing a woman to death. Admittedly this punishment has not been used in our lifetime, but it is still available and would be used, for example, in the event of a failed armed rebellion.

The other major work is the new power station. What you say about the value of small local schemes is good as far as it goes; but we will also have some pretty big coastal power stations and none more so than the one in the narrows of the strait. Eventually this will provide enough electricity to power a significant proportion of the Federation. To take proper advantage of this, a backbone grid is planned. Work has started on laying transmission cables to Routh and Louth as well as to the coastal villages. A later stage is likely to extend the network to Soubanc, Goddess City and Dambach with the power station providing seventy-five percent of the electricity in all but Soubanc where the provision will be thirty percent. Another coastal power station, being constructed near Soubanc, will provide for more communities in the south-west. According to the Geosians the strait station will more efficient and powerful by an order of magnitude than any 'natural' power station they have anywhere on Geos. With a sufficient distribution system they claim the strait source could me made to provide enough energy for the whole population of Duplos. I was given a tour of the construction site and progress is impressive. It will be several years before station becomes properly operational but an initial pilot is planned for next year with power to the coastal settlements between Islaview Market and Dunos that should extend to Routh shortly after. Louth should then be powered in 2617 or 18 and the next phase to Dambach in 2619 with Goddess City in 2620-21 and Soubanc in 2621-22.

Créezy is going to email Jezzie about her removal to Duplos and will cc you. We've had a board discussion on the best way forward and Astra had an informal discussion with Jero about the restrictions under the accords and the tax implications for Jezzie in the KNN. I'm sure you will approve our plans and we really look forward to having Jezzie over here.

I'm counting the phases to your return, with luck less than a selenth now.

Love

Arté

Louth Ph 4 Pd 10 (24/Spring) 2615

From zorro@wheels.co.wf.dp to rastu@camford.ac.knn

Electricity from Exercise

Hi Aimée

I was really interested in your description of the exercise bike and I agree we should develop a similar product which also acts as an electricity generator. Arté says he's sure he can produce a suitable design which he will run past you before producing a prototype.

From a WwW point of view one of the real advantages is that it would enable us to increase sales of all our various battery-run products. The main constraint on sales today is the ability for customers to recharge batteries. We do run recharging services but the take-up is poor because the service is inconvenient and expensive for the customer, and for WwW, it is a bit of a loss leader as we don't quite recoup the costs. If a customer can recharge their own batteries using a simple exercise machine the market for our products should expand significantly.

Your exercise bike also solves another little problem. You are aware how the act of cycling is often very stimulating for a woman. Part of this seems to arise from the sensation of speed and the fresh air against your face and body, but another part can be from the direct stimulation from the motion against the seat as yours legs rotate the pedals.

I have experimented with various attachments to the front of the saddle and I can confirm that it is possible to achieve seriously good sexual stimulation as you ride. The major downside is that it can greatly increase the danger of an accident, and such attachments should be forbidden on safety grounds. However, for an exercise bike, this consideration goes away. I propose to develop appropriate saddle attachments which would have the added advantage of making healthy exercise even more popular. If Jezzie could also include the smart lubrication technology developed for her vibrator we would be on to a real winner.

I'm writing to you directly because this subject is not really for Arté, or men in general, and when I mentioned my idea to Créezy she just said "Zorro, you're incorrigible." But actually it is much more than that. I'm very happy with Esau, but as yet not all women are so lucky.

Hope to see you in South Beach before the end of the Summer.

Love

Zorro

Louth Ph 4 Pd 10 (24/Spring) 2615

From creezy@wheels.co.wf.dp

to jezzie@peteschildconsult.co.knn

cc rastu@camford.ac.knn

Returning to Duplos

Hi Jezzie and Aimée

Hope you are both keeping well. Jezzie I'm sorry to hear about your seedparent, it must be very difficult for you, please accept the condolencies of all of us here. On the other hand we are all excited at the prospect of you coming to live here with your birthparent. We have been thinking about how best to proceed. Astra has identified a good plot of land bordering her property at South Beach. It has frontage to the beach and is large enough for a substantial house, offering a high level of privacy and also the opportunity to build a jetty for access to the sea by boat. I've talked to Jero about the rules under the accords and also the tax liabilities for you on Geos. Jero has confirmed that if you stay on Duplos for at least half the year then any income you receive and keep here will not be subject to KNN income tax and you will only be taxed on income earned on Geos or taken to Geos from Duplos. However, she warns that you won't be allowed to actually own land on Duplos.

We think the best way out is for WwW to buy and own the land and lease it to you for a peppercorn rent. You can then own the buildings, paid for by some of the money WwW holds for you. I'm sure we can come up with a comfortable house design to meet your wishes and arrange for it to be built ready for you. Astra now has proper indoor plumbing, electricity and network connection in her house and has the capacity to extend all the services to the neighbouring property for you, so you won't have to do without the comforts you are used to. As for work, as well as whatever the Geosians here can offer you, which I understand is quite a lot, we can also make use of your talents on a number of our projects with WwW.

You are not the only one to have noticed the potential of our lower gravity for care of the elderly. I have been in correspondence with Red Robin on the subject. She is planning to establish a care home here, also on the inner sea coast. We are finalising the details at the moment but the current plan is for us to form a separate company under the umbrella of WwW which will enter into a joint venture with Red Robin. We have identified a suitable site just west of Lanamont which looks ideal. Again we will buy and own the land which Red Robin's company will rent. There is a mansion already on the site which will be modernised and form the centre of the complex. At first we expect about a dozen patients together with a small Geosian medical team with other staff recruited locally. One Duplosian woman, who is currently on Geos undertaking nursing training, will also be joining the medical team. Eventually, if Red Robin is as successful as she hopes, the complex will include suitable homes for slightly younger retirees to be able to live more independently, while being able to transfer later to the care home when and if their care needs increase.

Lanamont is not all that far from South Beach; and it seems to me that the Geosian medical team there could also offer some service to you and your birthparent, which should make it much easier for you both to make the transition to Duplos.

18

The Empire Strikes II

Kingstown, New Norland: W ***1*** Pd ***B*** (***31***/Spring) ***161B***[5]

"They've done what?" The President was apoplectic.

"Mizzer President, we do believe it was a genuine accident. However, the Eastern space station went out of control and, as it broke up, a piece of debris has collided with one of ours and caused some damage to the station, with the loss of two lives, both New Norlanders. All the crew aboard the Eastern station will have died in the break-up."

"What in hell went wrong? I thought the Eastern Station was a copy of ours, based on their espionage. Does this also mean that all of our stations are vulnerable to a similar break-up?"

"Their station wasn't an actual copy of ours. They were able to accelerate their programme because of crucial material they stole from us; but there were many technical details entirely of their own; and there is no reason to suppose that we share their weaknesses."

"OK, good, but what was the problem?"

"Basically, it was their choice of orbit. You will recall that whereas we are orbiting outside the orbits of both planets, they were trying an inside orbit, that is one that went in a sort of figure of eight about the barycentre which enables them to fly much closer to the planets' surfaces. We had ourselves given careful consideration to such orbits but our expert, Wild Cat Waters ximself, had concluded that such orbits would be too

5 Recall that Geosian numbers are in duodecimal written in bold italic.

unstable to be of practical use. It appears that Wild Cat was right and although the first orbit was close to the design, the instability soon set in and, the third time round, the station went out of control. The various forces operating on the station then found a weak spot and caused the break-up. I guess we were lucky that only a small part actually hit us, and also that only one of our stations was in the way. It could have been a lot worse."

"Small comfort to those two brave crewmen we lost, or their families. Have we been able to recover their bodies?"

"Yes zir, a shuttle was sent from the station and the two bodies were picked up and taken to the neighbouring station, whence they will eventually be returned to Geos.

"They must be given a suitable reception with all honours. When the families have been informed in person, I will speak to them by videophone. We should then call a press conference and I will speak to the nation, but we must maintain a news blackout until the next of kin of the deceased have been informed."

"Yes zir, all the proper arrangements will be made. We will keep you informed and also prepare our protests to the Eastern Empire."

"Good, get our ambassador to make the protest to coincide with the press conference and call their ambassador here. You can leave xim kicking xer heels until I've finished talking to the nation."

"Yes zir, all will be done as you say. We will also bring Waters back from the KNN and get xim to the affected station to assess the damage and recommend the necessary remedial action."

With that, the official left the President's office to set the various actions in train.

Twin Worlds II

Camford W 5 Pd 11 (42/Spring) 2615

From rastu@camford.ac.knn

To arte@wheels.co.wf.dp; astra@wheels.co.wf.dp

Awful News

Dearest Astra and Arté

The most dreadful thing has happened. The Eastern Empire space station was in a highly unstable orbit and everything went haywire. The station flew out of control and broke up, killing everyone on board. Parts of the debris also collided with one of the New Norland stations causing serious damage and also killing two of the crew. Obviously, the whole thing has caused a tremendous stink here and various political actions are ongoing.

Wild Cat and Flying Eagle have both been recalled to Kingstown and Wild Cat is going to have to go to supervise the damage assessment and ensuing repairs to the station. Flying Eagle is also likely to find herself back in space for a while. In the meantime Roaring Deer is looking after Snow Hare in Camford and I am helping out where I can.

From our personal point of view, this incident is going to delay the launch of the two new stations and also our return to Duplos. I'm sorry to have to tell you this and disappointed over the extra delay before coming home and seeing you again. Meanwhile I will be able to learn more over here and Jezzie and Jo are planning some fun expeditions.

On yet another serious note, yesterwatch Jezzie and I had a visit of a very sinister sort. The visitor came from the KNN security service which Jezzie says is a rather clandestine organisation that looks after the national security of the country. Catching spies and disrupting terrorist organisations, that sort of thing. Anyway, it seems that there is a threat from some criminal or terrorist organisations against Duplosians here on Geos.

The security agent wasn't able to be very specific but said they were concerned that there could be attempts to kidnap me (or other Duplosians) and then blackmail the NN and KNN Governments for political motives. The security service have general intelligence about such threats, but aren't able to pinpoint precise targets or work out exactly who are behind the threats. Factions in both the Eastern Empire and the Grand Peoples Republic are implicated as are some organised criminal gangs.

They think that the most likely targets will be from the Duplos embassy staff or some of the exchange students in New Norland. However, they can't rule out an attack on me and Artur, as we are well known through the media coverage. As a result we are being provided with a bodyguard and there will be constant surveillance outside Jezzie's house and when we go out. It's all very scary but also exciting. I can't get my head round it or understand why I'm not just terrified. Obviously, I am very worried for Artur but somehow I'm less worried about myself. It's all very unreal.

On the other hand, Jezzie is properly terrified and has announced that she is going to sleep in my bed with me and with a gun under the pillow. I hope she doesn't snore, or end up shooting at ghosts. She has also re-arranged the furniture, moving Artur's cot into my bedroom and well away from both the door and the window. She insists he is not to be allowed out of our sight at any time. Actually I do agree with her on this.

I promise you I will take care and you can have confidence in the efforts of the security people. I'll keep you posted on developments as they occur.

love

Aimée

Louth: Ph 1 Pd 12 (29/Spring) 2615

From arte@wheels.co.wf.dp

to rastu@camford.ac.knn

LOOK AFTER YOURSELF

Darling Aimée

Astra and I are very worried for you over the awful news from Geos. Jero Dicks called on us earlier to assure us that everything possible was being done to keep you safe, but it is still very concerning. Of course you may be saying it's all very well for me to worry about you when Créezy and I are planning risky ventures of our own, but honestly, it is different.

Créezy went down to Soubanc and inspected the ship as it nears completion. We are planning the maiden voyage next period and after that will sail to the island that lies about sixty-five walks west of Soubanc. To comply with the accords we will have a mixed crew from the GSE and WF, but the plan is to seek a suitable harbour for a future staging port between Soubanc and West Isla. We both plan to be aboard for this voyage; but when eventually we make the second stage to Isla itself, I will stay away.

All four of us are setting off for South Beach next phase (actually five since Zorro has Esau in tow). Zorro and Créezy are planning a shopping expedition to Marcenza on the way. Créezy is being very secretive about their plans and I am quite intrigued as I believe it has something to do with our reconnection to Isla. All Zorro says is that it's girl stuff.

If we were dealing with the old Zorro I would have said they were going out on the razzle among the Marcenza fleshpots; but now it appears she has body only for Esau, and Créezy is largely celibate. I'll just have to contain my curiosity until they are ready to reveal all.

I'll write again once we have settled back into South Beach and perhaps I will have at last had my session with Jan.

Stay safe,

love

Arté (and Astra)

Part 3: Connections

19
Crazy

South Beach: Ph 1 Pd 14 (7/Summer) 2615

From ZORRO to RASTU

Créezy's killer outfit

Hi Aimée

Créezy and I stopped off in Marcenza on our way to South Beach so she could acquire an exotic outfit, which she says she needs for her planned conquest of Isla (her words!). The result is just incredible.

When we got here she gave the others a fashion show and the effect on the men just had to be seen to be believed. I thought they would both burst out of their trousers, especially Arté - Esau is not so well-endowed! I'm afraid Mummy and I found it very amusing, although we too were awed by Créezy. Poor Arté was rather embarrassed, while Esau fell to his knees and prostrated himself before the vision.

Well, Créezy is tall but she had shoes with extra thick soles and high heels bringing her up to two strides in height, which apparently will just top Thay and Shay on Isla. She then had a full length shimmering golden gown that is hemmed with sapphires. However the two sides are slit right up to her waist in an Eastern cut which is designed to accentuate her legs and affect men in the way that it did for Arté and Esau. To magnify the sensuality, the front neckline plunges in a steep V right down to her navel while the sleeves are a see through red silk. In her navel she wore a huge diamond and the points of the gown covering her breasts are set with rubies cut to emulate the nipples.

The whole outfit was topped by a head-dress with centre piece of three white tail-feathers from one of the rare flightless giant birds found on the margins of the desert to the south of the GSE. The centre one of these is a full stride long with the other two slightly shorter and perfectly matched. At the centre is an enormous emerald, and round her neck a ring of diamonds.

You really have to see it to appreciate it fully and the impression it has on others. I'd like to send you a picture but Créezy has embargoed all images until after her triumphant return to Isla. In fact she was somewhat hesitant about letting me describe it at all. She considers it to be Top Secret until used in anger so to speak. Like a weapon of war, which I suppose in a way is what it is.

After all that, I'm sure you'll be relieved to know that I was able to bring Esau back to reality and ensure his reaction wasn't wasted. I expect Mummy did the same for Arté.

Créezy has packed her war-dress away carefully and it won't appear again until she reaches Isla, so our men are safe!

I look forward to your return

love

Zorro

From ARTE to RASTU

Darling Aimée

Twin Worlds II

Astra and I are relying on 'No news is good news' regarding the dangers you are in on Geos, and we try not to worry too much since there is nothing we can do to help; but you and Artur are always in our thoughts and conversation.

As promised, Jan Martskind came to see us last period to present the findings of her study. (It now seems a bit strange for us to use the female pronouns for Jan, since we now know she is male, after we all went swimming in the sea, but we will stick to our convention). The outcome of the study is that there really is truth in our ancient myths about sons and daughters and also that there is a biological purpose for a bump other than keeping Zorro happy.

Jan says that in their biology the production of sperm by males is more-or-less continuous after puberty. This means that, unless there is some medical disorder, a male always has sperm available to fertilise a female, and also that the distribution of X and Y chromosomes is random in the sperm so that the likelihood of a son or daughter is approximately 50%. In actuality sons are slightly more probable because, apparently, female babies are stronger and before modern medicine infant mortality was higher for boys than girls. Somehow the net effect is for equal numbers surviving infancy. Immediately after ejaculation the sperm count reduces while the body has to build up supplies, which on average takes around a horum.

With us it's different. Male Duplosians don't manufacture sperm all the time but on a 'supply on demand' basis. The trigger for sperm production is the rubbing of the bump. This means there is a delay before there is sufficient sperm available to fertilise a female. The sperm count for a first ejaculation is very low. It is possible that a woman can get pregnant but rather unlikely and there is a danger that the sperm is 'old' which can affect the health of the baby. After the first ejaculation has flushed the 'old' sperm out of the man, the newly manufactured sperm is available for subsequent ejaculations.

Another difference is that in Duplosians the X and Y sperm are not produced randomly but there is a tendency for the male Y sperm to be manufactured first and the female X sperm to take longer. This means that the sperm from a second ejaculation has an abundance of Y chromosomes while that of a third ejaculation is predominantly X.

Jan's findings suggest that the probability of a son from a second ejaculation is about 70% while from a third the probability of a daughter is about 80%. Without deliberate intervention the net effect in nature is still to give a 50-50 distribution of boys and girls. However, as you know, we do interfere with nature by following the myth and preferring a daughter, which probably explains why there are excess females in our society both on Isla and on the continent. We'll just have to see whether turning myth into knowledge is beneficial or harmful to our society.

We also had a good discussion with Jan on evolution. She agrees with you that memes do not really give a satisfactory explanation for the evolution of speech and brains. In our discussion Créezy put forward the suggestion that the answer could be in war. People on both Geos and Duplos are incredibly warlike in a way that other animals are not and, regrettably, we are rather good at it, especially the Geosians.

Success at war is heavily dependent on command and control. This requires a high level of communication and similar team building skills. Furthermore the planning of tactics and strategy require significant mental ability and abstract thought. Basically without speech and brains we couldn't do war successfully.

On the other hand having the skills to be a successful war leader is of clear advantage in the mating game, with successful warriors likely to have first pick of mates, and indeed of other desirable resources. Those on their own side being flattered by the attention, and on the opposing side having no choice in the matter. It is easy to see how the development of speech, brain and war could form a positive feedback system driving the necessary evolution.

I think we managed to convince Jan who was also able to add the information that on Geos there are other primate species that also make sort of war on their own kind. These apes are nothing like as effective as people and it is easy to see that they are limited by their shortcomings in command and control. They do however manage to maintain social groups of up to about a hundred and fifty, and leaders emerge who engage in both offensive and defensive warfare with rival groups. Perhaps the terms we now use 'Homo Sapiens Geosa' and 'Homo Sapiens Duplosa' are undeserved and we should really be 'Homo Bellicosa'.

We also spoke to Jan about your friend Jo Jensen. She became quite agitated and tongue-tied. Zorro was able to pick up a lot from her body language and other reactions and we are pretty sure that Jan is in love with Jo but much too shy and embarrassed to show her feelings, or make any move in her direction. Indeed we suspect that coming to Duplos was partly influenced by her fears of a relationship with Jo. We must see if we can find a way of bringing them together. Jan is now on her way home to Camford for midsummer but says she fully intends to return here in the Autumn to take up a position at the University of Marcenza, which apparently she can do alongside her professorship at Camford, all because of the wonders of internet connectivity. She is interested in studying the Geology of the inner sea and also the Zoology of the tropical regions of the planet. Marouth/Marcenza are ideally situated as a base for these studies.

The other big event was Créezy's goddess-gown. I won't try to describe it, I'll leave that to a woman. I'm afraid I rather embarrassed myself with my reaction. A man's body doesn't always obey his brain. Créezy herself remained dignified, but, once they had got over their own shock, both Zorro and Astra showed their amusement at our expense (me and Esau). At least they then tried to make it up to us afterwards, and I don't really blame them, because I'm sure Esau and I made quite a spectacle of ourselves. I have to say though, I really would like to see one of those ostriches that have such feathers that went into Créezy's hat.

Morrow-phase I'm going to Montana to see your mother on my way to Soubanc. Créezy will come on later and we will meet up ready for the voyage to the off-shore island. As well as being the true maiden voyage of the new ship it will also be the first exploration of new lands under the accords. We will have back-up from the Geosians and always be in radio contact with them so there is no need for you to be concerned for our safety. They have already flown some drones over the island so we know it is uninhabited by people or large predators. There is a promising natural harbour on the north-east coast which is where we will be heading. Créezy tried to persuade the older Esau to come along as an experienced sailor; but he declined saying that he is now much too old for such adventures. We will have three of the Geosian exchange students with us who have sailing experience. Also we are not relying on wind power entirely but have electric engines to assist manoeuvring and to provide emergency back-up if required. Various generators on board, wind, solar and pedal-powered, will keep the batteries topped up.

The distance to the island is about a hundred walks and we are expecting the voyage to take about sixteen hora each way. We intend to spend a couple of phases on land, surveying the site and immediate surroundings. As there will be no roads suitable for our usual range of SPC we will be taking two of a new prototype with tracked wheels and partial electric power which are intended for use on rough terrain for construction and agricultural applications.

I will email you again after we return, when we will be going to Thayview to inspect the works for the power station and cable car and prepare for the drone survey of Isla.

Love from us all, but especially from me.

Arté

Camford: W 1 Pd 17 (28/Summer) 2615

From RASTU to ARTE; ASTRA

cc ZORRO; CREEZY

Dearest Arté and Astra

Thanks for your newsy email. I can't wait to see Créezy's Goddess outfit. Sorry, Arté, but I think I would have laughed too at the sight of you and Esau almost bursting out of your trousers.

At least that should have been a nice present for Astra and Zorro! The thought is certainly giving me an itch.

Fashions here are really rather boring. Most of the time people just wear shirt, trousers and a jacket or jumper. Everything is unisex and indeed quite unsexy. However in the warm weather I have allowed myself some of my regular short tunics which does cause a bit of a stir with the locals. Jezzie says I look indecent but fun. Actually when it's very hot the Geosians do change their styles and often wear a loose fitting gown with nothing underneath. Jezzie has some quite fetching ones which she wears when we go to the river, a swimming pool or the beach. Much easier to shed when going for a swim.

I, too, would like to see some of our more exotic animals. Here on Geos they have zoos which you can visit to see all sorts of creatures. As well as entertaining the public, these zoos have a serious scientific and educational purpose for the study of the animals and conservation of threatened species. as I think I said in an earlier email, some of the animals are analogues of those we know, like dogs and bears, while others are quite unlike any we know about. Most fascinating to me are the apes and monkeys. These primates are in a way related to people as they have a relatively recent common ancestor. Jo says that we might well find analogous species on Duplos living in the tropical regions south of the desert belt. Most of the non-human primate species on Geos are indigenous to the tropics and humans are the exception having spread across the whole planet. Jo's speciality is the study of apes and human evolution. I am trying to encourage her to come to Duplos and take part in our future explorations of the sub-desert lands and second continent.

Twin Worlds II

There are two other major animal families that don't appear to have Duplosian equivalents, felines and snakes. I mentioned felines in my earlier email. They are beautiful. They all have wonderful fur coats with interesting markings. Artur loves stroking our neighbours' two cats and they are very tolerant of his attentions. I'd love to bring one home with me but Jezzie and Jo both say it would be a bad idea. Settlers took them to New Hope and, with no natural enemies, cats devastated the local wild life, causing major ecological damage. I have been learning what a delicate balance there is between plant and animal life and how great care needs to be taken to conserve the natural order. People on Geos believe they have made terrible mistakes in their past and are desperate to ensure that we don't repeat their bad experiences.

In contrast snakes are very creepy. They have no legs, just a very long thin body and slither on the ground or in trees or swim in warm seas. They are predators and many species have a deadly poisonous bite. Others are extremely large and can even swallow large animals, including humans. I find them very scary and I'm glad we don't have any on Duplos.

Midsummer here is a major celebration and we partied long into the night on several watches. I have suffered some dreadful hangovers but it has been tremendous fun with booze flowing, fantastic food and unbelievable fireworks. Thousands of pounds are spent on just a few minutes of display. It's all quite incredible. At one party Jezzie went a bit wild and I lost her for a couple of hora. She hasn't said, but I think she was getting her itch scratched - they are so coy about it here!

Talking of which I have had a quiet word with Jo. It was a bit awkward because of their conventions but I think I helped her.

Fair Exchange

We've arranged a dinner party to welcome Jan back, just Jezzie, me, Jan and Jo. Jezzie and I are going to find some excuse to leave them alone and now that Jo knows that Jan has real feelings for her, she will find the confidence to make the first move. Both of them have been so scared of spoiling their existing relationship that they have not been prepared to risk a move towards greater intimacy. Very much like you and me, Arté. I think for some time I had known that I loved you, not just as a brother-like friend, but I didn't fully know myself and was unwilling to risk a rejection. I am so grateful to Zorro and Créezy for prompting the change.

Now I've gone and given myself another itch. I'm so longing to get back to you. You'd just better be ready to welcome me back properly. I promise to be good and not make you sore with my demands. (Sorry, Zorro and Créezy, I know these comments should be only for Arté - and possibly Astra).

Turning to the political scene, there was a minor incident when it appeared that someone was trying to get to me but the security guard managed to intercept her and make an arrest. The threat hasn't completely gone away but we have been told that the danger to me and Artur has lessened, with the terrorists more focused on New Norland.

The tensions with the Eastern Empire have increased further and a war has broken out between East and West Sylvania on the northern coast of the Sylvanian continent. In some way this is a proxy war between the Eastern Empire and New Norland with the Sylvanian countries as their respective clients.

New Norland moved a censure motion in the Forum of Nations against the EE for the incident with the space stations. The EE lost and was ordered to pay substantial reparations. The GPRG actually turned up and supported the EE but otherwise the only other country to vote with them was East Sylvania. I don't think the EE has actually paid the reparations, nor are they likely to, but it is nevertheless very uncomfortable for them politically.

Possibly as a distraction, a minor border incident has been allowed to escalate and East Sylvanian soldiers crossed into West Sylvania and have captured a major city which they have claimed historically. We see the most horrible pictures on television showing the destruction as the two countries bomb each other and fight on the ground. New Norland and KNN air forces are giving support to West Sylvania while the Eastern Empire is supplying East Sylvania and probably sending troops as well. It's all quite worrying and awful for the innocent people caught up in the fighting.

There is also a potential refugee crisis as thousands of West Sylvanian civilians are fleeing the fighting and crossing the narrow strait between West Sylvania and Souland in small boats. The Souland authorities are asking for help from their largely unresponsive neighbours and many of the boats are unsafe and refugees are being drowned as they attempt the crossing. The KNN and Midgeos have sent aid in the form of money and supplies to West Sylvania to establish temporary camps for refugees in West Sylvania itself. Camford University has held various fundraising events and Jezzie and I have both made donations.

There is a fear that the conflict could escalate into a world war but Jezzie discounts that as fear-mongering. We've also heard from Zir Jacky and in her opinion the conflict will be contained in the region, but the end is not in sight and fighting could well continue for years. Elsewhere on the continent the Central Sylvanic Republic has closed its northern borders and Equatoria has also closed its border with East Sylvania. Jezzie says there is some danger, albeit small, that unrest could spread within Sylvania. If it does, Jo is very concerned about the prospects for the very delicate populations of apes in Central Sylvania, where she has been involved in conservation efforts, and the animals are in danger from loss of habitat and poaching. War could not only disrupt this work but even cause the extinction in the wild of two complete ape species. Although every single human life is valued more highly than any animal, there are billions of humans on Geos but only thousands of even the most populous ape species.

On another topic close to home, Wild Cat has completed her report on the damage to the space station. Her recommendation is that repairs in space would be too expensive and the station should be retired from service. Some parts will have to be destroyed but the central units can be brought to a low Geos orbit and incorporated into one of the new stations. If Wild Cat's recommendations are accepted the first of the new stations will be launched in the autumn into a new slot midway between the now defunct station and one of its neighbours. The second new station will follow into the diametrically opposite slot and the third station due next year will replace the dead one, once it has been cleared away. The plan is still for me and Artur to return on one of the new stations. With luck this might be in late autumn, just a selenth behind schedule.

Love to you all

Aimée

20
Kidnapped I

Rastu woke with a headache and a sick feeling in her stomach. She was on a bed in a small room that seemed to be in motion, up and down while also rocking side to side. Where on Duplos was she - oh not Duplos, Geos! Still, where was she?

She tried to reach out but she couldn't. She noticed that her hands were tied. There wasn't much light, just a small amount coming through a round window high on the wall to her left. The window appeared to be just about a length in diameter, pretty small then. Every now and then it appeared to be splashed with water from the outside. Obviously it was sealed shut. The last thing she remembered was walking through a park on her way from Jezzie's house to college. She vaguely remembered that a man had approached and said something. Had she felt a prick in her arm? Maybe, but she couldn't recall anything more.

As her senses began to clear she became aware of a gentle sobbing emanating from the corner of the room to the right behind her head. Artur? No, he hadn't been with her. He was on a 'play-date' with Snow Hare being looked after by Roaring Deer. Jezzie was working at home and Wild Cat and Flying Eagle were both back in Kingstown. This must be connected to the threat the Security Service had warned them of. How long had she been gone? Would they have missed her, and was there any chance of rescue?

She managed to turn herself around and sit on the bed with her feet on the floor. Her head almost touched the ceiling. She wouldn't be able to stand up straight. She saw that the sobs were coming from a child, scrunched up in foetal position on a couch of sorts. She spoke in Norse. "Hello, we seem to be in a mess, my name is Rastu and I come from Duplos. Who are you and do you know anything about what's happening or where we are?"

Between sobs, the figure answered her. "I've seen you on television, and caught a glimpse of you at Grandpa's when you and the others were being honoured. I'm Prince Henry and my Mummy is the King's second child. I was going home after playing cricket when I was jumped on by two thugs and carried off. My security guard was shot. I'm pretty sure xe's dead. I don't know what they want but it's obviously political, or maybe they just want ransom money. There'll be a hell of a fuss, which is almost certainly why we're on this boat out at sea somewhere. The kidnappers will want to get us out of the KNN as quickly as possible."

Rastu was in shock, there was too much to get her head around and she knew she had to calm herself, clear her head and work things out rationally. Meanwhile she would try not to panic and take things as they came, dumin by dumin. Looking around her, she realised that she was the adult and would have to assume responsibility. "Right, Prince Henry, we've got to be strong and trust to the KNN security services to work things out. As things stand we're not going to rescue ourselves. We should probably assume that we are under surveillance and there is no chance of us escaping, and certainly not while at sea. If you can get up, come over here and sit next to me. We'll manage somehow. If they'd wanted to kill us they would have done it by now. Be a brave boy, and let's show them that we are not frightened of a few bullies. You are a boy aren't you?"

"Yes, I'm a boy but you're not supposed to ask that, it's rude. I'm not handcuffed like you so I can move freely in the cabin so I'll do as you ask. Do you think they're going to feed us? I'm starving. Oh and leave off the Prince - just call me Henry."

Rastu smiled at the last; trust a teenage boy to think of his stomach. "I'm sorry for the impoliteness, Henry. It's sometimes hard for me to remember how sensitive you all are to gender identification. On Duplos we are quite the opposite. But I was bound to find out pretty soon given the primitive nature of the ablutions in this cabin. I'm sure you'll get fed soon. I'm not sure that I could face anything myself. I'm not used to sea travel and am feeling a bit queasy."

Henry joined Rastu on her bed and also fetched her a bucket in case her queasiness got the better of her. Somehow that in itself made her feel easier. Shortly afterwards, they heard their door being unlocked and a man entered with two plates of food.

"Don't try anything silly", xe said in heavily accented Norse. I've brought you something to eat and," turning to Rastu. "If you promise to behave yourself and accept your situation I shall remove your cuffs. Sometime in the next few tocks we are going to transfer you both to a submarine to make it harder for the Royal Navy to track us. The submarine will be even more cramped I'm afraid but it can't be helped. It won't be for too long."

"I'll behave but tell me where are you taking us, and why?"

The man removed the handcuffs from Rastu. "You'll find out where you're going in all good time. Who knows, maybe we'll take you home! As for why, you can blame it all on the arrogance of New Norland and those one-sided accords. In due course the KNN and Duplos Governments will be notified of our just demands. For your sakes let's hope they see sense."

Fair Exchange

"As a prince of the blood I can tell you that XMG will never give in to blackmail, even at the cost of my life. And I fully support that policy."

"And as for the Western Federation on Duplos. We don't really have a government in the sense that you have here, and I am just a nobody with no influence whatsoever. My mother, and my few friends, both on Duplos and here on Geos, will undoubtedly mourn me. I will miss being able to bring up my baby son but it shouldn't harm his life. It is quite common throughout Duplos for male children to be separated from their mothers at a young age. Thus while you might cause great hurt and distress to us as individuals there can be no expectation of your actions assisting your so-called cause."

The man shrugged. "We'll see, but no matter, I think you both underestimate your weak-minded leaders." With that xe left them to eat their meal, locking the cabin door behind xim.

"I thought as much, the whole thing smacks of Eastern Empire hypocrisy. I may only be a twelve year old boy but I come from a long line of kings and despite my fear will pull myself together and defy their evil."

"Well said young man, we'll stick together and just do our best, OK?"

Camford: W ***3*** Pd ***16*** (***30***/Summer) ***161B***

From jezzie@peteschildconsult.co.knn to ARTE; ASTRA

Worrying News

Arté, Astra

I don't want to alarm you but I think you ought to be alerted to what is happening over here. There's no easy way of putting this but Aimée has gone missing. She set off for college as usual but didn't return at her usual time. I waited a while because there were lots of possible explanations. However, eventually I checked up and discovered that she hadn't arrived at college at all. I've contacted the police and all the local hospitals in case she's had an accident but there is no sign of her.

I hope my concerns are misplaced but it's not as if she is inconspicuous. I'll look after Artur in her absence, helped by Roaring Deer Waters and Jo Jensen. I'll keep you informed of all developments as soon as I know anything.

Jezzie

Camford: W ***4*** Pd ***16*** (***31***/Summer) ***161B***

From JEZZIE to ARTE; ASTRA; ZORRO; CREEZY

Really Awful News

All,

The worst has happened. I've had a visit from the security service. They are convinced that Aimée has been kidnapped by agents allied to the Eastern Empire. They don't know whether this has been sanctioned by their Government or whether it's down to some rogue elements of the EE military, which is deeply penetrated by organised crime.

As if that isn't bad enough there has also been a kidnap of one of the King's grandchildren. A guard was murdered as part of that kidnap operation. The security service are treating the two kidnaps as linked although they don't yet have positive evidence that they are. I don't know many details but Jero Dicks will be given a full briefing and will visit you to tell you what they know, and offer support.

All things considered, Artur is bearing up well. Obviously he's missing his mother but doesn't seem too distressed and of course doesn't have any understanding of what's happening. Although I'm very happy to keep looking after him here, I think it would be best if I brought him back to you on Duplos as soon as practicable. Other than that, there is not a lot that you or I can actually do. We just have to leave it to the authorities to do the best they can.

This is all so awful that I don't know what to say. Jo and Jan are being very supportive to me; and Wild Cat has called me from Kingstown to offer what support xe can, which at least will ensure that we get some high priority for bringing Artur home.

love

Jezzie

21
Kidnapped II

Jay searched through the park bins. Not a pleasant job but at least they hadn't been emptied so it should still be there. "Ah! There it is." Xe fished out Rastu's mobile phone. "Sloppy, the kidnappers should have destroyed it properly. Let's hope they continue to make mistakes."

Jay couldn't help but blame ximself for not keeping a closer guard on Rastu, despite the assessment that the threat had reduced. Later when xe learnt about the events at the palace xe reflected that it was actually a blessing. While it was possible that xe might have foiled the attempt, it was much more likely that xe would have been killed before xe was aware what was happening, like the unfortunate man guarding the prince. Then xe wouldn't have been able to do anything to help. As it turned out xe had some chance of following the trail.

Naturally, the kidnappers had assumed that the phone would have a tracker but hadn't realised the linkage to a beacon on Rastu's person. When the phone detected that Rastu was more than six twilomen distant, it alerted the agent's app. It was then a simple matter for Jay to geolocate the phone and determine that things were amiss. Xe realised that time would be of the essence and that xe needed to set off in hot pursuit - no time for needless bureaucracy, xe thought. Having xer hands on the working phone xe could get a rough fix on Rastu's location. Xe reckoned they would be about a **meal** ahead of xim, which would be tricky as they could be close to the sixtwy twilomen range of the device.

The good news was that he got a fix. The bad news was that Rastu appeared to be somewhere at sea off the south coast, heading due south. That meant they would be in international waters before anyone could catch up with them.

Xe wasn't prepared to risk unnecessary delays by trying to speak to xer superiors. Xe blagged xer way into taking one of the helicopters that the service kept at an airfield about twentwy twilomen South East of Camford and set off for the south coast. Xe dictated a report into xer laptop and sent it to xer HQ.

The prime minister had called an urgent joint meeting of the national security council and the privy council. Unusually, xe didn't chair the meeting but that honour fell to the King ximself. As well as the politicians from the inner cabinet, Chancellor of the Exchequer, Foreign, Home and Defence Secretaries, the leader of the opposition was included. Supporting them was the head of Royal Security, the permanent secretaries from the departments mentioned and the heads of the intelligence services.

The Director General of the Security Service briefed the meeting on the current situation.

"We do not have direct evidence that the two kidnappings are connected but nevertheless our current best assessment is that they are. One of our agents who has been advising the Duplosian, Rastu, has provided xim with technical monitoring equipment that has proved useful. Firstly the agent was alerted when it became clear that Rastu was separated from xer telephone and the agent was able to locate the phone in a waste bin in the park where xe had been abducted. Xe was then able to trace xim to the south coast and thence to a boat in international waters. Unfortunately the signal has been lost in mid-ocean. Nevertheless, our agent is on the case and assesses that the chances of finding xim again are good. Currently xe is engaged on identifying the boat and expects to make progress very shortly. As to the guilty party, our assessment remains that the operators are from the Eastern Empire and linked to their dissatisfaction with the Geos-Duplos accords. We are unable to say whether the EE Government is complicit, or even witting. We are confident in the assessment that elements of the EE intelligence services are involved; but its is probable that they are either rogue elements operating independently or under the control of organised criminals allied to extremist oligarchs who are known to have penetrated the EE military and security agencies."

"Thank-you, I'm sure your service will continue to do everything possible to locate and recover the victims. The question of attribution is crucial. We really need to know whether the EE Government is behind this or not as our response will be critically dependent on that judgement. Foreign Secretary, do you have anything to add from the diplomats."

"Yes your majesty. Obviously the Easterners were always going to deny involvement. However, the FO view is that on this occasion the denial is probably correct. The EE ambassador was visibly distressed and when the PUS and I met with xim we were convinced that at least xe had no knowledge of the situation. Our ambassador too, is of the opinion that the reaction xe has seen points clearly to the EE First Leader being caught completely by surprise. Intelligence from our usual trustworthy sources also suggests that the threat to Duplosian individuals was from hardline rogue elements within the EE services, but without official sanction. The Defence Secretary may want to amplify."

"Yes, the EE authorities might have just about contemplated an attack on a Duplosian, but would have almost certainly gone for one of the higher officials in the embassy in New Norland. Rastu, as a private citizen, just isn't the sort of target that the EE would go for. The Prince is an entirely different matter. Kidnapping xim is an act of war and the MoD just can't see that gaining official approval, or even a blind eye turned. The risks are just too great. If the two kidnappings are indeed linked, they must be down to rogue criminals. Even if they are not linked, it is still most unlikely that there has been any official involvement or even knowledge."

"Right, well thank you all for your views. I will leave the next steps to you Prime Minister. I'm sure you will allocate whatever resources are necessary to pursue the investigation."

"You can certainly be assured on that point, Your Majesty. The Foreign Secretary will work on our international response, coordinating with the New Norland and Duplosian Ambassadors. Meanwhile the Security Service will lead on the investigation seeing as their agent is in hot pursuit. The other intelligence services will give their support with whatever resources it takes as their highest priority. I believe the President of New Norland has already spoken to you to offer xer sympathies over Prince Henry. I shall be speaking to xim after this meeting and xe and Ambassador Gavos from Duplos are flying here morrow-watch for further discussions and to show solidarity with us."

22
Search

Jay looked down from the helicopter to the boat below. It appeared to be drifting with no sign of anyone on board. Xe was prepared to bet that this was the one. Xe ordered the pilot to descend and lower the rope ladder to allow xim to board. Xe took out xer gun, loaded a clip into the breach and lowered ximself into the boat. Xe was right, the boat had been abandoned. Xe put away xer gun and took out xer phone. Xe then set about searching the boat, taking pictures as xe went. One cabin was still locked. Xe broke through the door and entered. The cabin was shallow, barely three quarters of a **man** deep and completely bare, clearly used for cargo.

A sixth sense told xim this was not right. The boat was of a type commonly used by smugglers. Xe couldn't see the mechanism but xe was sure the cabin floor was false. There would need to be a professional search. Xe left a location beacon on board and returned to the helicopter. Then headed back to shore, radioing ahead for support.

Back on shore xe tracked down the boat's owner in a seedy quayside bar. Xe jabbed the nuzzle of xer weapon into the man's back and 'invited' xim outside for a chat about national security. "Your boat is being brought back into port as we speak. It is in your interests to co-operate and tell us how to get into your hidden compartment."

"I don't know what your talking about. I rented out my boat to a fishing party. There are no hidden compartments and, if you have indeed taken the boat, you must return it to me undamaged. I know my rights under the law."

"No you don't. You are a criminal and it is obvious that your boat is regularly used for smuggling. For that alone you could face a minimum of two years in prison. However in this particular case you can expect life or maybe even a rather grisly death as high treason is still a capital crime under mems old statutes."

"What do you mean, I deny any involvement in smuggling and, as for high treason, you must be out of your mind. I shall report you to the police for threatening me with a gun and.."

"The police won't get involved. I am from the security service and you are a suspect in the kidnapping of Prince Henry. That is high treason and if xe dies so will you. If you're lucky and we get xim back alive, you might get away with life imprisonment."

"I don't know what you're talking about. I want my lawyer before I say anything else".

"No lawyer, I don't have the time for that. You have just one chance to save your rotten skin and that is to co-operate. Maybe you can then convince my bosses that you are just a small-time crook who has been conned into allowing xer boat to be used in the kidnapping of the prince and the visitor from Duplos. Otherwise you'll be charged with the kidnappings. It's also possible that we might have to extradite you to Duplos. Their culture is still mediaeval by our standards. I'm sure they have a suitable punishment to fit your crimes."

Several tocks later Jay was staring at xer phone. The picture showed what looked like random scratchings on the underside of a bench from the cabin beneath the false floor on the boat. Xe was sure this was a message but meaningless in any script xe knew from anywhere on Geos. Xe sent it attached to an urgent message to Jezzie. Not long afterwards, xer phone pinged with a text reply.

Jay, I sent your picture to Arté on Duplos. Xe says it is written in Contish but using a transliteration into Islish script. As such, very few people would be able to read it. It says: "Rastu and Prince Henry were here, being transferred to submarine and eventually to EE. Captors hinted may be sent to Duplos. Demands are political. Don't give in. We are brave and determined." Yours Jezzie.

Submarine, that explains the loss of signal. Clever Rastu, we now have the evidence that the kidnaps are linked and that EE are involved. Jay could safely leave his bosses and the politicians to sort out the big picture. Xe would continue xer pursuit and try to rescue Rastu and the Prince. Xe took it personally, Rastu was xer charge to protect.

On Duplos, Zorro and Créezy had rushed to join Astra when the news of the kidnapping broke. Arté had travelled immediately to Montana to comfort Sturdon and bring her to South Beach, where they were all gathered together awaiting the imminent arrival of Jero Dicks with the latest update from Geos.

The very latest news, however, came from Arté himself when he was able to tell the others about Rastu's message found on the boat. "We must all be brave too, as Aimée would wish. There is nothing we can do from here and, especially with the Prince also being involved. We can be sure that the KNN Government will be doing everything they possibly can to find them and return them to safety. We must be ready to welcome Jezzie and

Artur here; but otherwise, must try to live as normal a life as possible and continue to work on our various projects."

When Jero arrived xe was able to explain everything that was being done back on Geos. "The security service agent, Jay, is still in hot pursuit. According to xer latest report the kidnappers are travelling overland through Midgeos, possibly heading for the EE border. Xe doesn't have a good enough fix on their route to enable the Midgeos authorities to intercept them but there is now a watch on all the border crossings with everyone being stopped and searched. If they attempt to cross by land or leave from an airport in Midgeos or the KNN it is highly likely that they will be discovered. Similarly the ports are being watched but there remains a possibility that a boat might be able to slip out from a remote part of the extensive southern coastline. It is Jay's expectation that that is indeed what will happen. Jay ximself is flying to the South Eastern corner of the continental KNN and will then make a clandestine crossing of the border into the EE from Midgeos. Xe hopes to pick up the trail from within the EE. Xe speaks the dominant language of the EE fluently and has appropriate field experience. Meanwhile the KNN Government are using all possible diplomatic channels with the EE. The current intelligence assessment is that the EE Government has been wrong-footed and had no knowledge of the plot let alone involvement in it. Nevertheless the Security Service are convinced that the plotters include influential elements of the EE military intelligence services and have access to significant official resources. Of late there has been considerable disquiet among reactionary forces in the EE concerning perceived liberalisation by the current Government; and the political undercurrents suggest that a number of plots may be in the offing. The EE ambassador to the KNN appears to be genuinely pushing xer Government to help and our own ambassador reports a more co-operative reception than usual, but wheels grind slowly in the EE and it's always a case of two steps forward and one back even at the best of times. The Foreign Secretary is making an emergency visit to the EE to escalate matters and their willingness to receive xim is a good sign.

Regarding the return of Jezzie and Artur, New Norland has given them the highest priority and they will set out as soon as Jezzie has sorted our xer affairs. Jan Martskind and Jo Jenson will accompany them to Duplos."

23
Travelling in discomfort

The submarine was unpleasant. For a start it stank, secondly it was very cramped for space which was particularly awkward for Rastu. When you are half as tall again as the average local, submarines are just not built to accommodate you. Mercifully, the journey was short. Thank the Goddess that they weren't travelling all the way to the EE in this diesel-powered cigar tube. Nevertheless she spent two miserable hora bent double over a bucket puking her empty guts out. Henry fared better. Xe could at least stand upright or lie down.

Eventually they surfaced in a sheltered, deserted bay on the western coast of Midgeos. A rowing boat then ferried them to the shore where there was a waiting ambulance. At least Rastu could now lie down as they were driven inland for about fiftwy twilomen. This turned out to be the most comfortable stage of the drive across the continent.

The kidnappers' plan involved several changes of vehicle to reduce the danger of being tracked and intercepted by the Midgeos police, who would surely have been alerted by their KNN counterparts. Although Midgeos was not as closely allied to the KNN as New Norland, they were part of a mutual defence pact against the threat from the EE. An outrage as serious as the abduction of a member of the KNN royal family would certainly be expected to result in a high degree of co-operation from the Midgeos Government.

Just over two hora, by Rastu's reckoning, into their journey the prisoners were handed some sandwiches and a drink which they were advised to consume during the next six tocks after which they would be transferred to less comfortable quarters. Accordingly, the ambulance stopped in a remote lay-by and they were put in a hold beneath the body of a long-distance lorry. This cramped space was where an off duty driver would sleep during a long haul. The space was wide enough for the two of them but too short for Rastu by a head. It was also unlit and there were no lavatory facilities. The prisoners were each handed an incontinence pad in case of need, just adding to their discomfort and humiliation.

This second stage of the overland journey was the longest, slowest, bumpiest and generally most miserable. Neither Rastu nor Henry had ever before felt so utterly disheartened. The only respite was that every **meal** during the three quarters of a watch they were in that lorry they stopped for a six tock break. Time to stretch their legs and grab a bite to eat.

The remaining two stages of the overland crossing were not much better, but at least were shorter and faster. After about six twundred twilomen they were unloaded from the lorry and transferred to the boot of a car. Inside, the car would have been comfortable, being as it was an expensive luxury model, but boots are not built for human occupancy. Let alone for humans of Rastu's size. She had to be curled around Henry and again they suffered in a cramped, dark space, feeling every bump of the road. At least much of this stage was driven on motorway, so progress was fast. About half-way they turned off on to a remote side road and stopped for the customary break before returning to the motorway to finish the stage.

Eventually they were transferred to yet another car for the final stage to an uninhabited stretch of coast. Their captors were not prepared to risk a land crossing as they were sure the border guards would be alerted. The final step to the Eastern Empire would mirror the departure from the KNN by fast motor boat.

At least Rastu now had enough space to stretch and they could both dispense with the humiliating nappies. Life on Duplos had inured Rastu to the privations of primitive ablutions but poor Henry had taken some getting used to the forced intimacy of their shared facilities as well as the in-your-face femaleness of xer companion. All things considered, xe was coping well.

The sea crossing was some three twundred and fiftwy twilomen and even though the boat was fast, much faster than the two craft that took them from KNN to Midgeos, it took them over half a watch to reach the EE shore. "Not long now," their captors said, when they all disembarked. Another ambulance awaited them and they transferred in relative comfort. After about two hora driving inland, they entered a compound surrounded by a high security fence and were taken to a single story building and locked in a cell, again too low for Rastu to stand upright. They were left with some food and drinking water. Toilet facilities were again minimal, a tap over a drain, a bucket and a jug and basin for washing. A sign over the tap in two of the EE languages stated that the water was not suitable for drinking. As neither Rastu nor Henry knew these languages they remained ignorant, though Henry was able to guess the meaning and inform Rastu of xer guess.

Jay was not without hope. Xe still had a Top Secret ace up xer sleeve. Although the app connecting Rastu to xer phone had a maximum range of sixtwy twilomen, there was an additional capability that could be triggered. Rastu's implant would respond to an appropriate signal that would then trigger a response giving some limited tracing capability. Both signal and response would be carried by a spread spectrum modulation below the noise floor. A constellation of low orbit satellites had the capability of sending the triggering signal and receiving the response. All Jay had to do was to switch on the app in the satellites and route the response to xer own phone. The system would not work while Rastu was inside the submarine but once they emerged on to the surface xe should be within range of one or more of the satellites. Normally the system would only transmit once per watch but for this application Jay was able to set every satellite in range to attempt a transmission twice per watch.

Just a couple of **meals** after Jay had returned in the helicopter xe got xer first ping. Thereafter the pings occurred regularly and xe was able to trace the approximate journey across Midgeos.

Xe had landed at an airport in the Eastern part on the continental KNN when xe was contacted by an analyst from home with the news that they had almost certainly identified one of the vehicles used to transport Rastu and the prince. They had spent long enough in this vehicle to yield more than one reading. They had been able to narrow the search down to just three vehicles, all long-haul lorries. Jay decided it was worth xer while to backtrack and see if xe could find out more from the owners/drivers of the lorries in question.

Xe was able to get a flight almost immediately to the nearest city to the most likely lorry depot. On arrival xe hired a fast car and drove with all haste to speak first to the owners and then, if possible, to the driver.

Unfortunately this first guess proved wrong. The lorry in question was part of a large fleet and the owners were able to give a sufficiently full account of its movements to satisfy Jay that it was unlikely to be xer target.

Xe took things a bit more cautiously after that and was able to discover that one of the possible candidates was owner driven and furthermore, there had been suspicion on the part of the Midgeos customs service that it was sometimes employed in smuggling cigarettes and alcohol between Souland and the EE, although they had never been able to prove anything.

That was enough for Jay. This lorry became xer prime suspect. After a quick call to the Security Service HQ they were able to put xim in touch with their Midgeos counterparts and arrange for the lorry to be traced, tracked and suffer a 'routine stop'. While the police conducted a thorough search of the vehicle, Jay was invited to join xer counterparts in interviewing the driver.

The police reported that the lorry was clean but they had noticed some fresh scratch marks in the sleeping compartment. There were also some soiled incontinence pads under the mattress.

Jay went to look at the scratchings and noticed the similarity with those from the boat. The message was much shorter and guessing from his recollection of the other just said 'Rastu was here' or something along those lines. Xe asked for the pads to be sent to the KNN for analysis; but reckoned there was enough here to confirm the use of the lorry.

Neither Jay nor the Midgeos agents were feeling in a gentle mood. There was no good cop, just bad cop and even worse cop. Unsurprisingly, the lorry driver confessed quickly. Unfortunately, xe knew very little. According to xim, xe had been caught smuggling into the EE and since then had been blackmailed into doing occasional jobs for EE military intelligence, or so xe thought. Xe had been approached for the current job some time ago but just told to be ready on call for whenever xe was required.

Xe told Jay that xe had been contacted a few watches ago and told to meet an ambulance about sixtwy twilomen from the west coast of Midgeos. Xe was told xe would be helping to exfiltrate two EE agents who had been in danger of arrest in the KNN. Xe never saw the two individuals. Xe was confined to xer cabin when the agents were loaded and unloaded or when they had a break, which they had once a **meal**. Eventually xe dropped the passengers and the two armed EE agents that accompanied them in a lay-by some six twundred twilomen further East. Xe knew that the party would transfer to another vehicle but xe was told to move along before it arrived so xe never saw it.

By this time Rastu and Henry had arrived at their prison in the EE. This meant that the signals arriving from the satellites showed no more movement; and the analysts were getting increasingly better estimates of their location. Jay decided it was time for xim to enter the EE and investigate the possibilities for a rescue. Xer superiors would be trying the option of official co-operation with the authorities; but, since collusion was not yet entirely ruled out, they also needed a clandestine alternative. Accordingly, xe drove back to the airport and caught a flight to a border town in the extreme south-east of Midgeos. Once there, xe sought out a safe house belonging to the KNN's foreign intelligence service, where xe was already known from an operation a twecade previously.

24
Action in the East

Signs from the Eastern Empire were encouraging. At least their ambassador to the KNN was being very positive about xer government's willingness to co-operate and as a sign of good faith had secured an invitation for Mz Lez Petersen, the KNN Foreign Secretary, to talks in the EE capital, to include a face to face meeting with the First Leader.

As a rule the politicians only get involved in negotiations of this sort once the spadework has been done by officials and the outcome is likely to be positive. Officials can be awkward, but politicians like to be seen as helpful. Thus the promise of a political meeting at this stage augured well. The First Leader of the EE was reformist by inclination and willing to build bridges to the West. This offer suggested xer star was in the ascendency with xer faction dominant within the ruling council. On the other hand, the old guard was still present and internal political turmoil is an ever-present danger. It was less encouraging that the EE were insisting on meeting on their home turf rather than somewhere more neutral like Gendalfo.

This could mean one or more of three things. Either the internal situation in the EE was precarious and the First Leader could not afford to be absent abroad for fear of a coup, or the outcome of the talks was sufficiently in doubt that the EE wanted tight control of the reporting, or even that a negative outcome could enable some political grandstanding aimed at appeasing the First Leader's opponents in the party.

Whatever! The PM decided that the Foreign Secretary should go together with Zir Marty Johannsen, the head of the Security

Service. The two ambassadors would also be present at the talks to support their respective teams. The KNN party was well-briefed on the progress made by the agent, Jay. The analysis of the material recovered from the lorry had been tested for DNA and confirmed the presence of both Rastu and Prince Henry. Artur had wailed somewhat when a sample was taken from him but in the end Jezzie had managed to calm him down enough for a nurse to take the sample to allow the positive identification of Rastu. The evidence of the link to the EE was incontrovertible and the geolocation of their present whereabouts, while inexact, firmly placed them within EE territory.

In a safe house close to the Midgeos/EE border Jay was preparing for a less official visit to the Empire. Xe was greeted warmly by xer old friend, the KNN resident. They enjoyed a convivial reunion with dinner and a bottle of the extremely good local wine. Jay explained xer need to enter the EE unobtrusively. According to xer calculations the captives were being held somewhere around a twundred twilomen from where the border meets the coast. Beyond that, xe had not laid plans but would be looking to rescue the captives and either return with them or deliver them to a co-operating authority within the Empire itself.

"It won't be easy," responded xer host. "I can furnish you with some identity documents, passport, driving license, car insurance etc. as a Midgeosian guest worker in the Empire." They won't stand up to detailed inspection but will pass muster with the usual local police authorities. I can also arrange to smuggle you across the border on foot, perhaps with a bike, but you would only be able to enter with a car through one of the official crossings, and that would be too risky. You will need your own vehicle to get to your destination. As far as I can tell, you are heading for a Top Secret air force base, originally built some thirtwy years ago for medium range missiles capable of hitting targets in the KNN, Midgeos and Souland. Our intelligence indicates that the base now includes space-launch facilities. It is believed to have been used most recently to send supplies to their erstwhile space station, but was not the site of the launch of the station itself. Recent imagery does show a rocket ready on the launch pad, but since the wreckage of the station there has been no activity. The base commander belongs to the reformist wing of the party and is seen as a supporter of the present First Leader. However, in this xe is in the minority on the base and the hardliners among both the officers and crew predominate."

"Thanks for all that. It will certainly be helpful in planning my approach. The problem of transport remains, however. I don't suppose there is useful public transport or that I could steal a car."

"Both those options are far too risky, and fortunately will not be necessary. Access to the surrounding area to the base is restricted and any stranger attempting to reach within twentwy twilomen by public transport will be stopped and subjected to interrogation. Getting you an identity and supporting papers that would pass the checks would take a couple of periods to organise and you don't have that long. Similarly any stolen car would be quickly reported and almost certainly traced by the police. The best bet is for me to arrange a car for you to pick up legitimately. I can spend the next watch doing that. I don't need to go into the details as to the how, but there is a small town about ten twilomen from the border. I can arrange for a pick-up truck to be waiting for you in a car park there. You and the driver leaving it will be dressed similarly and as far as the cameras or passers-by are concerned the swap will be un-noticed. I'll give you a set of keys and the license plate number. The vehicle will be full of fuel and the ownership documents will be in the glove compartment. The delay of just a watch really is the minimum I can manage."

Just one watch later Jay slipped across the border, cutting a hole through the fence in a long gap between guard posts. Xe was carrying a rucksack containing the coat and hat which would disguise xim when collecting the pick-up. Everything went according to plan. The walk into town took xer a **meal** but, once there, xe was able to find a quiet place to don coat and hat, pulling up the collar and carefully keeping xer face hidden from any security cameras. As promised, the pick-up was waiting in the car park. Jay approached the vehicle some nine tocks after it had been parked, carrying a shopping bag containing some food and other items, just purchased and holding a local newspaper in front of xer eyes, as if reading the sports pages. Xe got in the truck and drove out of the car park, stopping at the exit barrier to deposit the coins for parking charge. Xe then headed out of town and via a circuitous route approached xer destination, frequently checking that xe was not being followed.

Camford: W ***4*** Pd ***17*** (***37***/Summer) ***161B***

From JEZZIE to ARTE; ASTRA

Arté and Astra

I've just heard the details of our arrangements to come to Duplos. We are due to leave from New Norland in just over one period's time on ***7***/Autumn or W ***1*** Pd ***19*** or in Duplosian numbers Ph 1 Pd 21. So we should all be with you around a period later.

Fair Exchange

Flying Eagle will be in charge of delivering us safely to wherever you all are, South Beach or Louth? As well as Artur, I will have Jan and Jo with me. They'll be going on to Marcenza to take up their posts at the university. Jo says that despite the loss of Rastu's tuition, xer Pennish studies are going well, though Jan is somewhat behind xim. Mum is struggling a bit learning Contish but xe has agreed to give life in South Beach a try. I expect Créezy is up to speed with Red Robin's plans for xer nursing home near Lanamont. Anyway xe has offered to bring my Mum out with xim when xe is ready to move.

News of Rastu and the prince is still patchy but the agent, Jay, who was looking after us seems to have tracked them down to a secret location in the EE. The KNN Foreign Secretary is about to travel to the EE to try and get the authorities there to mount a rescue while Jay is also trying something less official in case the other route fails. We are all hopeful but there's still a long way to go before there is a satisfactory resolution. At least we know they are alive.

Getting positive confirmation required some DNA analysis and Artur had to supply a sample as he is the only relative of Rastu available here. Poor thing had no idea what was happening to him and without his mother was not inclined to be brave when faced with a 'nasty' nurse trying to take a swab. Eventually I got him calmed down and the sample proved that Rastu had been in the suspect lorry.

See you in just a couple of periods or so.

Jezzie

South Beach: Ph 2 Pd 19 (28/Summer) 2615

From ARTE to JEZZIE

Looking Forward to seeing you

Hi Jezzie

We are all looking forward to seeing you again and to welcome you to your new home; and to having Artur home with us. We will all be at South Beach for your arrival. Jero tells me that she will be at base island waiting for you and will bring you here after a short stop-over in Goddess City to sort out some paperwork at the embassy.

In the meantime, while Astra and Sturdon are staying here to make things ready for you, Créezy and I will go to Thayview to start the drone survey of Isla. It is difficult for us to concentrate on anything while we are all so worried about Aimée but we know that the only solution is to keep busy and not allow ourselves too much time to brood. Zorro and Esau are returning to Louth where Zorro is planning a major marketing campaign for the exercise cycle generators. Her plans are for a major sales drive throughout the autumn ready for the winter season's peak demand.

Best wishes from us all

Arté

The talks had started out affably enough. The Empire's officials pronounced themselves very willing to help in principle but were not sure what they could actually do in practical terms. They promised that, should either of the missing persons be found in the Empire, they would immediately be returned to the KNN embassy; and there would be no obstacles to them then returning home. However, the problem seemed to be that if the criminal gang concerned were indeed from the Empire, their identities were as yet unknown; and at the moment, they had no more information than the scant details that the Northerners had supplied. While they accepted that it was possible that the party had entered the EE, there was no record of them having done so, and it was surely possible that they were still in Midgeos, which after all was the last location of any positive identification.

There was a lot of pussyfooting about the issues. Neither side were willing to reveal too much of their secrets. From the KNN side the details of their tracking system were seen as much too sensitive to reveal and all they were willing to say was that they had been able to track the captives to a particular location in the EE, where they had now been held for several watches. Naturally they did not mention that they had an agent on the ground who was expected to be at the location shortly.

Apart from their wish to learn more of the KNN tracking capability, the Easterners were concerned about KNN espionage trying to uncover their military and space secrets. Bluntly, they said that the location mentioned was a Top Secret military base and it would be quite impossible for the captives to have been taken there without official detection. They were not prepared to allow KNN personnel access to the site and were not convinced of the case to order a search by their own security forces.

Later back in the embassy, the Foreign Secretary put Zir Marty under considerable pressure to reveal more details of their tracking capability, while Zir Marty tried hard to resist.

"Remember, " xe said, "we have an agent on the spot who would be at risk if we gave away too much detail. Now that xe is within sixtwy twilomen of the site xe will be able to locate Rastu precisely through xer link to xer mobile phone. Jay is very resourceful and once xe has the exact location pinpointed will be well placed to mount a rescue by ximself."

Lez Petersen was less optimistic about Jay's chances, but agreed that they should try again, perhaps just vaguely mentioning that the tracking system involved a beacon visible to satellites, hinting it was part of a secret royal protection system.

As it happened, the deadlock was broken first by the kidnappers themselves, and then events moved apace in response to a political crisis in the EE itself.

The kidnappers finally presented their demands to the KNN and New Norland Governments. Styling themselves the True Patriots of the EE (TPEE), they demanded the following concessions for the release of their hostages.

The Geos-Duplos accords must be disavowed and replaced by a treaty that is more favourable to Geos. This must allow for individual Geosian nations to make their own separate arrangements with Duplosian territories; and should allow for deals between them allowing transfer of land currently occupied by Duplosians, where that has been negotiated between the relevant Geosian and Duplosian authorities.

Current Duplosian ownership of such territory as is currently occupied by its people should indeed be confirmed; but uninhabited lands must be equally available for future occupation and ownership by Geosians and well as Duplosians.

Fair Exchange

The constellation of space stations in Geos-Duplos orbit should be taken over by an international organisation with representation proportional to the populations of the leventween countries in the Forum of Nations, and with similar proportionate rights for the countries to fill positions on board and take up space for passengers and freight.

Both Geos and Duplos should recognise the EE colony now in place on the otherwise uninhabited second continent of Duplos and accept EE hegemony over that continent.

The EE Government should recognise that its political reform programme is responsible for the recent setbacks in the Empire's standing in Geosian affairs. Accordingly, the First Leader should resign and hand over to someone more willing to roll back the reforms and uphold imperial traditions.

Until these conditions are met the Duplosian Rastu and the KNN Prince Henry will continue to be held securely in the aforementioned colony on the second continent of Duplos.

25
Coup and Counter-Coup

Rastu's phone pinged. The alert Jay had been awaiting. Xe was within the sixtwy twilomen range of the connecting app. Xe checked the phone, bringing up a map showing the estimated location. The roads shown on the map were typical for the sparsely populated rural hinterland in which xe found ximself. That is, they were narrow, twisty and potholed, but at least the traffic was light. Nevertheless progress was slow, averaging just about sixtwy tpm, the speed limit in built up areas back in the KNN.

After driving for almost a **meal**, xe came to a cross roads with a much wider well-surfaced road that had not been shown on the map. Funny that, xe thought the map had been derived from satellite imagery, which xe had assumed was from official KNN security service sources. Evidently not, the source must be commercial and subjected to EE military censorship. A sign on the junctions with the new road proclaimed it to be prohibited to ordinary traffic and limited to military or otherwise authorised vehicles; and the prohibition was enforced by cameras and aerial surveillance.

Jay was still about five twilomen from xer destination. Xe couldn't afford to risk detection so reluctantly moved the pickup off road and hid it in the surrounding woods, using some brushwood as additional camouflage. Xe then packed a rucksack with items xe might need and set off on foot. At least xer approach would be well hidden.

It was dark before xe reached the air force base. The trees had been cleared for about sixtwy **men** deep around the security fence, itself about two and a half men high and topped with coiled razor wire. Jay was convinced that the fence was alarmed. Xe also noted that the cleared area was being grazed by horses. Jay was an accomplished rider and knew that Rastu too could ride. Furthermore xe was accustomed to bareback from xer upbringing on Duplos. A possible plan for exfiltration to the pickup formed in xer mind.

Xe was at the point where the fence came closest to Rastu's pinpointed location. Xe moved carefully to the fence, took a digging tool out of xer rucksack and after a further eight tocks had succeeded in undermining the fence sufficiently to allow xim to crawl through. Xe observed that the guard towers along the fence were really too far apart and that xe had managed to find a good spot out of the range of the spotlights that occasionally swept the ground from these towers. "Imperial security is not as good as they would have us believe," xe thought.

Xe reached the building where the captives were held and pressed ximself against the wall while deciding xer next step.

The kidnappers' demands hit both negotiating teams like a bombshell. On the KNN side the PM had got the Foreign Secretary out of bed to give xim the shocking news. It was thirtwy tocks to midnight in the KNN but about ninetwy tocks after in the EE capital as their time zones were two **meals** apart. Lez roused xer secretary and then quickly got up and dressed. The embassy burst into life as the whole team held a hurried breakfast meeting.

The EE camp was even more disturbed. The kidnappers had delivered their ultimatum at the same time to the Presidential palace in Kingstown, the KNN Prime Minister's office and the EE embassies in both New Norland and the KNN.

It was afternoon on a working day in Kingstown and the first reaction came from the EE ambassador there. Xe urgently reported to xer superiors in the EE Foreign Office, who aroused the Foreign Minister and then the First Leader several tocks before the KNN Prime Minister had aroused Lez Petersen. Thus the EE team were soon in urgent session.

The intelligence chief was inclined to dismiss the demands as a hoax, possibly part of a plot by the KNN to further their agenda at the talks. The ambassador to the KNN claimed that was extremely unlikely. Quite a row was brewing between the two factions. The one seeking delay and the other immediate action.

After listening for a while the First Leader cut in.

"Stop now. I don't doubt the sincerity of either of you, but this is too much of a crisis for anything but unity of purpose. And, indeed the need for action is urgent. Quite apart from your argument, Mizzer ambassador, there are two specific details that incline me to accept the ultimatum as genuine. Firstly, while we may indeed suspect that KNN intelligence are aware of the space element of the base, they cannot know about our landing on the Duplos southern continent. Then, the demand for my own resignation and the halting of the reform programme suggests to me that this is very likely to be part of an attempted coup. We are all only too aware of the hardline reactionary forces that are still powerful within the government and military. Even achieving what we have done so far has been a considerable struggle to balance the various factions. We may make public claims of unity and probity amongst our public services but we shouldn't fool ourselves into believing our own propaganda. We all know that the whole Empire exists on a knife-edge with endemic corruption rife at all levels of society."

The room was stunned into silence, but several of those present nodded their heads.

The First Leader continued. "My reading of the situation is that in issuing this ultimatum, the plotters have got ahead of themselves. Perhaps they have already dispatched a spaceship with the hostages on board, but unless the launch has just occurred, I doubt it. I'm sure that any launch would have been detected and news would have reached us. It seems to me that a likely ordering of events would be, first the launch, which would then act as the signal for a coup, followed by the issue of the ultimatum. I suspect that there was an unforeseen delay to the launch. Maybe the base commander, who is one of us, blocked it, for example. If no-one alerted those due to send out the ultimatum, that could explain its premature release."

The intelligence chief then piped up. "I withdraw my earlier remarks, even if I were right, we can always pick up the pieces later, with minimal damage done. After all, our space launch site isn't all that secret. As you know, First Leader, we have been investigating various hard-line factions; and while we have as yet no hard evidence, we are very alive to the possibility of a coup, unfortunately, assisted by rogue elements in our own organisation. As our highest priority we must get you to safety and then take what actions are necessary to pre-empt any coup."

"Yes, yes. I accept that I must not go into the presidential offices this watch and indeed I look to you to lead the counter-coup. We also have to deal with the hostage crisis and the KNN. Let's hope that New Norland and KNN can manage to keep the ultimatum under wraps. I have to say I'm not very optimistic on that score given the extreme openness of their societies."

"We'll probably get a breathing space," opined the ambassador. "The KNN will be cautious and want to manage their public opinion. They always like to have this well under control where their Royal Family are concerned. And while the New Norland press can be a loose cannon, protocol suggests that the Government would at least consult the KNN before taking any significant step on this matter."

"Thank-you, that is helpful. As a first step we must investigate that damned air base. Can we get the police to raid it, find and rescue the hostages, and arrest the kidnappers. Get on to that straight away and ensure they have back-up and whatever authorities they need to get them on site."

"I'll get on to that immediately" said one of the supporting staff officers who then left the room.

"Now to deal with the KNN, with a potential coup in the offing we can't possibly meet them in a Government building. I don't like to go to their embassy, but I suppose that is the easiest option."

"Actually," interrupted the Foreign Minister, "some more neutral location would be better. Give me a few tocks and I'm sure we could persuade the Midgeos Embassy to accommodate us in their very luxurious conference facility. I also think we should invite the New Norland ambassador to join us."

"Erm, haven't we got that conference room bugged? I wouldn't want these talks to leak, possibly to the plotters."

The intelligence chief blushed. "Speaking professionally, I regret to say that we actually don't have a bug anywhere in the

Midgeos Embassy. They caught us out about five years ago. You may remember the fuss. Anyway, they have been most vigilant ever since and we haven't found a way back in. All our current intelligence on Midgeos comes from two-legged sources."

"OK Foreign Minister, please arrange it and then set things up with the KNN and the New Norland ambassador."

The former Secret Service Colonel stood outside the control building with xer phone held fast against xer ear.

"Fuck! Fuck! Fuck! Fuck! Those fucking morons, the fucking shit's really hit the fucking fan this time." Xer companions looked bemused. They were used to the Colonel's swearing, but this was rather more extreme than usual. As far as they were concerned things were going reasonably well. They'd got the hostages here safely; and surely they'd soon get to over-ride that poncy base commander. Before they knew it they'd be in space.

When xe had calmed down a bit, the now red-faced Colonel explained. "Those fucking morons have only gone and delivered the bloody ultimatum. We've got to get you all on to that spaceship and into space before someone twigs and gets on to us."

"Yes boss, but what about the CO?"

"Fuck the CO. Xe's only a Lieutenant Colonel in the poxy Air Force. I'll show xim who's in charge." XE pulled out xer gun. "You two get the hostages, get you all into the suits and get on board that ship, ready for imminent take-off."

"The two dashed for an electric utility vehicle while the colonel turned to go back into the control building."

Twin Worlds II

The orderly unlocked the side door and was about to enter to start preparing the captives' breakfast when xe was grabbed from behind and a knife was held against to xer throat. "Don't make a noise or move, or it's the last thing you'll do." It was all the terrified orderly could do not to drop the bag containing the breakfast things. Xe trembled. "Now, do you have a Duplosian woman and a young child in there?" The orderly nodded. "Right, you will go in first and I'll follow, just remember I'm right behind you with this knife. If you co-operate you'll suffer no more than being tied up and gagged while I make my escape with the prisoners. Otherwise, I slit your throat, got it?" The orderly again nodded and did as xe was bid.

But Jay was too late. When xe entered the building there was no-one there. Xe turned to the orderly, "where are they?"

"I don't know, they should be here. I'm supposed to be making their breakfast and then arousing them. I've got the food and plates here with me." Jay looked around. It seemed that the occupants had left in a hurry, very recently. The beds were still warm.

"What are the plans, where will they have been taken?"

"I don't know nothing, I'm just a skivvy here on the base. There were two men in charge of the prisoners. I'm not allowed to know their secret business. It's to do with the space ship out at the launch pad. There's been all sorts of kerfuffle going on ever since our space station was shot down by them New Norlanders. The space ship was supposed to be taking supplies up there I suppose, but no-one tells me nothing. It's all need to know. I never spoke to the prisoners. They didn't speak our language, I couldn't have understood them anyway. Please don't kill me zir, I've a partner and two children. I won't say nothing, just let me be."

Jay let xim be and walked through the building. All the signs were of a hurried exit. Xe then remembered to check the app on Rastu's phone. They were about half a twiloman away and moving at about fiftwy tpm towards the centre of the base.

"They must be in a vehicle," xe reasoned. Xe wouldn't be able to give chase, xe would just have to wait for them to stop and then try to track them down.

The front door was open. Jay left the building and noticed what appeared to be an office block about a twundred **men** distant across the tarmac. There were lights shining in the upper floors. "Control Tower ", xe thought. Xe made xer way towards it and noticed that a side door had been left ajar. Xe took out xer gun, slipped through the door and crept through the building until xe came to the staircase. As xe climbed the stairs quietly xe heard raised voices coming from the control room above.

"You're mad, you'll never get away with this. That space ship has been sitting on the launch pad ever since its mission was cancelled. We haven't heard from the party on Duplos since the accident to our space station. There need to be new checks carried out before launch. It could go horribly wrong. Think of the men you have on board. Whatever you say, the space ministry would never authorise your actions."

"The space ministry has no say in the matter, Lieutenant Colonel (xe emphasised the Lieutenant). This is a matter of national security. I am a Colonel in the Secret Service and outrank you. I've been patient with you but I've run out of time.

You are now under arrest for obstructing my orders. If you continue with your obstructive behaviour I will shoot you." To the others in the room, "continue with the launch sequence, Twentwy and counting."

Jay entered the control room, unnoticed, on the final count. "We have lift-off." On the control room screens the space rocket could be seen ascending as it sped on its way, leaving Geos behind.

There were cheers from those present but a glum face on the erstwhile base commander. "There's no more to be done here," announced the Colonel. "Let's get some rest, there'll be time enough to deal with the traitor when the new leadership takes over." The Colonel then left the room followed by the remaining crew, leaving the arrested base commander handcuffed to a chair. None of them noticed Jay hiding in the shadows.

Jay dispatched a quick report via a secure texting app on xer phone. 'Am at EE space port, too late. Space ship launched. Believe hostages on board. Base commander tied up by kidnappers, will interrogate. Possible coup in progress - Jay'.

Xe then approached the handcuffed commander. "I believe that space ship is carrying the KNN Prince Henry and a Duplosian guest, who were kidnapped recently. I tracked them here all the way from the KNN and was on the point of staging a rescue. I overheard some of your argument a few ticks back and want to know what's going on."

"I can't tell you much. I don't know about the captives but the man showing an ID as a colonel in the Secret Service arrived a few watches ago. Xe claimed to have essential supplies for a party that landed on Duplos' southern continent and demanded the supply ship be launched two watches ago. Although xer ID seemed genuine, I was suspicious and refused xer demands. There was indeed such a landing on Duplos, made when our recent space station made its second orbit of the planet. The station passed on a single report of a successful landing but later attempts to contact the party failed to get a response. Then the accident to the station happened and no more is known. The ship just launched was indeed due to send supplies to the landing party. This was in part experimental to ensure we could maintain a supply route independently of the space station. After the accident, attempts to communicate with the landing party have continued to fail and the supply mission was held in abeyance; but the ship has been kept in readiness on the launch pad. Of course we know about the kidnappings from the western news media but there has been no additional news received here on the base. What you've just told me is the first I've heard of any connection with the EE or with our unwelcome visitation from the Secret Service. Until about sixtween tocks ago, the Colonel and I were at stalemate. Then suddenly xe came into the control room, pulled a gun on me and ordered the crew currently on shift to launch the ship. Unbeknownst to me the regular duty roster had been altered and the duty crew were all somewhat old school in their views. They proved willing to accept the Colonel's orders without question. I don't know what's happened to my more trustworthy people, on whose loyalty I can depend. I am fearful that their absence augurs ill. Sorry I can't be more helpful. Can you help to release me from these cuffs?"

Jay's phone pinged. With an "Excuse me" xe looked at the message. "I've just heard from my superiors. There is an attempted coup in progress in the EE, but I understand that the authorities are staging a counter-coup and the prognosis is good.

I am ordered to get out of here as quickly as possible. Your police are on their way here with appropriate military back-up. While I could cut you loose, it might be better for you to remain as you are and wait for your police to rescue you, thereby avoiding some awkward explanations. It would probably be best for all concerned if you refrain from mentioning our conversation, or indeed my presence here. Just forget you ever encountered me."

"I understand what you're saying. If rescue is really on the way, I would indeed be better off staying put. I don't want to be implicated in a plot to overthrow the Government. OK then, leave me here and make your getaway. There are some honest people among the crew here and with the help of forces loyal to the First Leader we should all be OK and the see the Colonel and xer henchmen defeated."

Jay then crept out of the control tower and stealthily returned to xer tunnel under the security fence. Just as xe was emerging from under the fence xe heard the wail of sirens as a cavalcade of armoured police vehicles came on to the base.

Back in the capital the meeting in the Midgeos embassy had been short and to the point. The First Leader had no wish to be unnecessarily delayed. "I apologise for dispensing with the niceties but we are in a crisis situation. There is an attempted coup in progress. A hard-line reactionary faction is attempting to oust me as First Leader and then crack down on even the limited reform programme that I have been able to initiate. It is as much in your interests in the West as in mine that this coup should be defeated. It is clear that the kidnappings are closely bound up with the plot. As an Easterner I can only apologise that my countrymen have been responsible for this criminal act. They will be punished for it just as much as for the coup. I shall also undertake that any people over here who are implicated in the plot and not required for arraignment on even more serious charges in this Empire will be extradited to the KNN to face trial there. However, that is all platitude. I have already ordered a raid on the air force base which you have indicated as the likely whereabouts of the hostages. If they are found there, they will be returned to the KNN embassy here without delay. Beyond that, I and my team have urgent calls on our time to deal with the coup. The only thing I would ask of you, and the reason for asking the New Norland ambassador to be present, is that you do what you can to avoid, or at least delay, any public announcement of the kidnappers' ultimatum. Firstly, these demands are illegitimate and we will no more countenance them than will you. Secondly they would prove an unhelpful distraction here that will complicate our internal resolution of the crisis. Without them in the background, we will all be able to make much more progress in resolving our differences and coming to a mutually beneficial agreement on Geos-Duplos relations. Finally, I propose, that once we have overcome our present crisis, we hold a trilateral summit, perhaps in Gendalfo, where The EE, New Norland and KNN can move forward together."

Lez Petersen responded for the KNN, welcoming the First Leader's words and assurances and agreeing to get out of their hair to leave them to their task of defeating the coup. The New Norland ambassador expressed xer hopes for a speedy resolution to the crisis and promised to report back to Kingstown with a strong recommendation to maintain secrecy regarding the ultimatum and respond positively to the suggestion of a trilateral summit.

At that the meeting ended and the parties went their separate ways. The KNN party noticed the major military presence at the airport when they left and, before their plane took off, they could hear sporadic gunfire as rebel troops began an assault in an attempt to seize control of this strategic asset.

Jay approached the grey gelding that was munching away at the grass some six **men** from the security fence. Xe fished out some of the sweets that xe habitually kept in xer pocket and held them in front of the horse's nose. The horse in turn looked up sniffed at the sweets and gulped them down. It appeared that the horse considered this to be an adequate introduction to Jay as a friend. He allowed Jay to mount on to his back and slowly walk him towards the woods. It was fortunate both that Jay was an accomplished rider with bareback experience as well as in the saddle and also that it was common for horses in that part of the EE to be so ridden.

Thus Jay managed to return to where xe had hidden xer pick-up in reasonable time. Xe uncovered the vehicle, let the horse go and made xer way back to the border. Xe encountered no incidents on the way back, only noticing that there were long traffic queues at the approaches to border crossings as it appeared that the EE guards were being especially vigilant. That didn't bother Jay as xe had no intention of passing though an official crossing. Xe abandoned the pick-up about a twiloman from the point where xe had slipped through coming the other way and returned on foot. Xe noticed the hole in the fence had been repaired. This time xe again made use of xer digging tool and undermined the fence. Once on Midgeos territory xe phoned xer contact and arranged to be collected. Xe stopped long enough for a rest and meal and to complete a report for xer service and then caught a flight home to the KNN.

Xe was met at the airport by xer immediate boss and told to get over to New Norland as quickly as possible. Xe was to meet Flying Eagle Forest and travel with xim to Duplos to continue with the search and rescue of the hostages. Xe was also briefed that the service had agreed to release the details of the tracking systems xe had been using to the New Norland intelligence agencies. The developments were still considered experimental, and as such not normally shared with their allies. It was agreed that xe could give an outline of the capabilities and say that the developments were part of a programme for royal and VIP protection. The plan was to install the satellite end of the capability into the space stations under NN or KNN control (i.e. so far, all of them) and thereby enable the tracking system to be used on Duplos to help locate Rastu and the base on the Southern Continent.

This came as a surprise to Jay. Xe was tired and could really do with a holiday. Xe had expected to be stood down while someone else was assigned the duty of continuing the chase, possibly even that the task would be re-assigned to the New Norland agencies. However, despite xer tiredness, xe was pleased to be allowed to stay on the job. It was still unfinished business as far as xe was concerned. Xe was also excited at the prospect of the trip to Duplos, the first from xer service. After all, their real responsibility was internal homeland security. It was the more glamorous Foreign Intelligence Service (FIS) that would have expected to land the plum jobs involving travel to exotic locations.

Thus xe slept all the way on the plane and awoke fresh on landing at the Spaceport airfield, where xe was met by Flying

Twin Worlds II

Eagle accompanied by Jezzie and Artur. The last recognised xim as xe emerged from immigration and with squeals of delight threw xer arms about xim. Jay picked the baby up saying, "my you have grown tall."

26
Meanwhile on Duplos

"I'll stay here and continue working on the survey. Artur will not want to be overwhelmed with too many new faces. You, Astra and Sturdon will be quite enough for his reception committee." Créezy was as anxious as any of them, but very much felt that Arté would need space to get used to his new son, and that furthermore, Astra's hospitality would be somewhat overwhelmed with all the Geosian arrivals. In addition to Jezzie and Flying Eagle, there would also be Jan and xer new partner, Aimée's friend Jo Jensen. Then there would be Jero Dicks overseeing everything and to complete the party would be this security man, Jay, who didn't seem to have another name - or at least, hadn't divulged it.

"You don't have to, you know. You are always welcome at South Beach. We all think of you as family. Sure, we'll be a bit crowded, but Astra won't mind if you share our room. It's not as if we are in any way strangers."

"That's very sweet of you but really you must have some family time with Artur. It's not as if there's nothing to do here. The preliminary results from the North are most intriguing. I want to understand what's going on there and that means some carefully directed search, especially with all that river traffic coming south from the wild lands into the Lesser Estuary and beyond. I definitely detect the hand of Shay. She has been up to something and I'm determined to learn more."

There had been no surprises from the imagery from the survey of the southern half of the island. Everything seemed to be much as they remembered from when they had lived there, ten and twenty years ago respectively. Créezy reckoned she could slot right back in without a second thought. One of the smaller drones disguised as a blackbird had even flown low around her mother's house in Rivermouth and, although much aged, Créezy had no difficulty in recognising her mother and sister. "Craya's still ugly," she thought to herself, which was unfair and untrue; but Créezy always viewed her sister through whatever is the opposite of rose-tinted spectacles. On the other hand, she thought Cray looked good for her sixty-nine years. It took a bit of a mental leap for her to cope with the knowledge of her mother's age. True, her once blond hair was now silver but she was dressed in a very fetching gown and stood tall and straight as she strode across the street. Créezy thought the image was very attractive and she would frame a copy for her mantelpiece. Thay, too, she thought had worn well and looked every bit the lady about town when in Rivermouth, or the country squire on her estate, just a short distance across the strait from where she and Arté were working.

No, the south was unchanged, but the north. What was going on? The survey so far had stuck to high altitude but there were boats on what should have been dry land, some of which looked like they were being towed by huge horses. There were billows of smoke emanating from tall chimneys in the North-Eastern part of the Theocracy, and everywhere there were signs of gangs of people engaged in group activities. Even what looked like towns of tents in various places in the middle of the country. She needed some careful planning of low altitude imagery and then perhaps consulting one of Geosians. Jan is very knowledgable about geographical stuff, perhaps when she gets here she will be able to make suggestions.

Fair Exchange

Arté returned to South Beach, detouring via Montana to collect Sturdon. He marvelled how the journeys were made so easy with his electric car. Thayview to Montana is comfortably within the range of a single charge and he was able to recharge while having a meal and short rest at Sturdon's house. From there the rest of the journey to South Beach was comfortable, even allowing for the traffic jams that were now endemic in Marouth. Arté mused that they really must build a Marouth bypass. He reckoned that WwW could easily fund it and then recoup the cost through tolls. He was sure that Zorro could persuade the Marouth council to pass the plans. The current Mayor was an old friend of hers and WF society was primitive enough that their notions of civic corruption were rather more lax than those pertaining to advanced liberal democracies as they have in the KNN and New Norland on Geos.

"We're a small close-knit society," Zorro would explain to Jero when xe shook xer head in disbelief at the way things worked. "We don't need the sort of anti-corruption laws that are important for your huge populations. We all know each other and where you need lawyers to work things out, we can succeed with much less formality. A nod here and a wink there is all that's required to ensure everyone is kept happy and that the public interest is safe-guarded. The massive upheavals to our public infrastructure since first contact could never have been accomplished by civic bureaucracy. Yes, we in WwW have prospered enormously but those profits have funded projects that the taxpaying public want but would never have agreed to fund through increased taxation. The economy is booming as a result and living standards in the WF have never been higher. Male literacy levels are improving rapidly and as a result the matriarchal dominance of our society is diminishing. If we'd tried to do all this through party politics and legal bureaucracy we'd have made practically no progress and instead have become increasingly reliant on hand-outs from you on Geos. You tell me which scenario is more healthy for Duplosian self-esteem and a strong working relationship between our peoples?"

Arté and Sturdon reached South Beach a full phase before Jezzie and co were due to arrive on planet. Jero would meet them on base island and they would then all fly to Goddess City, where they would stay for various meetings and briefings in the Geosian Embassy. Flying Eagle and Jay would stay in GC a bit longer to arrange the next stage of the search for Rastu and Prince Henry. By the time of their landing on planet, half of the space stations would be equipped to send the triggers and receive responses from Rastu's implant, although the New Norlanders were not aware that Rastu herself was the host, nor indeed that the implant was inside her body. All they knew was that it was an experimental technology for Royal protection. Not unreasonably they assumed that the equipment was somehow linked to the Prince!

Jezzie, Artur, Jan and Jo would fly on the newly instituted service from GC to Marouth-Marcenza from where WwW would provide Jan with a car to take them to South Beach. Jan would be driving since xe had already worked in Marouth and so was familiar with the route. This all left Astra with about three phases to prepare for her guests. Sturdon set about tidying the house, making beds and all the other tasks that a good hostess likes to accomplish when entertaining visitors, even if they are family.

Astra, who as we know is not very domesticated, left her to it while she chivvied up the builders working on Jezzie's property next door. As seems to be the case with all building projects everywhere, the builders were behind schedule and ahead of budget. Astra threatened them with Créezy, of whom they were genuinely frightened, and under such threat they showed some improvement. Jezzie would not be able to move straight in as they had hoped, but there was a reasonable chance that the house would be habitable after a further two periods work. "Not too bad all things considered," thought Arté.

In his mind, Arté's role was to do as he was told by the women and give whatever help was needed. He would help Sturdon with any heavy lifting, moving of furniture and so on, but she was very capable and didn't require a lot of his time. She was used to working on her own and not accustomed to having domestic help. She was also somewhat in awe of this man who she regarded as a sort of son. They don't have a concept of son-in-law in any of the Duplosian societies, as relationships between women and their men tended to be transitory in nature. At least, Sturdon mused, we don't treat them as slaves here. She liked Arté, who was clearly good for her beloved daughter, and she recalled how she herself maintained a long-term relationship with the man who was Rastu's father as well as having been unusually maternal in regard to her own late son. In both these things her friends and neighbours regarded her as eccentric.

With Astra it was different. While she was scrupulous about not abusing her position, she had come to rely so heavily on Arté's assistance that asking him do to things for her became subconscious; and she scarcely noticed the way that he interpreted even her slighted whim as a direct order.

The current project of Jezzie's new home was right up his street. In reality Arté had worked as project manager for Thay's luxurious mansion on Isla. He wasn't prepared to indulge in the sexual diplomacy that back on Isla had enabled him effectively to give orders to the female contractor. Even though the place of men in the WF was much closer to equality than on Isla, that was only relative. There would have been considerable reluctance by the builders to accept any form of male authority. He had to behave much more subtly.

Astra was not good at the disciplined working required for a project of this nature and would miss important details, while being too ready to accept explanations for matters that she didn't really understand. Arté knew her well and understood her limitations perfectly. He would work out whatever needed doing and formulate the rebuttals to the inevitable excuses. He would brief Astra accordingly. Then she would confront the builders, with him standing in the background in a supporting role that had him seen as a secretary or general gofer, which fitted in with the cultural norms much more closely.

27
Return to Duplos

The imperial space supply vessel ISSV1 crash-landed on the southern continent of Duplos and activated its location beacon. The crash-landing was no accident. That was how it had been designed. It had not been expected to carry human crew or passengers, nor was it intended ever to return to Geos. The vessel itself was part of the supply, with its material designed for recycling into machinery for the earlier landing party. The makeshift modifications and installation of couches to accommodate the four passengers had been undertaken surreptitiously by crew sympathetic to the plot, under the supervision of the Colonel. The modifications were designed to enable the passengers to survive the crash landing; but they were untested and there was an appreciable risk of which the Captain and Sergeant were ignorant.

Rastu never learnt the names of her captors. They always addressed themselves by their former rank in the imperial secret service. Just as the leader back at the base had been the Colonel, these two, who had been with the captives throughout the journey from the KNN, were Captain and Sergeant. Neither Rastu nor Henry spoke any of the Eastern languages but Henry had known a few words; and eventually both had acquired some basic knowledge from listening to their captors. On the other hand, the Captain spoke good Norse and the Sergeant had a basic understanding. Rastu had managed to teach Henry some Contish, but they were severely reprimanded when they attempted to use it for private communication. However, once space-bourne, with the limitations on the shuttle there was tacit acceptance that the prisoners would so converse privately if they wished, just as the captors would conduct conversations in their own language.

When they entered the Duplos atmosphere the Captain instructed them all in Norse to brace themselves for the crash landing. This was the first Rastu or Henry learnt of that unwelcome feature of the spaceship design.

Fortunately the modifications more-or-less worked. At least, nobody died. Of the four, Rastu appeared to be in the best shape and managed to be first out of the shuttle. She was closely followed by the Sergeant, who moved to prevent her running off, as if she would have abandoned Henry.

Had she wished, she could have easily outpaced him. Despite the lack of opportunity in the zero gravity of the space shuttle, she had quietly exercised her muscles to the extent she could on the journey. Her brain and body were also evolved in the lower gravity of Duplos and she found her instincts quickly adapted. In contrast, the Sergeant stumbled around as his brain misinterpreted the unfamiliar gravity. The Captain had suffered a nasty blow in the landing and was somewhat dazed for several tocks. Meanwhile Henry was uninjured; but took some time to orient ximself and join Rastu and the Sergeant outside the vessel.

The shuttle had been designed to home in on the beacon from the original imperial landing craft. According to calculations, they were about two twilomen away. The crew should have received the alert from their own beacon and would be expected to arrive shortly to retrieve the supplies.

Once the Sergeant had patched up xer Captain's cuts and bruises and the latter had recovered from xer blow, they again handcuffed the captives and sat down to await the arrival of their compatriots, one of whom at least was party to the plot, if ignorant of the details as to how it had developed.

After about a **meal** hanging around, the Captain was beginning to get worried. Perhaps something had gone wrong after the landing. They knew that the party had reported a successful landing to the space station, but that had been the last that had been heard. After the accident with the station there was no possibility of further communication. On the other hand the lander was still sending out its locating beacon and the Captain was receiving a strong signal on his phone app, which decrypted to give the exact latitude and longitude on Duplos as well as the current date and time. Xe decided they would have to set out on foot. The Sergeant packed up four rucksacks with supplies, putting the heaviest load on to Rastu and the lightest on the Captain. They set off in single file with the Captain in the lead, followed by Henry, then Rastu and finally the Sergeant bringing up the rear. The captives were still handcuffed and both the others had their guns out.

They marched on until eventually they could see their destination, a small hill rising from the forest floor in the middle of a clearing. Nobody was about and the Captain sent the Sergeant to investigate. The door to the landing craft was unlocked and the Sergeant walked in to the empty cabin. There was no sign of anybody home. The Sergeant found and collected the ship's log for xer Captain to read.

The initial entries in the log following the landing were much as the Captain expected. Then on the third phase following the landing there was a hasty entry in a different hand. The writer had been left aboard to mind the ship while xer two shipmates had left on a recce of the surrounding area. They had last reported a whole **meal** previously and were now some thirtwy tocks late for their return. Xe had been unable to get a response when trying to make radio contact; but the location beacon was still transmitting and it appeared they were not moving. Xe wrote that xe was going to investigate.

There was just one more entry. Short and panicky. Xe had located the others. They were in another clearing in the forest surrounded by giant ape-men brandishing spears. They were still alive but bound and in hot water. Literally. They had been placed in a giant cauldron which was itself held over a fire. They were being cooked alive. The writer had returned just to make the entry and collect weapons and ammunition to enable a rescue.

That was it. No more entries and no more information. The Captain entered the ship and ransacked it for what weapons and ammunition xe could find. It was growing dark and the Captain decided they should rest until first light. They entered the ship where the Captain and Sergeant occupied two of the beds leaving the captives to make do with the third between them. The handcuffs were used to secure them in such a way that they could enjoy some restricted movement while being unable to escape.

As light dawned, the Sergeant made breakfast for them all, after which they prepared to set of again. They stowed such of their supplies as the Captain felt they could do without in the short term and repacked to ensure that both Captain and Sergeant were free from the encumbrance of baggage, leaving just the captives still handcuffed and burdened. The party then set off to explore further.

Fair Exchange

As they entered the forest surrounding the landing ground they found their way barred by a large feline, somewhat resembling a cheetah. The Captain pointed xer gun and fired.

On base island Flying Eagle landed the SS Norland President Wheatfield, the prototype first in its class of aerospace shuttle. There had been much sucking of teeth in New Norland about the use of this craft on Duplos. Quite apart from it being still at the experimental stage, it was also nuclear powered. The technology had been adapted from that used in nuclear powered submarines and was still seen as a military secret. The allies in the KNN were aware of much of the development, as indeed they had contributed to the total design, with none other than Jezzie Peteschild having overall responsibility for all the AI in the system. However, even they were not privy to the detailed design of the nuclear power source.

Quite apart from the experimental nature of the prototype and the secrecy of the project, there remained the policy to prohibit the export of nuclear technology to Duplos. Sending this craft was in clear breach of that policy. One that on NN insistence had been endorsed by none other than the Forum of Nations.

However, this was an unforeseen emergency. All aircraft available on Duplos had a maximum range of about three twundred twilomen before needing to recharge batteries. The distance from the WF to the southern continent was around four twousand five twundred twilomen, which would require at least fiftween recharging breaks en route. As each charge would take around three **meals**, depending on wind and solar strength, the time taken would be far too long to satisfy the urgency of the mission. The nuclear craft did not need recharging and would accomplish the journey in one hop. There really was no choice. The one restriction that the New Norland authorities were able to stipulate was that both Flying Eagle Forest and Major Bald Eagle Sky should be on board for all flights and that one of these two should remain aboard whenever the craft had to be left without an armed guard. Also, only these two or, in emergency, Jezzie Peteschild should be allowed to pilot the craft. The unmanned pilot mode must be disabled while the craft was on planet. The concession regarding Jezzie was made reluctantly in the light of strong remonstrance by Flying Eagle. They had to have extra cover in case of injury to ximself or Major Sky and, after all, Jezzie had been intimately involved in the design of the craft and was knowledgeable about all of its operational capabilities.

On landing, the required guard was set and the passengers disembarked to be greeted by Jero Dicks on behalf of the Geosian Embassy. The passengers remained on base for a rest and dinner while Flying Eagle showed Bald Eagle around the craft and familiarised xim with the controls and capabilities. Before xer selection for the Duplos landing mission, Bald Eagle was the premier test pilot for the New Norland Air and Space Force. There was no-one better qualified than xim to learn to pilot such a craft at short notice. Flying Eagle was delighted to have xim as xer deputy and co-pilot on this mission.

When all were fed and rested, Major Sky took on the task of flying them all to the airport outside Goddess City. Xe then remained on board, despite the presence of two embassy guards. The rest proceeded to the Geosian embassy for their meetings, with Jo Jensen detailed to look after Artur.

Stripy Tiger, as ambassador, opened the meeting, welcoming them all. Xe explained that this was a KNN show and the role of the New Norlanders was to lend technical support. While Flying Eagle was to be in charge of the shuttle craft and Major Sky would provide back-up, the political leadership would come from Deputy Ambassador Jero Dicks and the operational command on the ground from Jay.

Xe continued saying, "when the rescue was first mooted I was to be included in the party in case of encounters with native Duplosians. However, I realise I'm not necessarily the most suited for the task if native beings are at a much more primitive stage of development, as we now believe. Recent satellite imagery suggests that the local animal life includes some large ape-like creatures that appear, at least, to hunt co-operatively. When we discovered that Jo Jensen would be arriving we've changed tack and now prefer for xim to accompany the party. I think xer expertise with ape populations as well as xer established reputation in primitive anthropology makes xim well-suited to the task. It is a bonus that xe is a KNN national."

Finally, before handing over the meeting to Jero and leaving to brief Jo, Stripy Tiger introduced a Duplosian woman who had been sitting quietly at one end of the table. "This is Major Mikhaila of the Shadowlands Union. She is here in Goddess City as the personal representative of Dictator Petrova and special envoy from the Shadowlands Union to the Geosian Embassy. Although this mission is search and rescue rather than exploration, it has been agreed between the WF and SU that a presence from the SU is politically expedient. Major Mikhaila will be joining the party to provide that presence."

Jay was able to brief the meeting that xe had obtained location data from the hostages. They were being held at around latitude twelve degrees south of the equator, longitude one twundred and fortwy-five point eight degrees east of the meridian through Louth. That is about ninetwy twilomen inland from the west coast, just north of the southern tropic.

Flying Eagle added further to the brief by announcing that xe had brought another piece of useful new technology. This was also still officially a Government secret but shared with the KNN and not embargoed for use of Duplos. Indeed the exploration of Duplos was very much a driver for the technological development.

"This is affectionately known as a flying saucer. It's official uglier name is a long-range drone hub. The disc-shaped hub is about two **men** in diameter and has a range of seven twundred twilomen between charges. It can hover over the ground or travel at up to one twousand tpm. The hub contains Jezzie's latest AI software and is fully autonomous, while also being capable of accepting remote control. It can charge itself by solar or wind power, or take an external charge, for example from the mains or from a ship, vehicle or aircraft. The hub has all the imagery capability of the most advanced drone, but also carries a dozen small drones attached to its body. These can act autonomously or be controlled via the hub or externally. The drone family automatically return to the hub for recharging when necessary. This is a highly flexible tool for planetary survey. All imagery or other data acquired by the drones is transmitted to the hub, and from the hub passed on externally for examination. However, the hub itself contains automated processing features enabling intelligent data evaluation. With this tool we should be able not only to identify the location of the hostages exactly but also to evaluate the environment and plan their safe extraction. With

Jezzie's expertise we have the greatest chance of exploiting the technology to the maximum extent."

The meeting then went into planning mode and an initial operational plan was agreed. The team to travel to the southern continent would consist of nine members. From New Norland would be the two Eagles, Flying and Bald; from the embassy, Jero and from the KNN, Jay, Jezzie and Jo. Then there would be three Duplosians, Mikhaila from the SU and Arté and Créezy from the WF. Knowing, as xe did, the norms on Duplos, Jezzie took Mikhaila aside and explained that Arté was not there to provide sexual services to the Duplosian women; but was a full member of the search and rescue mission in his own right. Mikhaila is a good soldier and readily accepted the position but was quietly pleased when Jezzie offered to acquire her one of the intelligent vibrators on sale in xer name.

The team would first fly to Marouth along with Jan Martskind and baby Artur. Majors Sky and Mikhaila would remain at the airport with Flying Eagle and the nuclear shuttle. Jan would go into Marcenza to find somewhere to live and arrange xer affairs with the university. The rest would be driven to South Beach, where Artur would be united with his family, and the WF members of the party would be collected and briefed.

They would then all fly on to the easternmost point of the main continent. The flying saucer would be dispatched to the northern tip of the second continent, just over six twundred twilomen away. It would recharge and fly south to the indicated destination just north of the southern tropic, to conduct a drone survey of the target area. Guided by the intelligence gained from the survey, they would then travel to the target and undertake the rescue. Simple really!

The cheetah dropped dead. Then all hell broke loose. Spears flew out of the trees and impaled the Captain where xe stood. Huge ape-men dropped down on to the party quickly overwhelming the Sergeant and capturing the others who, after all, were in no position to offer any resistance. The spears were retrieved from the Captain's corpse that was then stripped of xer possessions and left to rot where xe had fallen. The ape-men carried off the three captives to their camp, just a short distance further into the forest.

Rastu observed that the ape-men lived on platforms in the trees surrounding a small clearing in the forest. In the centre of the clearing was a fire and what was clearly cooking facilities. She could smell an antelope being roasted over the fire, being turned on a spit by two ape-women.

The captives were taken to one of the platforms about five strides above ground. The platform was surrounded by a cage made from a wood that Rastu had not seen before. Inside the cage was a Geosian dressed in rags. The three were pushed into the cage; but clearly from their body language, the ape-men were puzzled by the handcuffs and the evident physical difference between Rastu and the Geosians.

The existing prisoner and the Sergeant immediately engaged in rapid conversation which neither Rastu nor Henry could follow. Obviously, this was the third member of the imperial mission to Duplos. The one who had written those last two entries in the log. If she was still alive, reasoned Rastu, there was still hope for them all. She was on the thin side and sported various yellowing bruises and healed cuts. This suggested to Rastu that she was being fed a somewhat inadequate diet, but otherwise was not being mistreated. The injuries were old and presumably inflicted during capture rather than afterwards. Rastu then settled down together with Henry in a corner of the cage away from their erstwhile captor. She took the opportunity to observe her surroundings, and especially the comings and goings in the clearing below.

She was astonished to observe that several cheetahs wandered in and out of the clearing. At one time she counted four of them in the clearing at once. The ape-men seemed quite unconcerned at their presence. Rastu was not familiar with felines. There were none in the Duplos known to her civilisation. However, as mentioned earlier, she had encountered domestic cats in Camford and some of their more ferocious wild cousins in zoos. Everything she knew about the larger felines told her they were dangerous carnivores and ruthless hunters at the top of the biological food chain. The seemingly tame interaction between the cheetahs and ape-men was just not natural.

Natural or not, it was a fact. There were food bowls dotted about the clearing, but none too close to the fire. The wandering cheetahs appeared never to approach the fire more closely than about six strides. But there was one large male that was lying on the ground at about that distance, seemingly enjoying the warmth and allowing a smaller ape, a female child, to stroke his fur and scratch his head between the ears while cooing gently at him. She also saw one of the male apes using his spear to cut off a portion of meat from the antelope and take it to one of the bowls. He called a noise, and about a dumin later, a female cheetah came in from the forest, stood by the bowl and lowered her head to start eating. Rastu found it hard to believe but clearly the ape-men were keeping these cheetahs as pets. No wonder there was such a violent reaction to the killing of one of them by the late Captain.

Later, after the ape-men and cheetahs had been fed on the roasted antelope, and for the ape-men also some boiled roots and vegetation, there appeared to be a conflab going on in the centre of the clearing, with much waving of arms and legs and hooting or other vocalisations by the ape-men. While this was going on, some younger ape-women, ape-girls really, came up to their cage with some food for them. An accompanying adult male came as guard and pointed a spear at the Geosian pair while the ape-girls gave food to Rastu and her companion, a task made harder on account of the handcuffs. The girls occasionally turned and glared at the Geosians while this was going on. Once they were satisfied that Rastu and Henry had been able to enjoy the choicest meat and drink their fill of a vegetable soup, they gave them each an orange-like fruit. When this was also eaten, they placed the remaining, smaller portion of the food on the floor in front of the others and retreated along with the guard. There was no fruit for the others.

For the first time the Sergeant addressed xer former captives in broken Norse. "They have obviously decided to fatten you up for the table. My friend here tells me they fed xer two colleagues to the cheetahs; but that they made them ill and xe thinks this is why xe has avoided being put in the pot ximself. It's clear they realise you are not one of us and therefore might be safe to eat. They probably think the Northland child is yours, and also not one of us. Bon appetit suckers."

"Don't take any notice of xim, Henry, xe doesn't have any idea about what the ape-men are planning. And those girls seemed genuinely solicitous of our welfare, and showed considerable antipathy to the Easterners. They've noticed that we were being held prisoner and perhaps are viewing us as their enemy's enemy, who is therefore their friend.

In this, Rastu was not far from the truth. All the gesticulation below was indeed occasioned by the apes debating what to do with them.

Eventually there was a resolution to the debate. Obviously, not everyone was happy but a decision had been reached. Three ape-men came up to their cage. One of them held back the Geosians while the other two carried Rastu and Henry out of the cage and thence down to the ground.

The ape-men were indeed giants. They were proportioned much as Rastu herself but with relatively much longer and stronger arms. They were also completely covered in orangey-red hair with only the centre of their faces, soles of their feet and palms of their hands hairless. Female breasts were relatively smaller than those of Duplosian women, but larger than those of Geosians. The hair on these breasts was also much thinner than on the rest of the body or the male chest. The shaft of the male penis was also bare and the bump (yes, they had one, but small, Rastu observed with a smile) was less hairy than elsewhere. Finally, their feet were a bit more like hands than her own. Clearly, they could be used for gripping as they moved through trees, holding on with both hands and feet as they swung through the branches. They were natural tree climbers and it was unsurprising that they made their homes there. In height, Rastu was surprised to observe that, unlike her own species, the males were slightly larger on average. She reckoned the average ape-man was about two and a half strides tall, a third as much again as herself. The average ape woman was slightly shorter, perhaps by a similar amount (around three divisions) as the opposite difference between male and female Duplosian people. Her observations accorded with her guess that males were dominant in ape-man society.

Once on the ground, they were taken to the pile of objects taken from the Captain and Sergeant and, through sign language, were invited to inspect them. Rastu pointed to a set of keys and then to her handcuffs. One of the ape-girls understood immediately and picked up the keys and handed them to her.

Rastu couldn't unlock herself but called on Henry to hold out xer arms and she found the right key and undid xer cuffs. She then handed the keys to xim to return the service. It was so good to have their hands and arms free again. they both rubbed their wrists and turned to the apes to sign their thanks and appreciation. The girl who had fetched the keys then led them to her tree, where they were helped up to a platform and shown to somewhere to sleep. There was already a sleeping cheetah on the platform. Perhaps noting her guests body language, the girl went up to the cheetah, woke it up and hooted in its ear making shooing gestures with her hands. The cheetah growled, but got up, climbed down to the ground and looked for somewhere else to sleep.

When Jezzie and the others arrived in South Beach they were greeted with elation. Sturdon held out her arms to Artur who took his first steps as he almost ran to her. From being held back from walking by the Gravity of Geos, he found that his legs were strong enough to propel him on Duplos. He also saw someone so like his mother. Not his mummy, he knew that, but like her. Taller and thinner than Jezzie and the Geosians who had hitherto been all the other people he knew; and also seeming very familiar. Sturdon scooped him up into her arms with a cry of "you little darling, come to Granny."

Artur's thoughts if he could have articulated them would have been something like "Yes, just like Mummy." Instead, he threw his little arms around her neck and squealed with pleasure. Looking on, Arté and Astra both beamed.

Eventually Sturdon handed Artur to his father saying. "This is your Daddy, you must let him hold you for a bit. It's so wonderful for us all to have you home at last."

For the next few dumins Artur endured playing the title role in pass the parcel before Astra remembered her duty. Passing the baby on to Zorro, she ushered the Geosians in and ordered tea, which was brought in by one of the young men from the village who she had hired to help with the domestic chores.

Jezzie properly introduced Jo to everyone and they settled to enjoy their reunion over tea and cakes. About a horum later Créezy arrived and, after paying due homage to the baby, joined in the general conversation.

Artur was put to bed in a cot in Sturdon's room while the others partied well into the night. Créezy couldn't help but notice how Jero was paying attention to Jezzie. Clearly becoming smitten, she thought. Pity it was so close to winter and a bit cold for a swim. Those two need to find out each other's sex. How stupid that they are so coy about it. And even when they know, like Jan and Jo, they make such a to-do over getting together that its a mystery how there came to be so many billions of them on Geos.

Twin Worlds II

After they had all risen, breakfasted and attended to any incipient hangovers Arté took Jezzie off to inspect the progress on xer new home and talk to xer about Aimée.

"I'm so worried about her. I try to be strong, especially for Sturdon, but sometimes I just despair. Astra and Créezy have been wonderful throughout; and have done everything they can to keep me occupied and take my mind off brooding, but Aimée is so young and vulnerable. She must be in the most terrible state with nobody to care for her. I know everything possible is being done for her and Jay has been exceptional, well beyond the call of duty but, oh Jezzie! I love her so much and feel so helpless." By then the tears were flowing despite himself.

"Aimée is strong, much stronger than you give her credit for. That note scratched on the boat was so brave. She is indeed exceptional and you can bet that she has taken on the burden of supporting the twelve year old Henry. That in itself will strengthen her resolve further, and keep her mentally fit. She is now on Duplos and Jay has assured me xe has proof that she is alive. You will be with us when we rescue her and you will be the one to restore her to her son and mother."

Xer words put the heart back into Arté and he resolved to put his fears behind him and try to adopt a more positive outlook. "Changing the subject, what do you think of the house?"

"I love it. You and Astra have done so well, and the quarters for my mother are so right. Oh, for when this is all but a distant memory and we can settle down as neighbours. Aimée and I will have such fun together. I just can't wait to splash about in this gorgeous sea together, teaching Artur to swim, and just everything. I'm sure I'm going to learn to love you and Astra almost as much as I love Aimée. We may be of different species but Aimée and I often say to each other that we are just like sisters. And talking of the sea, it's a beautiful bright phase. Why don't we stop here a go for a swim."

"Because it's fucking cold, that's why - whoops, sorry I meant freezing cold. I do apologise for my bad language. Please forgive me. And well, Aimée has always wanted a sister, she even tried to make me into one. She has overblown romantic notions about the relationship. I think it helps that you are from different planets. Your relationship will prosper much better than any two real Duplosian sisters. They are poisonous, just ask Astra."

"I can easily forgive the language. I'm an engineer and swearing is part of the job description. We Geosians are not as prim as all that. Anyway, I confess I was being naughty myself. I have seen Créezy's depiction on Aimée's bedroom wall and also on the ceiling above her bath. Part of me just wanted to see the reality. Otherwise, it isn't anything like too cold here for someone brought up with the seas around the islands in the KNN. They can be cold even at the height of summer." Xe fell into a giggle. "I recall the squeals when we went to the beach and Aimée rushed into the water for the first time."

"Well, perhaps you should ask Jay or Jero. They're both kingdom people. They should be similarly inured to the Autumn winds over the inner sea."

"Perhaps I will, and there are no Autumn winds tophase."

When they returned to Astra's house house Jezzie borrowed a towel from Astra, found an opportunity to speak to Jero on xer own and whispered in xer ear. Jero nodded and the two of them snuck off for a walk along the beach together.

28
Rescue

Rastu observed her new friends carefully. The girl who had so befriended her was about her size and was clearly intrigued by her. The child was as yet sexually immature, or at least Rastu thought, her tits haven't developed yet. Perhaps equivalent to nine years of age. Naturally Rastu realised she knew nothing about the ape-men's lifespan or developmental stages. Gradually the girl began to teach Rastu some of their sign language and the meaning of some sounds. Rastu studied hard and, being highly intelligent, began to communicate with her hostess. She also included Henry in the lessons as much as she could, although the girl really wanted Rastu all to herself. It amused Rastu to realise that Henry was being seen as an annoying younger brother in the way that nine year old girls tended to regard six year old boys. The necessities of nature ensured that their sexes were quickly discovered.

The apes were fascinated by the peoples' clothes and clearly found them hard to understand. The climate at twelve degrees latitude is hot and in the southern hemisphere it was mid-spring. Probably the most pleasant time of the year. Life was good to the apes. They appeared to have no natural enemies. They worked in a sort of symbiotic partnership with their pets. They would hunt together with the cheetahs chasing down the faster prey and the apes keeping larger predators at bay through organisation and numbers. The apes also carried the kills back to camp and cooked the food. Although the cheetahs would and could eat the meat raw they seemed to prefer it cooked. They also enjoyed the warmth of the fire while keeping their distance to avoid sparks flying into their coats.

The apes also gathered fruit and nuts, dug for roots and collected certain leaves and fungi. These they would cook for themselves or eat raw as appropriate. They made use of elementary wooden and stone tools and could even make clay pots that they would bake hard, and which, if not too close to the flames, made serviceable cooking pots.

Rastu noted that they didn't have any metal technology, nor had they invented a wheel, domesticated any animals other than the cheetahs, which were not really domesticated in the way of dogs, horses, sheep or cattle, nor did they cultivate crops by way of farming. In Geosian terms Rastu thought they were early paleolithic.

The girl found Rastu's hairlessness both intriguing and worrying. She would poke under Rastu's clothes at any opportunity and stroke her skin and make concerned sounds and signs. Was Rastu ill, had all her hair fallen out? If so why was her head covered luxuriously and her pubic area and underarms immune to the hair loss? Even more puzzling, why had her tits grown already, and so big and soft? Until Rastu stopped her the girl grabbed one of her nipples and started to suck to see if there was milk. "A good thing Artur is weaned," thought Rastu. If Rastu would let her, as she occasionally did, the girl would lift her gown and stroke her pubic hair with a smile of satisfaction on her face. She liked it if Rastu would groom her in return, not in the pubic area, but on her back, tummy or arms. She seemed to like nothing more than Rastu combing through the hair of her back or tummy with her fingers. The girl would then throw her head back and croon softly. Rastu had noticed how such grooming was an important ritual among the apes; and had realised that the girl's concern at her hairlessness was linked to such grooming. Hair seemed to be an essential ingredient, hence Rastu's occasional acquiescence in the girl's desire to stroke her upper pubic area. Rastu smiled to herself when the thought arose in her mind that the girl would have preferred Arté's hairy chest.

Her time was not all spent with the girl and her mother who shared the sleeping platform with them; but when on the ground in the clearing, the girl would introduce her to her friends for some mutual grooming, and on occasions they were summoned to meet an adult. On such occasions Rastu took special care to be on her best behaviour. She always gave due deference and took great trouble to groom the adult, especially the large male who had demanded her presence and was obviously an important leader. He was often in the company of a large cheetah that was obviously the alpha male among its kind, judging by the deferential behaviour of other cheetah's both male and female.

Generally Rastu observed that the apes were what she regarded as semi-monogamous. That is that for the most part they lived in family groups with the older adults sharing with a regular partner of the opposite sex. Just occasionally a larger male would have two partner females, and in the single case of the dominant leader, three. There was also quite a lot of cheating going on by both sexes. Whenever someone was caught out by their partner there was generally a fight and clear disapproval by the cheated partner. But that didn't prevent either of them from having some sneaky sex behind their partner's back. Younger unattached males appeared to be especially in demand by older partnered females, while as far as most males that she observed were concerned, she thought any sex they could get was always welcome. "Rather like the Zorro of old," she thought.

Apart from trying to avoid being caught out by their partners, the apes didn't seem to have any inhibitions about public sex and were not at all bothered by Rastu observing them. She was interested to see that for the most part intercourse was from the rear. Thus the male bump rubbed the female between the buttocks and not on the clitoris as is the case for human Duplosians. "Strange," she thought. "Are the girls missing out, and do they know it?"

After a full period with the apes Rastu was feeling confident in her communications with her hosts and set about trying to explain her situation, first to her friend and her mother then, with their help, to other adults who were prepared to listen.

Obviously, she couldn't go into such details as the life on Geos. But she could explain that she came from a distant land and that she and Henry had been brought here by force by some bad men of a different race. Not all that race were bad. Most were good and friendly and she expected that one day the good people would find out where she and her brother were and come and rescue them. She thought it easier to explain Henry as her young brother than anything else. As far as she was concerned she didn't care what happened to the bad men. All the time she had made no effort to speak to the Easterners, nor to enquire into their welfare. This had rather shocked Henry who had been brought up in a more liberal society that had abolished capital punishment and sought to reform rather than punish criminals.

But however enlightened her outlook in Duplosian terms, Rastu was not the product of a liberal democracy. Kidnapping an innocent female for political motives would earn the death penalty in any of the three territories on continental Duplos, or according to Arté and Créezy, on Isla. Furthermore the kidnapping of someone of the status of Prince Henry would ensure the charge was High Treason and the death would as gruesome and painful as could be imagined. As far as she was concerned if the apes wanted to cook them up to be fed to the cheetahs that was fine by her.

"Please tell me you're not serious!" Poor Henry backed away from Rastu in shock. "How can someone as lovely as you be so callous. "The Easterners are human beings, and must be treated humanely even though they have committed a serious crime. They deserve a fair trial, and even then capital punishment is barbaric. The Sergeant deserves life imprisonment but the other Easterner is innocent of our kidnapping and should merely be sent back to the EE. Much as I love and respect you, it is important to stand up for civilised values."

Rastu thought carfully. She had to acknowledge that Henry was right about the other prisoner, but she still thought a death sentence was appropriate for the Sergeant. She bent down towards Henry and hugged him, speaking softly. "Oh, Henry I didn't mean to upset you. I do agree with you about the other Easterner, xe has done us no harm, but xe has broken laws in coming here and should be held accountable for that. However, here on Duplos a death sentence is considered appropriate for the Sergeant's crimes in kidnapping us and exposing us to danger. And that's without consideration of your special status or the political dimension. It seems to me that those aspects count at least as terrorism, and possibly as high treason in your country.

I know that the KNN has generally abolished capital punishment but I was led to believe that high treason was still an exception. And in the Sergeant's own country, xe would definitely face a death penalty for these crimes.

Henry, I really don't want us to fall out over this. I'm afraid I will hold to my opinion. In my view, life imprisonment is even more barbaric. However, I'll keep my opinions to myself and will say nothing to our hosts or do anything to encourage them to punish the Easterners. On the other hand, you must realise that there is nothing we can actually do to help them escape. If the eventual outcome is that the prisoners are extricated and sent for trial either here on Duplos or in the KNN then fine; but do you really think we can accomplish anything from our present predicament?"

"Oh Rastu, I don't want us to fight. I still love you so much. But I know my duty, and that must come first. Civilised values must be protected. What you say about our ability to do anything or influence their fate is true. Also these people have indeed brought that fate upon themselves."

Xe looked up at Rastu with tears in xer eyes, "please are we still friends?" Xe received the assurance of a hug. Xe buried xer head into her bosom as Rastu carried xim to the platform in the trees, where xe curled up next to her and, and feeling her warmth about xim, fell asleep.

At the same time as Rastu was explaining her situation to the apes, her would-be rescuers took off in their nuclear-powered craft from Marouth-Marcenza airport. The flight would take them about twenty-two hora. They would fly with pilots in four hora shifts with Flying Eagle first shift, Jezzie second and Bald Eagle third and then in rotation. The next shift's pilot would be co-pilot for xer predecessor. After each shift the pilot would go to rest, the co-pilot would take over as pilot and the resting pilot would take over as co-pilot. It was a tough schedule and certainly needed the three of them to pilot the shuttle. At least they would be flying high enough to avoid any mountains, and for much of the middle part of the flight, the pilot's job would be to monitor the instruments while the dumb autopilot flew the craft. (The smart autopilot being disabled to comply with the conditions placed on them by the New Norland authorities).

As anticipated, there were no incidents en route and Bald Eagle Sky put down the shuttle safely close to the eastern tip of Duplos' main continent. Flying Eagle and Jezzie then prepared the flying saucer and dispatched it over the sea to the southern continent to conduct its close survey of the target site.

Some hora later the first images were returned along with the analyses carried out by flying saucer's artificial intelligence computer.

The drones had found both the imperial craft and ascertained that they were unoccupied. One of the drones had even entered the main craft through an open doorway and clearly shown it to be uninhabited. Another drone found what looked like the remains of an adult Geosian. They were able to estimate that these remains were around a period old placing them close to the time when the kidnappers had landed.

Later on, the drones were able to locate and photograph the ape-men's camp. One drone came close to being caught by the ape-men, to whom it looked like a strange bird, never before seen. Indeed there was heated discussion between the apes as to the meaning of these strange birds that seemed so intent in exploring their camp. Rastu was also interested. She and Henry were pretty sure of the identity of these birds and made a point of being as visible as possible to them. She took her friend's mother aside and did her best to try to explain that she was very sure that her friends from far away would very soon arrive to find her. She took great pains to explain that these strangers would be her friends and would be no threat to the ape-men although they might be wary of the cheetahs.

She was very worried that, just like the Captain, one of her rescuers might attack a cheetah and thereby set the ape-men against them and undo all her good work. When next a drone bird appeared she made a point of going up to the female cheetah that sometimes shared their sleeping platform and deliberately petting it within sight of the drone. She just hoped the drone was filming and would forward the pictures to her putative rescuers.

There was great excitement when Jezzie came upon the first pictures that showed Rastu alive and well and walking freely among the ape-men. Xe was all for setting off immediately, but Jay advised caution. "We want to know as much about the set-up as we can. We've seen one corpse but we don't know if it was one of the kidnappers or from the earlier imperial landing party. We know there were two kidnappers in the ship with the hostages but we don't know how many Easterners were already here. Judging by the size of their shuttle, it wouldn't have been many but could be anything from two to five. We also want to see if the prince is there and to learn as much as we can about these ape-men; and indeed, the cheetah-like animals that we see in some of the film footage."

Jero endorsed Jay's cautious approach and the whole party bent themselves to the task of examining the latest material. Jo was particularly fascinated. After all, the study of apes is xer speciality. Xe was able to detect a high degree of organisation and it was clear that they communicated through a sophisticated sign language, probably augmented by a limited vocabulary of sounds. Xe made a point of trying to interpret and learn what xe could of the signs and sounds and also to observe the social interactions between the apes.

From this study Jo was able to learn a great deal of what Rastu had already discovered from her observations. Xe was given the task of pulling together all the intelligence from the observations and compiling a report for the expedition leaders.

The result was quite amazing. The ape-men had a primitive early paleolithic technology and lived in a community of family groups with a symbiotic relationship to a small colony of cheetahs, in an approximate ratio of one cheetah per ape family. With a few exceptions, the apes were basically monogamous but adultery was rife with both males and females all too willing to cheat on their partners behind their backs. Males were dominant and larger than the females. Social cohesion and the hierarchy of status was supported by mutual grooming and other rituals. Rastu had clearly been adopted by one of the families and was generally tolerated by the others. She was often in the company of a female ape child of her own size with whom she slept at night. Prince Henry shared the same sleeping quarters and was also free to come and go. One platform was surrounded by a cage and housed two Geosians who were evidently prisoners. Jo advised that they should now be in as good a position as any to approach the apes; but they should do so with caution and show no armament or other indicator of hostility, other than xe will mention later. Xe should take the lead in company with the Duplosian members of the team, especially Arté, who should walk slightly in front of her. The impression she recommended they try to make is of Arté as leader, the two Duplosian women as his consorts and the Geosians as servants, with Jo ximself acting as Arté's personal secretary and mouthpiece. Also Arté should be bare-chested and carry a spear, the exception to the no visible armaments rule.

Xe illustrated xer report with a number of stills taken from the film footage. Of particular note was one showing Rastu with her hand resting between the ears of a reclining cheetah. "This is an important message which Rastu has taken a risk to ensure we understand. The cheetahs are important to these ape-men and under no circumstances are any of us to attack or threaten them. It is clear to me that Rastu believes that were you to do so you would provoke the hostility of the ape-men and endanger the mission fatally." Other images included examples of Rastu grooming her child friend and also adult apes. Rastu curled around Henry as they sleep and the cheetah asleep on the same platform with them. One film clip that xe deliberately excluded had caused xim great mirth. Xe quietly shared it only with Jezzie. This showed Rastu lying down with her pubic area exposed while her girl companion carefully groomed her hair. "This is precious but we must expunge it from the official records. I'll keep a copy on my personal phone to give to Rastu later. It'll then be up to her if she wants to share it with Arté, keep it privately for herself or destroy it. I will of course destroy my copy once I have shared it with her."

"I don't know," responded Jezzie. "Duplosians are not at all puritanical about these things. Even though Rastu is unusually modest for a Duplosian woman, she might well be quite proud of this clip and want to share with her friends just to demonstrate her closeness to this ape girl. You know, don't you, that Duplosian women frequently share their sexual partners with their female friends. Threesomes are very common. If I were her actual sister she would be very hurt if I didn't join her in bed with a man on occasion. She was very proud that Astra was present for Artur's conception and even took her turn with Arté. She tried to hide it, but she was quite shocked when I recoiled at her suggestion that I should enjoy a threesome with Flying Eagle and Wild Cat."

"Responding as an anthropologist, I can adopt a neutral stance; but I too am a creature of our culture and, yes, I do find what you say to be quite appalling. I can see that I have a lot to learn and a lot of attitudes to rethink if I'm going to fit in here. However, let's be clear; much as I love you, I'm not going to invite you to share Jan."

"No indeed, all we have to do is accept that things are different for Duplosians and we shouldn't judge them by our idea of sexual morality."

Two phases after first sending out the flying saucer the party took off for the southern continent.

They landed next to the original imperial craft. The two Eagles remained on board to look after the shuttle; and to provide military back-up should it ever become necessary. The flying saucer was also ordered back on board, but a couple of drones were sent flying high above the seven walkers making their way steadily to the ape-men's clearing.

Fair Exchange

The signal reached the camp that the party of strangers were approaching. The watchers from the trees gave the message that there were seven of them. Three were like Rastu and the other four from the same race as the two prisoners. But they all seemed to be servants of the taller people and were carrying the party's burdens. It was just as Rastu had predicted. The leader was a male somewhat taller than Rastu but still much shorter than any adult ape-man, even the smallest female. At least this leader had some hair on his chest even if it were patchy by their standards.

Their approach to the clearing was unimpeded but the ape-men lined the route to where the largest male stood, flanked by two females, with Rastu standing to one side and a pace behind. Her right arm was held protectively around Henry, drawing xim into her side. Just behind Rastu stood her ape-girl friend with her mother.

"The impression we make now is crucial," whispered Jo to Arté, "remember what we we have rehearsed."

Arte came to a halt two strides in front of the ape leader, bowed and then sat on the ground cross-legged but sitting upright and looking straight at the ape-man. He then made a motion to the rest of his party. Mikhaila and Jo knelt beside him and started to groom his chest. Créezy turned to the Geosians and beckoned one of them forward. Jezzie responded, bringing a box which xe handed over with a low bow. Créezy took the box which was full of ripe fruit, carried it over to the ape and, kneeling before him, laid it in front of him keeping her head bowed.

When the ape took the box and gave her a signal, she rose, took a step backwards, bowed again and then moved beside one of his females and started to groom her side.

After a short interval the female began to stroke Créezy's long hair and the ape sat down, bowed to Arté and stretched out his arms. Arté reciprocated the gesture passing his spear to Jo, who in turn, turned and beckoned Jay over to take it away. The ape also relinquished his spear and his two females came over to kneel by Arté and started stroking his chest, inviting Mikhaila to join Créezy beside the ape where they then both knelt to groom him in their turn.

The ice was broken and the atmosphere in the clearing visibly relaxed as the assembled male apes put down their spears and sat down in groups while females and children dashed around fetching bowls of food to hand round, not forgetting to take some meat that had been stewing in a large cauldron to fill the bowls for the cheetahs that had come to observe the goings on.

The ape leader then beckoned to Rastu and her friend's mother. They were invited to help interpret to enable the dialogue to proceed. Arté summoned Jo for the same purpose. Rastu's ape-girl was left to look after Henry and the two of them joined in the task of distributing food to the assembled adults.

That first session was mainly limited to pleasantries. The preliminaries were completed and the stage set for later more substantive sessions. The subject of Rastu's repatriation was not even mentioned. Progress was slow, not just because of communication problems, but also of the demands of complex protocol beyond the experience of the visitors. All things considered, Jo Jensen did remarkably well in judging the import of the various gestures from the ape-men, and Rastu too gained in confidence and insight into the social niceties of ape-man culture.

One less satisfactory outcome for Rastu was that her friend's mother came to realise that Rastu was fully adult and to treat her with more respect. She also took much more interest in the relationship that had developed between her daughter and Rastu and clearly had what we would describe as 'a quiet word' with her daughter. The consequence was to put some distance between them. The daughter became more inhibited on account of Rastu not being seen as a playmate of her own age but an adult with wide experience of the world. Rastu missed the ease of their former friendship as their relationship grew into one more appropriate to an adult woman and pre-pubescent girl. The girl's grooming of Rastu was now limited to a respectful stroking of her hair, and avoided the more intimate contact of her former ways.

When the 'formal' discussions resumed, the status of the captives was raised. Communicating through signs, hoots and grunts make it impossible to reproduce the precise 'discussions' but what follows is a gist of the meaning inherent in those communications as later described in the report that Arté, Jo and Jero put together for the KNN Government.

Through Jo, Arté was able to explain that Rastu was his favourite woman who had been taken from him by men intent on challenging his leadership. Henry, on the other hand, was not her brother but the grandson of a very powerful leader and had also been captured for political reasons. The Geosians present were servants of that great leader and had been sent to serve Arté in the task of apprehending the criminals and recovering the stolen hostages.

He explained the roles of the members of his party. Créezy and Mikhaila were women of his court as (effectively) 'ladies-in-waiting' on Rastu. Jo Jensen was the great leader's head of protocol and was his mouthpiece for all dealings with outsiders. Jero was the head of his household while Jezzie and Jay were trackers, responsible for determining the whereabouts of the hostages. He, Arté was himself the leader of a great tribe of people and was a close ally of Henry's Grandfather. When they discovered that the kidnap of the two hostages had been perpetrated by the same criminal gang intent on driving a wedge between the leaders' and peoples' friendship, Arté took personal charge of the expedition to pursue the gang.

All this gave the ape-man much food for thought. In his turn he explained that some while ago his camp had been attacked by two unknown ruffians with weapons that spat fire and killed at a distance by magic. Two of their pet cheetahs had been killed and three ape-men had been killed and several injured before the invaders were overwhelmed and captured. One of the dead men was the partner of the female now speaking for the leader and father of the girl that had befriended Rastu. The captives had been duly punished by being cooked alive in the great cauldron and then fed to the cheetahs. However, their meat was not palatable for the cheetahs, many of whom fell sick afterwards. After that, the remains of the stew were taken far into the forest and thrown into the brambles. Just afterwards, a third man was spotted also carrying a fire-spitting stick. He was quickly ambushed from above and even now is locked in a cage overlooking the clearing. He hadn't personally taken part in the earlier attack and had not killed or injured any of the ape-men or their cheetahs so was not deserving of immediate death; anyway, the cheetahs would not want to eat him. As a result, and also because he was too stupid to understand any of their signs or sounds, they were at a loss to know what to do with him.

While they were still debating the issue, a second party of strangers arrived. Two of these were clearly of the same race as the prisoner while the others, the 'spokeswoman' had pointed to Rastu and Henry, were different and appeared to be captives. One of the cheetahs stood before them to bar their way until a warrior could be fetched. "Perhaps if one of us ape-men had stood with a spear beside her, things might have gone differently," she offered as an aside.

The leader of the new party pointed his wand at the cheetah and the magic killed it immediately. Ape-men then dropped from the trees, killed the cheetah-murderer and captured the others. The body of the murderer was left to rot where it lay.

We were puzzled by the status of your friends. When we locked them in the cage their hands were still bound by devices that we could not untie. We noticed that these two moved away to the opposite corner of the cage from the others. We also saw that the new captive appeared to be known to the existing prisoner. They exchanged noises that we now know is how you and your servants communicate with each other.

While the warriors were debating what to do here in the clearing, the women prepared food and the spokeswoman's daughter by the previously murdered man and her cousin took the food to the prisoners. When they returned they and their guard reported their findings and the warriors were convinced of the newcomers' respective guilt and innocence. "We thought Rastu was a child from a race similar to our own and that perhaps Henry was her baby brother. She proved to be very intelligent and was able to show us how to release their bonds. She also made friends with my daughter, which I encouraged, believing her to be a child of similar age and my daughter was able to teach her many of our signs and sounds. She was a remarkably quick learner and has behaved well as a guest in my household and our tribe. She has even lost her initial fear of the cheetahs and has been welcomed by my family pet. Now that I know she is really an adult I have told my daughter that she must treat Rastu with more respect and not take the liberties that are indulged between children."

The discussion of what to do next was scheduled for the next phase, to follow a celebratory banquet and drinking session. The apes made a pretty powerful fruit cider, which the males especially drank in copious quantities. There were several hang-overs in Arté's party when they awoke on the sleeping platform that the apes had constructed for them.

The ape leader's suggestion for the way forward came as a shock to Jo Jensen. Xe had to fight hard to retain xer objectivity as an anthropologist and abjure from xer own cultural reaction. Yet to the ape-men the suggestion was a signal honour to Arté, recognising his high status on a level with the ape leader himself.

The spokeswoman explained that, as we all know, it is good for everyone, but especially those of high status, to publicly renew their partnerships at critical times in their lives. Rastu being Arté's favourite was ideal, and the new-found friendship between their tribes was surely a proper occasion for such a celebration. There should be a joint ceremony where both the ape leader and Arté should renew their principal partnerships. Then after the celebrations, when it came time to depart, it would be right and natural for Rastu and her servant to accompany her master to his home.

Fair Exchange

This outcome appeared to be better than their wildest expectations. However, joy turned to dismay in Jo's mind when Rastu explained to her the nature of the ceremony, having in turn been told the details by her friend's mother, who had to explain that her daughter must not be allowed to attend the ceremony on account of her youth. She could look after Henry while the adults all enjoyed the spectacle. She was at great pains to enlighten Rastu as to the considerable honour being bestowed on them by a joint celebration with the leader himself.

The bottom line was, Rastu explained to Jo and Jezzie, she and Arté would have to have sex in public before the assembled adults from both tribes. Jo's immediate reaction was: "you can't be asked to do that. We must find a way of declining without causing offence and seek an alternative path to our objective."

Rastu was then blunt. "No, Jo what must be must be. I'm up for it and, if necessary, I will exploit Arté's inner slave to order him. We just have to do it, the stakes are too high to piss around. We need to meet up to discuss the practicalities, we three plus the other Duplosians. We don't need to bother Jero or Jay."

When they all got together, Rastu spelled it out. "Arté, you and I each need two female supporters to help prepare us, you take Créezy and Mikhaila and I'll have Jo and Jezzie. Jo, stop looking so coy, we all know you are both female; or is it that you want to have some fun with Arté, I won't mind if you do! I thought not, now pay attention. It will be easier for your Geosian sensibilities to support me. After some initial ceremonial waffle and much boozing by the spectators. You two will lead me to the platform where I have been staying and the ape-woman there, as head of family, will greet us and oversee proceedings. There won't be anyone else present except the cheetah, as she has no partner and children are forbidden to see the rites; although I strongly suspect that my ape-girl friend will find a way of slipping the leash and peeking. Apparently that's by no means unheard of with older children. You two will then prepare me. It's not difficult. You undress me, wash me and give me a nice massage until I'm really hot for it. Do either of you have one of Jezzie's vibrators?" Both the Duplosian women nodded. "Good, lend one to Jezzie for me. We can explain that this is our way, and that will excuse you any intimate contact. When I'm ready the master of ceremonies will be told and when all four of us are appropriately aroused, you will take me down to the clearing to await Arté. The ape leader's partner will be brought down at the same time. After that, you move out of the limelight. You can go away and hide or stay and watch, whatever you wish. I don't mind."

She then turned to the others. "You two will prepare Arté. You take him off to your platform where there will be a couple and a cheetah to greet you. You then prepare him in a similar way. That is, you undress him and groom and massage him. But, there's no getting away from it, you will just have to do the intimate bit - the work but not the fun. One of you must massage his bump, using your hands, while the other other brings him to the first ejaculation, again with hands. I told you you can't have the fun bit. Then when he's ready and I'm in place you bring him out and you, Créezy, must help him couple with me from the rear. Once he's in, you too can step out of the way and join the crowd. Arté and the ape leader then just have to get on with it. For the best protocol, Arté, you should wait for him to disengage and then immediately do the same. Got it all of you?"

Arté was first to say, "I don't like it. My love for you is a special and private thing and not for general public spectacle."

"Man up and get over it. This just has to happen. You wouldn't have argued with Thay and you won't argue with me. You have lots of experience with Créezy and you still love her anyway and I'm sure it will be no hardship to be massaged by Mikhaila. She's very pretty and you'll enjoy seeing her tits. Oh I forgot, you two have to strip off to support Arté properly, which is another reason why it's better that the Geosians support me. They can keep their clothes on, or not, as they choose."

With great reluctance all was agreed. Jero and Jay were spared the gory details and told they had to make themselves scarce during the ceremony. This was excused to the ape-men by claiming that it was not fitting for servants to view their masters at such a ceremony; and the exception for Jo and Jezzie was necessarily force majeur to provide Rastu with the supporters she needed.

In the end, the ceremonies went off without a hitch, except that Rastu's ape-girl did get to peek at the proceedings and was goggle-eyed at the time and in awe of Rastu when they next met. "What's it like, please tell me, and more in the same vein, some of it quite crude and graphic. Their relationship had not completely transformed to that between child and appropriate adult!

Eventually it came time for the visitors to depart for home in the WF. Before leaving they raised the question of the other captives. There was much haggling but secretly the ape leader was pleased to be rid of a problem that would really only otherwise be resolved by the death of the captives. However, there was form to be kept.

The captives were brought before Arté and thrust to their knees before him. First he turned to the earlier captive, addressing him in Norse, with his words translated into the man's own language by Jay. "You are charged with theft of technology from the Government of New Norland of Geos, the illegal entry into Duplos in contravention of the Duplos-Geos accords and the further entry to the southern continent in contravention of the same accords and the laws of the Western Federation, the Great Southern Empire and the Shadowlands Union. These are serious crimes and you will be taken to the WF for initial trial and punishment for the offences on Duplos. After your punishment here you will be extradited to New Norland to face their justice."

"He then turned to the Sergeant. "You are charged with even more serious crimes. Take down your trousers."

"Certainly not, why should I do such a thing."

"It is for you to obey, not me to explain. However the nature or one of your crimes is more or less serious depending on whether you are male or female. Now take them off or Major Mikhaila here with take them off for you and she will be neither gentle nor careful of the fabric."

The Sergeant reluctantly dropped his trousers until his male genitals were exposed to view. Mikhaila made a dramatic gesture of disappointment.

"Male I see. In addition to the relatively less serious crimes against the accords as your colleague has been charged, you are also here-by charged with the forcible abduction of a female citizen of the WF, being yourself male, and of various acts of assault on her person, and also of exposing her to unacceptable risk to her life by transporting her through space in a vessel that was not designed for human transport. This is a serious crime under WF law and carries the death penalty. You are also charged with the abduction of a child, a member of the KNN royal family with political intent, and furthermore exposing xim to risk as with the previous charge. This is also a serious charge, and it is open to the KNN to determine whether your actions also amount to terrorism or high treason. The authorities of the WF and KNN will need to negotiate to determine the most serious charge and thus the priority of your trials. What is certain is that you will be tried either in the WF or the KNN, and the sentence handed down will undoubtedly last for the rest of your life."

"He turned to Jero, "I hand these two over to you for custody." Jero and Jay stepped forward and cuffed them with the handcuffs previously adorning the wrists of Rastu and Henry.

While this was going on, Rastu and Jo provided an edited translation of the charges for the benefit of the ape leader, without mentioning any concept of interplanetary travel. He was well seized of the gravity of the offences and the likelihood of proper punishment of both offenders. He turned to his warriors and, in effect, pronounced. "My warriors, you have seen the gravity of the misdeeds of these two creatures. Should we continue to feed them and give them protection or should we give them to these new friends of ours to take away and punish as they deserve?"

There was a resounding response that amounted to "Good Riddance." And thus it was arranged; and all the humans returned to where the Eagles were waiting for them with the engines ready to depart. The only other codicil was that Jo Jensen had secured an invitation to return in the future with a few friends to live amongst the apes and learn their ways.

29
Life Resumes

Goddess City Ph 3 Pd 25 (23/Autumn) 2615

From rastu@wheels.co.wf.dp to MUM; ASTRA; ZORRO

I'm back! This is my first email from my new account at wheels which Arté has set up for me. I could have used my Camford account but now I'm on Duplos it seems right for me to use a local email address. We landed at Goddess City late yesterphase. Jero and Jay took our former captors to jail to await a preliminary trial hearing and the rest of us had a good rest. Tophase we are going to have some formal debriefing meetings with WF and Geos Embassy officials and then we'll be allowed to fly home to South Beach. I can't wait to see all the improvements you have made, as well as Jezzie's new home.

Before you ask, I'm well, although coming down from what Jo says is an adrenalin high. I've so much to tell you all and, you know, despite the awfulness of the experience, I wouldn't have missed it. In the end I was actually a free guest of some ape-people and I have made some lovely friends with them. That experience has truly enriched my life.

You would have been amused to see Arté in action. He was cast as leader of us all and, basically, King of the WF. Créezy and Mikhaila had to act as his subordinate concubines, but without getting any of the associated fun, and the Geosians were cast as lowly servants. Jo Jensen orchestrated it all and everyone played their part superbly. In the very last scene, my former captor eventually complied with Arté's order for him (as it proved) to publicly demonstrate his sex under threat of Major Mikhaila forcibly removing the man's trousers. Her dramatic show of disappointment at being denied this treat just had to be seen to be believed.

She was given the compensation of being the prisoners' chief guard on the way home. They both spent the journey in terror of her, especially when she waved a knife about in a way that implied she would just love to collect their genitals as a trophy. Sorry if it is wrong of me to gloat; but the Sergeant who captured me deserves anything he gets and I know the KNN judicial system will be far too merciful and let him live.

We had a video call from the King of KNN soon after our arrival here. After talking with xer grandchild, xe thanked me profusely for looking after Henry during our ordeal. Xe is going to appoint me as a Knight Commander of the order of the Royal Household (KCRH) - just ask Jezzie who is awestruck! On formal occasions you will have to call me Zir Aimée which is definitely one-up on Dr Arté - (imagine a smiley here). Anyway, Henry begged xer Grandparent to be allowed to delay xer return to Geos and see some of the sights here on Duplos, it being such a wonderful opportunity for xim. As a result you must prepare for a Royal guest and xer protection officer, i.e. Jay, and then Jero to follow later after xe has finished with the paperwork etc. arising from our adventures.

Créezy is just itching to get back to the Isla survey and plan her triumphant return. I can tell that Arté, too, would like to get back to the project; despite him promising to devote himself to me exclusively for as long as I need to recover; and then for us to have a holiday together to reacquaint ourselves properly.

Well, I'm a great deal stronger and more robust than he gives me credit for. I have grown up a lot in the past year for all sorts of reasons, my partnership with Arté and Astra, life on Geos, motherhood, my kidnapping and life with the ape-men. All these have contributed to the new Rastu and I am quite ready to resume normal life. However, a holiday is a good idea and after a short time in South Beach, I propose to take Arté to Thayview to join Créezy on their Isla project. I really want to inspect the new power station, anyway. While there I'll be able to take Henry (and Jay) on a number of short trips, Soubanc, Montana, Louth and Routh all spring to mind as obvious destinations. I do hope that you, Astra will also have time to join us. After all we do need to catch up on some sex with Arté - I'm getting as bad as Zorro!

Love to you all, I'll be with you so very soon now.

Zir Aimée Rastu BA, MM, LN, KCRH

The Kingdom of Northern Nations

Royal Proclamation

By order of Xer Majesty King Willem, this watch the Twentwy-eighth of Autumn in the year One twousand, six twundred and eleventeen.

We are delighted to inform our people of the safe return of our beloved Grandchild the Prince Henry after xer kidnapping and removal to the planet Duplos by criminal elements from the Eastern Empire, intent on blackmailing our Government and that of our eternal ally, New Norland; and also of overthrowing the legitimate Government of the First Leader of the Eastern Empire.

At the request of the prince, xer return to this planet and country and our family will be delayed while xe takes the opportunity to visit and get to know some of the people of the planet Duplos.

When xe does return to us, our Government has been pleased to decree a special public holiday throughout our Kingdom to allow us all to celebrate together.

We owe much to so many for their support throughout this difficult time for the Prince's family and even more to those who enabled xer survival and rescue.

We especially acknowledge the support from the President of New Norland and the First Leader of the Eastern Empire, in addition to the efforts of their officials. Among individual officials we would mention our Foreign Secretary, the Head of our Security Service and our Ambassador to the Eastern Empire. Of the foreigners, Eastern Empire's Ambassador to our court is worthy of singular mention.

For those who have made their contribution at a personal level we, with the agreement of our Prime Minister, have decided on the following special honours list.

The Order of the Royal Household:

Knight Commander: Aimée Rastu of the Western Federation of Duplos and also a citizen of this kingdom;

Scientific Companion: Dr Jo Jensen of Camford University;

Companion: Unnamed officer of our Security Service;

Lieutenant: Mz Jezzie Peteschild of Camford;

Honorary Appointments for non-citizens of the KNN:

Honorary Companion: Dr Arté, of the Western Federation of Duplos;

Honorary Lieutenant: Mz Crayza Créezy, of the Western Federation of Duplos; Major Mikhaila, of the Shadowlands Union of Duplos; Honorary Captain (NNN) Flying Eagle Forest; Major Bald Eagle Sky both of the Republic of New Norland.

The order of Service Overseas:

Knight Commander: Mz Jero Dicks, KNN Special Ambassador to and Deputy Head of the Geos Mission to Duplos.

On our behalf, Zir Jero will supervise the Prince Henry for a special investiture to be held at a convenient place and time of xer choosing in the Western Federation of Duplos to present the recipients resident on Duplos with their insignia. Zir Jero and the Security Service officer will be invested at a ceremony here when next convenient.

"So we're all getting honoured," said Rastu.

"Yes, but yours is by far the most important," responded Henry. "They had to give Jero a knighthood because anything less would be an insult to xer office, and xer order is just a regular one in the gift of the Government to reward its more distinguished people. Jero would have been bound to get one sometime just for being the first KNN ambassador on Duplos, unless he fucked up that is. The order of the Royal Household is in the personal gift of the King and is specifically for service to the Royal Family. I'm so pleased and excited to be allowed to do my first proper Royal duty. My siblings and cousins will be so jealous. You normally have to be at least twenty-four (that is the right decimal number for twentwy, isn't it?) to do royal duty on you own. And it is exceptional for anyone not in the direct line to be allowed to do an investiture." He rushed over to Rastu and hugged her closely. "I do so love you."

"And I love you, Henry; but do calm down, and I should tell you off for using the 'f' word. I'm sure princes shouldn't use such language."

"Phooey, you should hear my co-parents sometimes. I know we shouldn't swear in public or where journalists might catch us; but you are not public. You are my dearest specialist person in all of both worlds. What we've been through together must bond us for ever. If I'd seen any other girl like I've seen you, I'm sure I'd be made to marry them. As I see it, if you've seen each other as intimately as we have, you are allowed to use swearwords."

Rastu laughed, shook her head and ruffled Henry's hair. "You are incorrigible, as bad as Zorro. I'm sure you'll get on with her when you meet."

Although both Arté and Zorro did a lot to help, Rastu couldn't but feel that most of the burden of all the guests fell on Sturdon. As usual, Astra just took things as they came, seemingly oblivious to the frantic activity around her. But Sturdon showed herself as much at home with Astra in South Beach as in her own home in Montana. She was just so overjoyed at having her daughter back, with the added pleasure of Artur, that she didn't seem to mind any domestic chore. And anyway, the Geosian Embassy had been prepared to give lavish funding for domestic help from the village. The accommodation was also much eased by the use of Jezzie's new house, which was now sufficiently habitable to house Jezzie, Jo and Jero. Henry insisted on being as near to Rastu as allowed and Jay needed to be in reasonable proximity to the Prince. The two of them shared a bedroom in Astra's new extension. Rastu and Arté shared an enormous triple bed in the main room, in which, at Rastu's insistence, Astra joined them most sleep-times. On the rare occasions when Rastu allowed her to leave them as a pair, Astra would move into a spare bed in Sturdon's room. Zorro and Esau occupied Zorro's old room and Créezy had already departed for Thayview with Jan Martskind.

Jan showed Créezy the footage from the Isla drone surveys taken while she had been away on the southern continent. They had also been discussing the adventures. Jan had been kept up to date via emails from Jo, but xe was interested in hearing Créezy's perspective, especially her descriptions of Jo's contribution, as Jo ximself had been modest about xer achievements. "You know that by custom on Geos, Jo will be entitled to name the species, although perhaps really, since she is a KNN citizen, that honour should go to Rastu. It's a moot point. Anyway, Jo had decided on Pongo Gigantus Australis Duplosae as the formal appellation for the apes."

"Pongo sounds rude to me, surely they should be Homo, or Hominida or something like that."

"No it's not rude. As with the great apes on Geos, they will be part of the Hominoidea superfamily; but there would have to be considerable study before they could be reclassified as genus Homo. As of now, only our two species have that classification. Jo thinks that the closest Geosian analogue to your ape-men is the orangutan, which is an endangered species with small populations on Haven and the north cape of New Hope. There used to be some in the south-east of the GPRG but it is believed they are now extinct there. Their established genus is Pongo. As for the rest, Gigantus is a direct reference to their size relative to Duplosian humans, while Australis Duplosae means 'of southern Duplos'. Once Jo has undertaken xer proposed research and published a scientific paper I expect they'll become known informally as Jensen's Apes. However, back to the subject at hand. All the evidence points to industrialisation in the North of Isla. From what you say, this is all after your and Arté's time, which means inexplicably rapid development over just ten years. And in terms of some developments, leaping ahead of the continent."

"Well, you mentioned the canals as a particular sign. I do know that there has been some canalisation in the Lesser delta region for some generations. Primarily this was for flood management, but has also provided transport. I guess the technology was there and certainly would be known to Shay from her estate near Barton. I suppose she might have thought to employ the same technology to river navigation, once she had river-transport business on both the Lesser and Second rivers. Arté told me, that after she was given the Barton estate, she developed the Lesser transport considerably, making herself a fortune and extending the navigation as far as Knot-on-Lesser. She also had a trading post on the main river from the north flowing into the Lesser Estuary, and was developing peaceful relations with some of the wild tribes up there. Otherwise, Isla did know about coal and how to make some steel, but there wasn't really anything much of an industry with either. The canal technology around Dambach and the use of coal for heating or limited steel-making in the north around Kongholm here in the WF, are much greater than anything that used to be done on Isla."

"Well, the scale and organisation we see here are considerable. Canalised parts of the rivers extend navigation throughout the Lesser and Second river catchment areas. Most significantly, navigation is now possible all the way from the Lesser to the Second estuaries. Principally, this is down to a canal linking the two rivers aided by their tributaries. Furthermore, there is a new canal from the Lesser going south towards Midborough. Construction seems to be halted just outside the Midborough boundary where there is quite a concentration of people camped. Even further south, there are other construction signs including a couple of isolated canal stretches that suggest a plan to extend from Midborough to Cattlebridge. Presumably, it is planned to link to the Great River." Jan pointed all this out on a large map xe had drawn, and illustrated xer points with photographs taken from the drone film footage.

"Wow, Thay won't like that! My guess is that work has halted because of a spat between the sisters. Any hint of Shay muscling in on Thay's near monopoly of the Great River traffic will cause one hell of a rumpus. And I bet my Mum will be left trying to keep the peace between them. Poor Mummy, I actually feel sorry for her. Those people in the camp, a lot seem to be men, and some, both men and women, are carrying what seem to be huge spears and are engaged in some sort of military drill. I can't understand them having men in an army, other than in minor supporting roles. Charioteers and members of the phalanx would only be female. Islanders don't train men in war-fighting. They're only there as camp-followers to do various supporting tasks and do a bit of skirmishing on the side to cover retreats or follow through on a rout. Their chief role is to provide a sexual outlet for the soldiers. With the adrenalin rush of a battle, the women are really gasping for it. A losing enemy's men have been known to be raped to death, and even those of the winning side are expected to service several soldiers each. It's a good thing that full-scale battles are extremely rare."

"Ouch, you Duplosian women are brutal. The use of rape as a weapon of war has been outlawed on Geos for centuries. Our primitive northland ancestors did have a reputation for such behaviour; but even then I think it was much more a case of pillage than rape. In a modern conflict, like the one unfortunately going on in Sylvania, there's killing and destruction; but I haven't heard of any allegation of rape of the enemy. And as for one's own colleagues, such a thing would be quite unthinkable."

"Yes, but then you lot are so squeamish about even a hint of sex that I can't understand how there are so many of you. That aside, we do seem to be seeing signs of military preparation in the north. There are also quite large encampments on both sides of the Lesser, which is unusual. Raiding parties are rarely more than twenty or so strong. Fifty is the most I've heard of. Also they wouldn't hang about on the north bank of the river. That's wild land territory. I'm puzzled; but it's got to be down to Shay somehow."

"Leaving that aside, we've also got all those smoking chimneys. Look at these pictures taken from very close in. I'd say this was steel manufacture on quite a grand scale, fuelled by coal. Both coal and the iron ore are being brought down from the north by barges along that northern river, across the narrow end of the estuary and into the canal system through the Lesser delta." Xe pointed out the route and showed pictures of the barges and the huge horses pulling them downriver and within the delta system."

"Using horses like that is new to me. Those are cart-horses, used on farms for heavy ploughing or moving large loads. They use great oxen for similar tasks in the east of the GSE and SU. What can Shay want with all that iron and steel? They only need so many knives and swords. I can't begin to understand it. And what's more, trade with the wild lands in metal goods is forbidden. They don't have, or at least don't exploit, metal technology themselves. Educating wild people in anything remotely connected would be considered a serious crime. On this scale it could even amount to treason. I wince at the thought of what they will do the Shay if she's found guilty of that."

"What will they do?"

"You really don't want to know, given the squeamishness of your culture; but you asked, so. They would hang her upside down by her ankles with her legs about half a stride apart and then split her in two with an axe or, if feeling particularly vindictive, a saw." Jan's hand went to xer mouth as xe ran to retch over the sink. "I told you you didn't want to know." Créezy called after xim. She wasn't proud of herself, but needed some cathartic release as she absorbed the implications of their analysis."

30
Return to Isla & the Thayview Conference

When Arté arrived with the party from South Beach. There was a serious discussion of the situation. Jero was adamant. "We Geosians cannot and must not interfere with what is clearly an internal matter for Isla."

Créezy responded. "I'm not asking you to interfere, but I must get to Isla somehow. If you can't fly me over, can you lend or sell me a microlight? That isn't you interfering. I'd ask for something more robust like a helicopter but I can't pilot it."

"Really I do want to help, but it is at best a moot point whether such help would be in keeping with the accords. I can't allow any Geosian Diplomatic or Government personnel to take any active part, which rules out our accredited pilots and, I regret, Jay. I suppose you could hire a microlight but it would be very dangerous for you and I don't see how you could do much entirely alone."

Jezzie interrupted. "OK, I think we are morally obliged to help. I am not a Government employee, nor do I have any diplomatic status here on Duplos, or anywhere else for that matter. But I do hold a pilot's license on Geos and am accredited to fly on Duplos. Don't look so worried, Flying Eagle. I'm not planning to pinch the nuclear shuttle. WwW could hire a helicopter or one of the older VTOL craft and employ me as pilot. For all Jay's expertise xe's of no use unless xe interferes. I take it, Créezy, that you have a plan once you get there."

"Yes, I have a plan, and it would certainly help if I could bring someone else with me."

"I'll come" said Zorro and Rastu simultaneously.

Arté wanted to object.

"Don't worry, Rastu will be in no danger, I promise. With three of us my plan will work, I'm sure. Zorro must play a slightly riskier part; but Rastu's only role is to give cover to ensure that Jezzie doesn't have to do anything that could be construed as interfering with Duplosian politics. How's your Islish, Zorro?"

"Not good, Rastu's is better. I'll practice hard between now and departure."

Jezzie spoke. "I can help with that a bit. I've got a translation machine here that I've been developing. It's still at the beta stage, but is a phone app that allows you to get a translation in close to real time. With an earphone only you can hear. Or you can broadcast through the phone's speaker. You speak into the phone in one language and the translation comes our through the speaker or earphone. It relies on the best artificial intelligence I know. Apart from various Geosian languages, it knows Contish and Pennish and has a smattering of Islish. Based mainly on your input, Rastu. With help from one of you islanders we can quickly improve its Islish capability by an order of magnitude."

In the end it was agreed that Jezzie could be a chauffeur as long as she didn't get involved in any battle or war, only carried a gun for personal defence and only carried non-lethal ammunition.

"That's sufficient," said Créezy. "I will also be carrying such a weapon. It is probable that I will need to send someone to sleep by way of demonstration. If all goes to plan nobody will be killed. Let's all get on with it."

Fair Exchange

Not long before they were ready to depart, there were more shocking pictures from Isla. Quite clearly a substantial army was gathering just outside Midborough, while inside the town there were signs of defensive activity, almost certainly in preparation for siege. Further south, a second army was marching from Cattlebridge. Were both armies allied, intent on capturing the Island's second town, or were they opposing, ready for a 'Battle of Midborough'? There was no way they could tell but both Créezy and Arté were convinced it was the latter.

"And you really are betting your life on it."

"It won't come to that. I'm just going home to visit Mummy and my cousins. The only fly in the ointment is that I might have to see my sister."

Once the VTOL aircraft arrived and had been checked over by Jezzie, four passengers boarded. Esau the younger was a last dumin addition.

As Jezzie and Flying Eagle both knew, xe could have flown the aircraft remotely from Thayview, but they weren't going to admit that to Jero. Jezzie didn't want to miss out on being the first Geosian to tread on Isla. Xe was also intrigued to learn more of what xe termed 'the crazy plan'.

About two hora after they had left for Isla, Jezzie landed the aircraft in front of Arté's tower and Rastu and Esau emerged bearing a stretcher. They took the stretcher into the tower and deposited its occupant on a bed in an upstairs room. Esau then stood guard, while Rastu returned downstairs. Jezzie and Rastu then collected a car and drove back to Thayview farmhouse to join the others.

"That was quick," exclaimed Astra. "What's happened and where are the others?" She looked worried when she realised that Rastu and Jezzie were alone.

"Sorry we've been so long, we had to wait for our prisoner to turn up. Esau's guarding her in the tower," replied Rastu. "Zorro and Créezy are still on Isla and will be for a while. Jezzie will return for them when they need her. Right now Créezy is on her way to Midborough while Zorro is bound for Rivermouth to collect Cray and then rendezvous at Midborough." All this as if her audience were privy to the crazy plan.

Arté was bemused. "What prisoner, do I know her? Just what is going on? I thought Créezy was going to Rivermouth to see if her mother could do anything to help defuse the situation and not dash off into the middle of the potential battlefield all by herself."

"She's not by herself, one of your daughters is with her. And, yes of course you know the prisoner. She's Thay and you are not allowed to see her without either me or Astra present to keep you under control. And I will brook no argument from you on the subject. She'll be asleep for another couple of hora yet. Esau will advise us when she wakes and we can visit her then. As of now she is under arrest on the charge of conspiring to your attempted murder. It's all part of the crazy plan and you are required to co-operate."

"But I will not consent to Thay being punished for what is past and has turned out so much to my benefit."

"She will not be punished, or at least not in the sense you mean. You must trust Créezy, and me. I have approved her plan which I believe to be masterly. She has the tits to carry it off, and unless you mess it up with your misplaced loyalty to Thay, we will all benefit, including Thay and Shay." Turning to Astra she said. "We must make arrangements for both a trial and a conference here. We need to identify a neutral chairman to preside over the trial. You will be one of the judges but have to be regarded as partisan. Do you think Fermos could be persuaded or should we perhaps ask the Mayor of Islaview, as she is local? The trial itself is really a formality and the real job of the chairman is to ensure that justice is seen to be done. You and the third member will ensure the outcome accords with our requirements."

This was a new confident Rastu speaking. Astra was impressed. Arté was gobsmacked. Much as he wanted to argue he decided it was politic to fall back on his Islish roots to 'know his place' and 'keep her commandments'. Accordingly, he kept his smacked gob shut.

For the next couple of phases they were kept busy furnishing a barn as a temporary courthouse and conference room. Jezzie organised the necessary technical support: video, microphones recorders and all the paraphernalia of modern facilities. Jan and Jo were invited to be observers and facilitators as necessary. Such roles were in no way seen as breaching the prohibitions of the accords regarding interference in local politics.

Following a more private discussion between Rastu and Astra, it was agreed that the Mayor should indeed be appointed to chair the trial tribunal; but that Fermos really was wanted for the conference. Among other things, this was intended to address the relationship between Isla and the WF. Rastu didn't know exactly who to expect from Isla but it would certainly include Shay and Cray. They had learnt that Cray was now president of Isla's Superior Wapentake and currently chair of the Parliament which was the supreme governing body of the Theocracy, consisting of the Superior Wapentake and Arch Convocation acting in concert. Thay and Shay were both members of the Wapentake representing Chalcliff and Strait Hundred, and Oakbridge and District Wapentake respectively. Cray was the member for Rivermouth Central Hundred. Within the Superior Wapentake, Thay and Shay each commanded major factions. Between the three of them they had the power to speak for the entire Wapentake and, with such supporters as they had, would be able to make commitments that would comfortably pass through the parliament. Rastu knew all this as a result of Créezy's dialogue with Thay before the latter's arrest.

Thay woke with a headache. It took her a while to realise what had happened to her. Was she dreaming, or what? The last thing she remembered was coming home from parliamentary business in Rivermouth to be greeted by an excited Thar saying they had some really special visitors. She went in to find herself confronted by her dead cousin Crayza with two strange women, a strange man and a midget. It must have been a dream because Crayza had died at sea nearly twenty years earlier, yet here she was larger than life, certainly looking older than the eighteen years when she died, claiming to be herself and asking questions about her mother, and about the current state of the Theocracy. After that, Crayza drew out some sort of wand and everything went blank. Now here she was with a headache in an unfamiliar room with Crayza's strange male companion by the door, talking to his hand. Perhaps she'd died. That seemed the only explanation.

A few imins later the door opened, the man walked out and let in one of Crayza's female companions, another strange woman and an older-looking ARTHAY. She screamed his name. She must be dead. "Oh my Arthay. Am I really dead? Are we re-united in the house of the Goddess? Is there really a Goddess. I'm so sorry about what I did, about what happened to you."

Arté looked at his former owner and tears welled up in his eyes. "I am or was Arthay, your former slave and lover. But you are not dead, nor am I. All the things we learnt from the priestesses are wrong. We are on the continent, just a few imiles across the strait from your home. You can see it from the top of this tower, I will show you later. Here I am a free man, there are no slaves. I am no longer Arthay but Arté, the people here aren't very good at the th sound. And I am no longer yours, not will I be. These two women here are Astra and Rastu and they are my life partners. I am exclusively theirs for as long as they wish. After I was marooned here, I was helped by the father of the young man who has just left us. He had been a fisherman from the Great River who had been shipwrecked. Thanks to him I received an education here. Rastu was my study partner and best friend. Astra then became my employer. She is a distinguished astronomer. Much later, we three developed our present relationship and Rastu has recently presented me with a son.

There is one more major shock you must face. We are not alone. Geos is another world just like ours, but its people are more advanced. So much so, that they have learnt how to cross from their world to ours. The short person who brought Crayza back to Isla, and then you to the continent is one of the Geosians. I know this is a lot for you to absorb in one go, but we will have time for you to learn and understand more.

We had hoped to approach you much more gently and have been preparing for Crayza's return to Isla for some time. Then just recently we observed changes in the Theocracy that caused us to act so precipitously. I hope Crayza, by the way over here she is called Créezy, arrived in time. We fear a great battle is about to be fought and she hopes to stop it."

"Oh Goddess, this is much too much for me to take in. But Crayza won't stop the battle. The reason I was in Rivermouth was to await news. Early reports were of heavy defeat with much loss of life. I had rushed home to collect Thar and then return to Rivermouth to give my support to Cray and to beg her forgiveness. Oh, where is Thar? She shouldn't be left on her own. There is only an elderly slave in the house. She's your daughter too, all I had left of you." Thay then uncharacteristically burst into tears.

Rastu responded. "Thar is with Créezy, she will keep her safe. Our friend, and Astra's daughter, Zorro, has gone to Rivermouth to find Cray. We expect them back here in a couple of phases or so. A period at the most."

"I should be happy that Crayza has carried off my only child to a battlefield! Shay will capture her for sure and then what?"

"Shay will not capture her and Thar was very happy to go with Créezy once she had been assured that you were not dead, but just sleeping, and that you would be looked after. I was there. Thar will be fine."

"And Crayza by herself will succeed where her sister failed with an army. An army of the finest troops the Theocracy has seen in at least two generations."

"She will succeed. She won't be pleased if she has to see her sister, though. I don't know what it is with you islanders. I have longed for a sister all my life. Yet there you are: You and Shay and

Créezy and Craya bent on destroying each other. I can't understand it. Don't smirk Astra. You are almost as bad with your attitude to your own sister. I tell you this Thay, we might not succeed in reconciling you and Shay but I will not allow you to pass the feud on to your daughters. For their father's sake, I will protect them even if I have to steal them from you and never let either of you see them again."

Thay's mouth dropped open. She couldn't believe what she was hearing. This chit of a girl was threatening her as a headmistress might a naughty schoolgirl. And she, Thay, the leader of half of the Isla Theocracy believed the threats and realised that in Rastu she had met her match. She had indeed lost Arthay to this girl. If this was to be Thar's stepmother the child would at least not be abandoned.

Thay was not allowed out of the tower but did not lack for visitors or occupation. She marvelled at the telescope and the view of Isla and her house. She learnt so many things and began to study the language. Arté visited often and willingly answered questions or talked of the old days or of his new life. She learnt some of Astra's and Rastu's histories including Rastu's recent ordeal and she began to warm to them both and get to grips with her new reality. The negation of her religion didn't bother her. She hadn't believed in the Goddesses deep down, but otherwise the revelations were disturbing. She was proud of Arthay's achievements but couldn't really accept that this was anything but a freak. "Men are inferior that's how it is," her brain kept telling her. "And without male slavery how can society function, wouldn't we all die out if men could choose not to have sex?" It was a puzzle. "Strangely, Shay would be OK about no slavery. One of the causes of the war was Shay's new laws in the north outlawing slave raids in the northern wild lands, freeing all non-criminal female slaves and allowing men to be freed by their owners or even, when it suited the local wapentake, to allow for the compulsory purchase of male slaves who would then be given their freedom in return for some public service. Wasn't that how Shay had attracted so many men for her navigation projects and to swell her armies? On the other hand, while I can manage without sex without too much difficulty, Shay's appetites are legendary. How will she cope when she can't just order a man to indulge her?" All this thinking of ifs and maybes was making her headache come back. She needed to relax and let whatever will be, be.

In the fullness of time, Jezzie got the call to return to Isla where she picked up Créezy and her party. Thay was fetched from the tower and taken to the conference barn. Jezzie landed, dropped four passengers at the tower and then took the remainder to the barn. Jezzie and Zorro entered with three Islander women, namely Cray, Shay and Valray. Thay and Shay tried not to look at each other, but Zorro brought Cray and Valray to be introduced to everyone.

When they came to Arté, Cray shook his hand formally and told him she was pleased to see him again after so many years and that he looked well. Valray was overtaken with emotion. "I never expected to see you again after you left Oakbridge. We don't think about our sons on Isla, but your accomplishments are enough to make any mother proud. Cray's daughter has told me so much about you. How I have been catapulted into meeting with the great and the good, I don't know. Shay has been good to me in the last ten years since she inherited Elmhouse. And it seems that all my good fortune is because of you. I am a woman of my times and culture, and that can't be changed. You know, you are the image of your father, Edgar. He escaped from me, which is as well, as I would have been unable to keep him once back in the Theocracy and by then it would have broken my heart. His partner Wilja has forgiven me for her capture and separation from Edgar. Please can you find it in you also to forgive me."

"You gave me life. What is there for me to forgive. I was happy at Oakbridge where you sent me. I think I recall Wilja. She was a slave in the kitchens and often gave me some extras when the priestesses weren't looking. If I've got the right person, she had a daughter who joined the order and was also very kind to me but never tried it on with me. I can't recall her name, but she was in trouble on my account when I went to join Chay so I never got to say goodbye to her."

"I don't know what her name was then. She changed it later to honour her heritage. She is now Wilda and Abbess of Oakbridge. She is also Edgar's daughter and your half-sister. Her lack of sexual interest in you followed a warning from her mother. While we are all here, Wilda is in charge in Rivermouth as Shay's deputy."

This last was news to Thay who realised that Craya must have lost, not just a battle, but the whole war. Things were serious. She must talk to Cray and find out more of the goings on since she was abducted.

Créezy made her entrance. Shay had seen it before and some of the others had some inkling. But for Thay and Rastu it was new. Rastu knew enough that she kept an eye on Arté's crutch.

Créezy was dressed in her Goddess outfit. It's been described in full already so the details will not be repeated. With her heels, she was taller than the twins and they are taller than any woman that most of those present had seen. Then the ostrich feathers that crowned her brought the total height to over three strides. The richness of the dress filled all the women with envious thoughts while the cut had the anticipated effect on the two men, which Rastu's eye confirmed. Even the Geosian males present, Flying Eagle and Jan, found they were also affected, much to their embarrassment. Fortunately Jo and Wild Cat were amused rather than hurt. The latter had arrived just a couple of hora earlier. She had landed from Geos not long ago and just deposited Snow Hare with Sturdon in Montana where the latter was also looking after Artur.

Flanking Créezy, but half a pace behind, were the near-twin sister-cousins, Thar and Shar. They too were dressed in spectacular long dresses of silver, but of an age-appropriate cut. Bringing up the rear was a man that only the recent arrivals from Isla had met before. He was also tall, actually about half a division shorter than Arté, and with similar features. He was carrying a bow equal in length to his height and on his back was a quiver full of arrows.

The overall effect was indeed of a Goddess, accompanied by her nymph attendants and her champion. The whole room gasped. Thay wanted to rush to her daughter and hug her but she didn't dare move. Neither nymph looked at their mother or their aunt. But had their eyes focused on their father. They had been well drilled and enjoyed their role in this magnificent piece of theatre.

When they came within a short distance of said father, the Goddess halted. The nymphs stepped forward and knelt before him. The Goddess took a step sideways and beckoned the champion. Then she spoke in Islish.

"My dear and beloved friend, son of Valray and Edgar, Arté, Master of Mathematics and Doctor of Philosophy of the University of Routh and Honorary Companion of the Order of the Royal Household of the Kingdom of Northern Nations, Greetings. I have the honour of presenting to you my nieces and attendants, Shar and Thar, your daughters by Shay and Thay; and also my lover and life partner, your brother, Edwin, the son of Wena and Edgar. On behalf of these your family I ask you to acknowledge them and henceforth be their protector and friend as is fitting for your blood relationship. Will you do that?"

Arté was stunned. All he could think of was to say, "I will."

The Goddess then turned to Astra and Rastu and continued, this time in Contish. "My dear friends, Astra and Rastu, as the life partners of the father of these my nieces will you accept them into your home on such occasions as is convenient for them. Will you look after and protect them and support their father in his obligations towards them?"

Taking their cue from Arté's previous response, they each answered, "I will."

While this was going on Jezzie circulated round those present handing out copies of Créezy's words written in all three languages, Islish, Contish and Norse.

The formality over, Créezy removed her headgear and the sword slung by her side and handed them to Edwin. She then scooped up her nieces and said loudly. "Now we've got that over let's all have a drink and nibbles while we await the Mayor for the next formal part of the proceedings." She addressed the girls, "You two can't have any booze, but you'll love the lemonade and ice creams that I've arranged for you. Isla has nothing like them. Now as arranged you'd better go to your mothers."

There was clearly a code here. Each girl first approached her aunt and curtsied to her, telling her that she would not continue the feud and would hope to come to know and love the aunt and would certainly be close friends with her sister-cousin. They then went to their own mothers and hugged them before telling them how much they adored their glamorous Auntie Créezy.

Half a horum later the Mayor arrived. The twins were made to stand next to each other before the tribunal, the Mayor in the centre, Cray on her right and Astra on her left. Zorro then acted as counsel. She invited each of Thay, Shay and Arté to give their account of the events leading up to Arté's fall into the sea. She then asked Thay and Shay to describe briefly how their mutual enmity had brought war to Isla. The tribunal members were then given the opportunity to ask questions of any of them. Next, questions were invited from others in the room. Finally, Shay and Thay were invited to make a statement to enable them to air their current thoughts, acknowledge their errors and to express remorse or regrets.

Arté then asked if he too could make a statement. In this he reminded the court that the final outcome had been entirely beneficial to him. That even at the time, he bore Thay no ill-will, that Shay had tried to save him at personal risk, and that his dearest wish was for the reconciliation of the twin sisters. He wanted no punishment to be inflicted on either of them. They were the mothers of his two fine daughters. And now all he wanted was the privilege of sharing in the upbringing of these lovely girls.

Each of Astra and Cray then gave their comments before the judges retired to consider the case. After a short break in which tea and cakes were served, the tribunal reconvened. The Mayor pronounced their findings that the twins were equally to blame for the mutual antipathy between them. "You allowed your personal feelings against each other to cloud your judgement. Shay, your initial assault on Arté was wrong. Thay, your reaction was both disproportionate and mistargeted. That the outcome was beneficial to Arté was just good fortune. We are pleased that you each now acknowledge that, and have shown remorse. From the point of view of the WF, we hope you will both work to bring about the changes in Island society to meet the conditions that Arté has set for him to set foot there again. That is all there is to say on that matter. We are unanimously agreed that there is nothing to be gained by ordering any form of punishment. In this judgement we have been strongly influenced by Arté's own statement. Before leaving the personal matters, we order that the sister-cousins must be allowed contact with their father here in the WF. We comment that, without prejudice to the proceedings of the conference in which you are all about to engage, the world had changed. Isla is no longer isolated just as Duplos itself is no longer alone. A broader education for all of us is vital to prepare for this brave new world. We strongly recommend to all three of you parents of these girls that a considerable part of their education should be spent outside Isla. The offer by Rastu of places at the Federation Grammar School in Marouth should be given serious consideration. At the very least, it will be important for them both to become fluent in the Contish language and be introduced to the ideas of modern natural philosophy. We turn now to the serious events that have occurred this period on Isla. War is always a tragedy and civil war is the worst. This tribunal orders you both on pain of arrest for treason to work together tirelessly to heal the rift between north and south of the island and to make a peaceful settlement. Cray here assures me that between you three, you have the power to do so.

That's all. I wish you every success in your conference due to start on the morrow-phase. I understand that Professor Fermos will be coming out of retirement to represent this Federation and the conference will address both the peace process on Isla and the future status and relationship between Isla and the Western Federation. This tribunal court is now at an end."

Cray took her daughter aside. "I trust you took on board the comment about sisters. I am so happy that you are alive and I have you back even though you are now living so far away. Please, I don't want to find you only to lose Craya. You were so cruel to her."

"That's not down to me. You will sort it out with Thay and Shay. Shay would not have carried out the execution. I knew that even before I bought her commutation. Shay had already promised Shar that she wouldn't go through with it. Can you say the same for Craya had the battle gone the other way. She had stood in the public square in the centre of Cattlebridge and vowed to split Shay in two with a saw. You must admit it to yourself. She would have ordered the grisly execution. There is no blame to Shay for stringing her up by the ankles and letting her fear her fate. It was for you that my first deed was to buy her commutation. I paid the were-guild for the seventeen of Shay's soldiers who died. I whacked her a couple of times on the fanny, so what! Even after receiving the were-guild, Shay would have been within her rights to march her naked from Midborough to Rivermouth with a whipping in every half-horse village on the way. As it is, Wilda didn't even make her walk. Face it Mummy. Craya is a coward as well as being incompetent. She didn't just lose that battle. It was a massacre. She should have surrendered as soon as she saw Shay's superior tactics and weaponry. Instead, she saved her own skin while condemning her soldiers to die. Even I would have had trouble paying the were-guild for her army. The real danger for Craya will come from the relatives of her own army, not from me. I don't want to inherit from you, but Craya is not worthy of it and will only lose what you have worked for. Find another heiress, or heir. Leave Craya with a regular pension to keep her from starving, but get someone else to administer it. Thay could do it and be a lot more indulgent than Craya deserves."

The conference lasted for three phases. Thay and Shay at least acted as if they would try and tolerate each other. Thay agreed to support the ban on slave-raiding, to end full-life enslavement of women and to bring in an act to recognise free men and to support a nationwide ban on sacrifices to Nepa. Shay in turn accepted that the time was not yet come for total abolition. Thay further conceded that individual Hundreds and Wapentakes could make their own abolition laws. The incorporation of the Isla Marches into the Theocracy was recognised and the status of the Northern Wild Lands revised, with a path to full incorporation to be negotiated, and the ban on trade of metal goods to be lifted. Finally, the three secular leaders agreed that it was time to limit the power of the convocation. For a start there should be no more abbeys or temples admitted to Arch Convocation, while the Superior Wapentake should be expanded by adding constituencies as the Theocracy expanded (or is that 'Former Theocracy').

On relations with the WF, Créezy was confirmed as Isla High Commissioner to the WF and representative to the Geos Embassy. With reluctant acquiescence by Cray, Arté was appointed deputy High Commissioner.

Subject to re-confirmation in five years time, Isla formally agreed to become an autonomous region of the WF and to conduct all Foreign affairs through the WF diplomatic service. In the other direction, all universities in the WF would be required to admit students from Isla and special bursaries would be set up in the WF to fund such students. The WF would also be open for immigration from Isla; but Isla would be entitled to set quotas limiting immigration in the opposite direction. Some other minor but practical agreements were also reached.

Finally, the Isla representatives welcomed Arté's initiative over the cable car and Thay agreed to the construction of the island end. They also welcomed Créezy's plan for a Western sea link and would explore the possibility of electrification and of air links to be provided through WwW, with the help of Geos.

31
Epilogue: Loose ends tied

After the conference Rastu was able to have her long chat with Valray to compare Arté with Artur as babies. Jezzie took Cray and the twins back to Isla, where they had much work to do. The other islanders stayed on for a further two periods to get to know something about the continent and to acquaint themselves properly with their new-found family. After that, Jezzie again borrowed the VTOL and ferried them home, together with Créezy, who also had work to do to help sort out the political and religious upheaval on Isla. However, she made it clear that she and Edwin would settle into her permanent home in the WF.

The girls enjoyed their stay with their father but it was agreed they would return home to spend a year or so at the boarding schools they were due to start. They would have short visits in the holidays and then, at the beginning of the first autumn term following their tenth birthdays, they would enrol in the Federation Grammar School. Valray would also make regular visits to maintain contact with the grandson she now adored. Arté estimated that the work on the Isla side of the cable car would take about two selenths and WwW would hire suitable air vehicles for both manned and unmanned cross-strait operations as required for the works. Jezzie took charge of all the air logistics. The WF parliament endorsed the political agreements made at Thayview. They had little choice, as Astra explained bluntly to a few dinosaurs who thought they could just march in and assert the WF's long-claimed sovereignty over the island and all its people. "Do you really seriously think we could win a war across the strait. The Geosians won't assist with transport or, indeed anything else. And you will never get the support of our own population. Our negotiations are a win-win for both peoples."

Jezzie's house was complete for New Year and Red Robin was planning to open xer nursing home outside Lanamont during the first period of Spring ***1620/***2616. Jezzie arranged that xer mother would move to Duplos at the same time.

2615 had been a hectic year for all of them and as they celebrated New Year they all looked forward to a less stressful 2616.

Jan and Jo set up home together in Marouth where both had generous contracts as full professors. Jo immediately got to work on xer projected study of the ape-people, now officially termed Pongo Gigantus Australis Duplosae. Xe was planning a long field study in the the southern hemisphere for two selenths starting in the last period of their winter, and was recruiting postgraduate students to assist. Jan was planning a geological study of the continent at the same time. "Should that be duplological here?" Xe mused.

On Geos, the politics were also stressful and negotiations were a lot more complex than those engineered by Créezy to end the war of the twins and manage the reconnection of Isla and the continent. It was well into ***1620*** before matters were resolved. However the outcome was far better than anyone would have predicted during the previous year. Indeed, from the point of view of Geosian politics, a great deal of good came from Rastu and Henry's ordeal.

Fair Exchange

Henry returned to a tumultuous welcome from the people of the Kingdom, and a lot of jealousy from xer siblings and cousins of xer good fortune to spend time of Duplos. One sibling really, really wanted to go and live with the apes too. They looked so big and cuddly with all that fur.

The trials of the two Easterners proceeded in the way these things do. The Sergeant was convicted in the KNN and sentenced to life imprisonment. Xe was lucky. The WF would have executed xim, as would the EE who made a rather half-hearted attempt at having xim extradited to face charges connected with the coup. Xe was expected to serve xer whole life. One of the conditions set for xim ever to be paroled was the agreement of the WF authorities.

But it was on the larger international stage that matters improved. The defeat of the attempted coup in the EE enabled the First Leader to push through reforms with little resistance, and also enabled xim to take a much more pragmatic stance in negotiations with NN and the KNN. The Gendalfo summit was extraordinarily productive. The results included a partial acceptance of the accords by the EE, with just some qualifications regarding trade. The EE abandoned all territorial claims on Duplos. An offer by NN for the EE to participate in the satellite constellation was somewhat grudgingly accepted. The EE would not buy space stations from NN; but would supply twelve stations of their own design to fill slots in the existing orbit bringing the total future capacity to thirtwy stations in total. The EE programme to complete their share of the constellation would be spread over a twecade. After much argument, they agreed to design and build to internationally recognised safety standards and be subject to inspection for compliance. The 'international' was a bit of a face-saving formula. Everyone knew that in practice the standards and inspection regime would be set by NN.

The EE would also appoint a Chargé d'Affaires to the Geosian Embassy in Goddess City as a first step to fuller diplomatic participation. Finally, to the relief of the whole international community, both superpowers agreed to end military support to the conflict in Sylvania if the EE succeeded in persuading their East Sylvanian client to end its incursions. As this was very much a proxy war between the superpowers, the outcome was assured and a suitable face-saving formula was found to end the hostilities and return to the status quo ante.

After those momentous achievements, the progress with the new space stations seemed somewhat ordinary. But progress there was. The first two new stations launched in the **work** before New Year; and two more plus the restoration of the one lost in the accident were on schedule for ***1620***. It would now be easier and more comfortable, especially for the larger Duplosians, to travel between planets.

Appendix 1: Personalities and Relationships

In this appendix I give a brief list of the main personalities in the first two books of the Twin Worlds series and their relationships to each other. I would have liked to draw a family tree but it is much too complicated for depiction in only two dimensions.

From Duplos:

Principal/Major Characters

Arté b. 2574 Isla (formerly Arval, Arthay): marooned in the WF 2606, principal character in both books, a mathematician and scientist. Son of Arval and Edgar, variously slave/partner of Thay on Isla, later partner of Astra and Rastu in the WF. Half brother of Wilda and Edwin, father of Shar, Thar and Mikos Artur and, unknowingly, of Thay's goddess-daughter.

Aimée Rastu b. 2588 WF: principal character in both books, Arté's study partner and friend, later partner. Daughter of Sturdon and mother of Mikos Artur.

Astra b. 2562 WF: major character in both books, an astronomer, Arté's employer and then business partner and later his co-partner with Rastu. Mother of Zorro.

Thay b. 2569 Isla: one of Isla's elite, twin sister and rival of Shay, daughter of Chay and owner/lover of Arté, mother of Thar.

Shay b. 2569 Isla: see above, twin sister of Thay, also goddess-daughter of Cray, mother of Shar.

Créezy b. 2578 Isla (formerly Crayza): marooned in the WF 2595, major character in both books, daughter of Cray and sister of

Craya, took Shay's side on Isla, sometime occasional lover of Arté, eventually partner of Edwin.

Zorro b. 2579 WF: daughter of Astra, sometime occasional lover of Arté, eventual partner of Esau II.

Duplos: Lesser characters:

Esau I b. 2543 Isla (formerly Efray, Eshaw): Isla Fisherman shipwrecked and marooned in WF 2566. Beachwarden who rescues both Créezy and later Arté, father of Esau II.

Esau II b. 2580 WF: Son by Esau I of an archaeologist, later partner of Zorro.

Chay b. 2540 d. 2606 Isla: Mother of Thay and Shay, cousin of Cray, leading politician and businesswoman, bought Arté as coming of age present for Thay.

Fermos b. 2542 WF: retired politician and magistrate, distinguished amateur mathematician and Professor at University of Routh. Director of studies for Arté and Rastu. Still influential in WF.

Cray b. 2546 Isla: leading politician on Isla, President of Superior Wapentake from 2612. Mother of Craya and Crayza, first cousin of Chay, goddess to Shay.

Craya b. 2571 Isla: daughter of Cray and sister to Créezy, took Thay's side against Shay.

Valray b. 2548 Isla: Farmer, mother of Arté.

Sturdon b. 2560 WF: mother of Aimée Rastu and her late brother Mikos Urdo.

Mikos Artur b. 2614 KNN, Geos: son of Rastu and Arté.

Thar & **Shar** b. 2607 Isla: respectively Thay and Shay's daughters by Arté.

Gavos b. 2563 WF, Duplos ambassador to Geos.

Petrova b. 2577 SU, Colonel then Major-General and then Dictator of the Shadowlands Union.

Mikhaila b. 2583 SU: Major in the SU army.

Billini b. 2564 GSE: GSE representative in Geos-Duplos negotiations.

Wilda b. 2573 Isla: daughter of Wilja and Edgar and sister to Arté, rose to become Abbess of Oakbridge.

Wilja b. 2554 Isla (wild lands): enslaved to Oakbridge Abbey, mother of Wilda.

Edgar b. 2547 d. 2613 Isla (wild lands): escaped from capture by Valray, father of Wilda, Arté and Edwin.

Edwin b. 2576 Isla (wild lands): son of Edgar and Wena, later partner of Créezy.

Wena b. 2555 d. 2615 Isla (wild lands): sister of Wilja, mother of Edwin.

From Geos:

Principal/Major characters

Wild Cat Waters b. 2576 NN: engineer and one of the two leaders of first contact landing party, child of Roaring Deer Waters and Bunny Rabbit Rock, partner of Flying Eagle Forest and co-parent of Snow Hare.

Flying Eagle Forest b. 2576 NN: engineer and one of the two leaders of first contact landing party, child of Basking Shark Forest and xer partner, partner of Wild Cat Waters and co-parent of Snow Hare.

Jezzie Peteschild b. 2582 KNN: engineer and one of the original landing party. Had a brief affair with Flying Eagle in 2610. Rastu's friend and host on Geos.

Lesser characters.

Jan Martskind b. 2582 KNN: Professor of Geology and former Zoologist, one of the original landing party. Later partner to Jo Jensen.

Jo Jensen b. 2586 KNN: Zoologist/Anthropologist specializing in great apes. Former student of Jan and later xer partner. One of Rastu's tutors at Camford University.

Jacky Jackson b. 2572 KNN: Colonel (later Brigadier) leader of KNN contingent of original landing party.

Wise Owl Cornfield b. 2566 NN: Professor of Astrophysics. One of original landing party.

Bald Eagle Sky b. 2581 NN: Major in NN Air Force, test pilot, one of original landing party.

Stripy Tiger Svensdot b. 2580 NN: Psychologist/Anthropologist, one of original landing party later NN ambassador and head of Geos mission on Duplos.

Mountain Lion Mountain b. 2571 NN: Colonel in NN Military Police, head of security on original landing party.

Dancing Bear Grasslands b. 2574 NN: Doctor on original landing party.

Great Whale Ocean b.2577 NN: Doctor on original landing party.

Red Robin Garden b. 2587 NN: Nurse on original landing party, plans to establish retirement/nursing home on Duplos for elderly Geosians to benefit from lower gravity.

Snow Hare b. 2614 NN: Child of Wild Cat and Flying Eagle conceived on Duplos mission.

Roaring Deer Waters b. 2547 and **Bunny Rabbit Rock** b. 2548 NN: co-parents of Wild Cat Waters.

Basking Shark Forest b. 2546 NN, birthparent of Flying Eagle Forest.

Polar Bear Meadows b. 2538 NN: Founder of Meadowcraft Aerospace inc. that invented and developed the first space shuttles.

Gnawing Beaver Meadows b. 2569 NN: Took over Meadowcraft Aerospace from xer parent.

Jero Dicks b. 2574 KNN: KNN ambassador and deputy head of Geos mission on Duplos. Chaired the negotiations for the Geos-Duplos accords.

Lord Rivers b. 2556 NN: First head of political mission to Duplos.

Jay - b. 2584 KNN: security service protection officer assigned to guard Rastu.

(Prince) Henry b. 2603 KNN: a grandchild of the King.

Anders Stevensen b. 2580 KNN: gynaecologist and obstetrician.

Les Mairdot b. 2585 KNN: mid-wife.

Lez Petersen b. 2560 KNN: KNN Foreign Secretary.

(Zir) Marty Johannsen b. 2559 KNN: Head of the KNN Security Service.

Xer Majesty King Willem b. 2545: King of the Kingdom of Northern Nations.

Appendix 2: Duodecimal numbers

On Earth we count and express our numbers using the decimal place value number system, that is we work base ten. In continental Duplos they use the same system so there is no difficulty there. On Isla, the isolated island culture on Duplos, which is more primitive than the continent, they use a system more akin to Roman Numerals. This is covered in more detail in appendix 6 in the free download of book one's full appendices available from my web-site.

On Geos they have adopted a duodecimal system. This makes a lot of sense in many ways, but can be confusing for us. Rather than introduce twelve completely new symbols, I have decided to use the ten we are familiar with and two additional ones, A and B to denote ten and eleven respectively. In order to limit confusion I shall put a number in ***bold italics*** whenever it is to be interpreted as a duodecimal number. Thus while 10 will mean ten, ***A*** will also mean ten and ***10*** will mean twelve.

Powers of twelve are the numbers consisting of a one followed by a number of zeros. Thus ***100*** is 144, ***1000*** is 1728 etcetera. The number ***1728*** is the duodecimal for 2768. ($1 \times 12^3 + 7 \times 12^2 + 2 \times 12 + 8$). For fractions, the familiar form of numerator/denominator is the same as we are used to, it's just that the numbers have to be interpreted as duodecimals. However when we use the analogous notation to our decimals, we have to remember than now it is not a decimal point but a duodecimal point and the duodigits after the point represent twelfths, one hundred and forty-fourths and so on. Thus ***3/4*** is the same number as 3/4 but if we want to put it in the 'decimal' notation it won't be ***0.75*** but ***0.9. (***9 twelfths is the same as three quarters, ***0.75*** would be 7/12+ 5/144 = 0.618055555..). Just as with decimals, all rational numbers (fractions) in the duodecimal form will either stop after a finite number of places or eventually the last part will be recurring. The fractions that give finite duodecimals will be those which in their lowest terms have only factors of powers of 2 and 3 in the denominator (just as for decimals, the denominator has to only have factors of powers of 2 and 5).

One of the common usages in the books is for dates on Geos. The events that are being described occur around the year ***1600*** in the Geos calendar, which is close to 2600 decimal. In book 1, Duplos doesn't have a calendar for us to number its years. Later and in book 2 the adopt the Geosian datesbut using decimal numbers. The events in book 2 occur in the years ***161A*** - ***20***, or 2614-6.

Finally on language. The numbers one to twelve are as in English. However, after that a different set of number words is required. Instead of the teens, we have the tweens; onetween, twotween, thirtween to ninetween, tentween, leventween. Then we go through the twentwy's to leventwy's until we reach a twundred for ***100*** or 144. Finally a twousand for ***1,000*** $=12^3$ = 1728 and a twillion for ***1,000,000*** = 12^6.

On Earth we use micro, milli, kilo, mega as prefixes to denote powers of 10^{-3} and 10^3. On Geos they have a similar system for powers of 12^{-3} and 12^3. Thus swega, swili, twilo and twega means respectively multiply by 12^{-6}, 12^{-3}, 12^3 and 12^6. Finally we have pertwent and pertwentage for the base twelve version of percent and percentage.

Appendix 3: Weights and Measures

This is extracted from a fuller version available from the free download on my website. The latter includes fuller conversion tables from the three cultures, whereas here I just include brief details of those measures used in the text.

People on Geos and Duplos

Just as on Earth in ancient times our systems of weights and measures owed some reference to measurements on people, the same is true on each of these planets. By way of introduction, I will cover the basic dimensions of Geosians and Duplosians.

On Geos there is no gender dimorphism, apart from the obvious. Both males and females have an average height of 1.53 metres (a tiny bit over 5 ft) and an average mass of 75 kg (165 lb). That is, on Earth, an average Geosian would tip the scales at 75 kg, and a 75 kg Earthling would weigh the same as the average Geosian on Geos (nearly 84 kg weight).

Geosians have a thickset stocky build compared to us on Earth, and female breasts are small. Fashions of both clothing and hairstyle are unisex. So it is impossible to tell male from female when dressed. Variation in height, girth and natural weight[6] are lower than on Earth. Height is approximately normally distributed with standard deviation of just 3.5 cm (1.38"). Thus 68.3% of Geosians are between 1.495 and 1.565 metres tall and 95.44% are between 1.46 and 1.6 metres tall.

On the other hand Duplosians are tall and thin and do show gender dimorphism. Their limbs are also proportionately longer

6 Just as on Earth some Geosians (and indeed Duplosians) are fatter or thinner, lighter or heavier due to lifestyle choices.

than ours. Duplosian men have an average height of 2.2 metres (7' 2.6") and average mass of 72 kg (159 lb). Duplosian women have an average height of 2.3 metres (7' 6.55") and an average mass of 73 kg (161 lb). The standard deviation of height for both men and women is 10 cm (4").

Measures in general

On Geos, as on Earth, the traditional definitions of measurement have been replaced by references to physical constants in a way that preserves the old nomenclature, while ensuring the exact quantities are precisely defined. Geosians also make use of prefixes for powers of 12 as we do for powers of 10. Commonly used prefixes are:

swega = 12^{-6}, swili = 12^{-3}, y7twilo = 12^{3} and twega = 12^{6}.

Duplos is less advanced. On the continent they have exact standards based on standard physical objects. On Isla things are a bit more rough and ready, but there are standard rulers and weights kept in the more important temples. Those in the principal temple at Rivermouth are increasingly seen as the base standard.

Time

The **year** and **period** are common to both planets. The period is the time that Geos and Duplos complete their orbits around each other at exactly 12 Earth days, while the year is 359.999 Earth days, almost exactly 30 periods long. Most other time units are divisions or multiples of the period, influenced by binary, decimal or duodecimal divisors. The only exception is the **selenth**, based on the orbit of Selenos, at 89.614 Earth days. On Geos and continental Duplos, the selenth has been decoupled from the motion of Selenos, and refers to a quarter of the year. (90 days).

Fair Exchange

On the island of Isla, they stick to the lunar calendar but adjust at New Year to maintain reasonable alignment between the seasons of the year and selenths.

Main time units are as follows:

In all three cultures the base is the period with 30 periods in a year. The selenth is also used for the quarterly seasons.

Geos:

The smallest unit is the tick which equates to 2.778 seconds.

72 ticks = 1 tock, 72 tocks = 1 meal, 12 meals = 1 watch, 6 watches = 1 period, 5 periods = 1 work.

Longer timescales are 1 life = 72 years and 1 mem = 144 years.

The terms meal and work derive from a meal being a historic 'standard' interval between mealtimes and a work being the usual time period for payment of salaries, although casual labourers are often paid per period. A watch is also the length of the Geosian day. Because of possible confusion I put the words **meal, watch and work** in bold typeface when used as a time unit. Inconveniently for us there is no obvious equivalent to an Earth hour which is 18 tocks or a quarter of a meal.

Duplos continent:

The smallest unit is the dusec which equates to 2.025 seconds. 40 dusecs = 1 dumin, 40 dumins = 1 horum, 80 hora = 1 phase, 4 phases = 1 period. As on Earth they use a century for a hundred years. A phase is also their day and a horum is exactly 54 minutes.

Isla:

The smallest unit is the isec which equates to 0.989 seconds. The phase and period are the same as on the continent.

64 isecs = 1 imin, 64 imins = 1 ihor, 64 ihors = 1 phase.

Thus an ihor is 1.125 hours or 1.25 hora.

Length and Distance

The base unit of length and distance in all three cultures was set by reference to people, in the way that such units as foot, yard and mile were established on Earth. On Geos the base standard is the 'man' which was defined by the average height of a Geosian. 1 **man** = 1.53 metres = 5' 0.236". All the other length and distance units derive from this via multiples of 12.

On Duplos the base unit is the 'stride', like the Earth yard. The value of a stride on the continent is slightly longer than on Isla. Where I need to distinguish I shall write the Isla version as 'istride'. A **stride** is 1.25 metres = 4' 1.21", an **istride** is 4' = 1.2192 metres. All other length and distance units are derived from these by simple multiples or factors. On the continent these tend to be mixed binary and decimal. On Isla, binary is the norm.

Geos:

The important units from the narrative are the man and twiloman which is 12^3 men equating to Earth's 2.644 km or 1.643 miles.

Duplos Continent:

The units mentioned in the narrative are the division, length, stride and walk.

10 divisions = 1 length, 4 lengths = 1 stride, 2000 strides = 1 walk. In Earth terms the walk is exactly 2.5 km (1.554 miles). It is also the distance covered at average Duplosian walking speed in a quarter of a horum.

Fair Exchange

Isla:

The units mentioned in the narrative are the smidge, thumb, foot, istride and imile. The foot (isla length) is exactly the same as Earth's.

8 smidges = 1 thumb, 8 thumbs = 1 foot, 4 feet = 1 istride, 1024 istrides = 1 imile. Thus an imile is about 1.248 km (0.776 miles).

Speed:

Geos: speed is measured in twilomen per meal (tpm) or races per tock (rpt). In most towns the speed limit is ***60*** tpm which works out as 118.31 miles in 4 hours or 29.58 mph. Converting from tpm to rpt is simple, just divide by six - very easy in base twelve. As seen in chapter 10 of book 1, twilomen per tick (tpt) is also used for some astronomical velocities).

Continental Duplos uses 'walk' as a measure of speed as well as distance. Walk's actual derivation was from the typical distance covered in a quarter of a horum. As a speed, walk means four walks per horum (= 11.11 kph = 6.94 mph). Similarly Duplosians use the terms Jog and Run for eight and sixteen walks per horum respectively.

Isla doesn't have any specific terms for speed.

Volume

All these societies have adopted some volumetric measures from historic liquid measures otherwise they will use cubic, as we do, in the same way as square for areas. Volumes are not referred to much in the narrative. Mention is made of cup, scoop and doop. In Earth metric units, 1 cup (Geos) = 172.72 mls; 1 scoop

(Duplos) = 238 mls; 1 doop (Duplos) = 4 scoops = 954 mls or 1.678 imperial pints).

Mass & Weight

These two quantities are linked on Geos just as on Earth. Of course on Geos their local g defines the relationship. Surface gravity on Geos is 1.119 times that on Earth or 10.98 m/s^2. This translates as 55.38 $men/tick^2$ which in the Geosian duodecimal system is ***47.47*** *$men/tick^2$*.

As with linear measurement the measurement of weight and thence mass is based on a 'standard' person at 75 kg. Confusingly, Geosians use the same term 'man' as for linear measurement, relying on context to distinguish. For smaller and larger quantities other terms are used for some duodecimal multiples/factors of the base man. The text also mentions 'weight' and 'rock'. 12 weights = 1 rock, 12 rocks = 1 man.

For astronomers, **1** Geos = 1.4588 Earths, 1 Earth = 0.685 Geos.

Continental Duplosians have not yet worked out the physics of weight and mass, their science is pre-Newtonian. However they do have the concept of weight under Duplosian gravity[7]. On the continent their standard weight is that of a doop of water (1 dupound - dp), which under Earth gravity would be 976.5625 grams or 2.152 lb. (On Duplos this weighs 1.82 lb or 0.825 kg). The average mass of Duplosians is 73 kg (Female) and 72 kg (Male) which under Duplosian gravity weighs 61.65 kg and 60.8 kg. However because the gravity factors cancel out these averages in Duplosian units are 74.752 dp and 73.728 dp respectively.

---

7 *Surface gravity on Duplos is 8.28 m/s^{-2} or 0.8445g.*

There are colloquial terms for other weights but nothing that is universally recognised.

On Isla weight is based on an arbitrary (religious based) standard object - a near spherical ball of iron, of mass 1.823 kg. Thus the average Duplosian woman weighs 40.04 balls. For more domestic convenience, island Duplosians use the quarter, which as the name suggests is a quarter of a ball.

Angular Measurements

The value of π is universal and the natural radian measure of angle is used in Geosian scientific work just as on Earth. A common approximation to π on Geos is the duodecimal value π = ***3.1848***. Geos has adopted the same degree as Earth (360 = ***260*** degrees in a circle). However further subdivisions are by 72. Thus 72 gemin = 1°, 72 gesec = 1 gemin.

Educated Duplosians are aware of π as the ratio between the circumference of a circle and its diameter and of the area to the square of the radius. They have not developed the concept to include radian measurement of angles. The continentals divide the circle into 60 equal angles, Thus 1 dudeg = 6°. There is no other universally accepted term for angular measurement other than a right angle which is 15 dudeg. Those wanting more precise measurements use various subdivisions, usually by powers of 2 or powers of 10 or a mixture of the two.

On Isla all divisions are by powers of 2. In the temples they divide a right-angle into 64 idegs. Circular measure is based on practicalities. Those that need to know about such things know that the ratio of the area of a circle to the square of its radius is greater than 3+1/8 but less than 3+3/16. Working with fractions is limited to dividing by 2 (or its powers) and they lack the mathematical notation to deal with fractions.

Temperature

Temperature on Geos is measured on a scale of ***100*** (144) divisions (div) between the freezing point (***0***) and boiling point (***100***) of water at sea level on Geos. The Earth Kelvin is 1.44 div Geosian. Geosian science is aware of Absolute Zero.

There are no standardised methods of measuring temperature on Duplos.

Currency

New Norland, the dominant country on Geos, has a three unit duodecimal currency system, for convenience I shall denote them by penny, shilling and pound[8]. As there is no trade between Geos and Earth conversion to Earth currency is pretty meaningless but in terms of wages the pounds are close to 'parity'.

Duplos is even more difficult to compare. Isla's money is issued by the temples, and much of its use is for religious purposes. Much of the economy is based on barter or exchange of obligations. Some money does also circulate, however, and some people are paid wages.

On the continent the various territories have their own currencies. I shall only give details of that of the Western Federation.

Geos: New Norland/KNN £1 (pound) = 12 s (shillings) = 144 d (pence).

---

8 The KNN also uses £sd. The exchange rate fluctuates. On the **watch** of the first contact the official rate was **£1** (NN) = **£1.16** (KNN), or **£1** (KNN) = **As 8d** (NN).

Fair Exchange

In New Norland the minimum adult (24+) wage is £3,456 per work (£691 2s 5d per period), (£20,736 pa). Average adult wage is £30,096 pa. Typical salaries for school leavers and new graduates are between £13,824 and £19,008 pa and £24,096 and £31,104 pa respectively. Wild Cat and Flying Eagle started on £41,472 pa. But then they did have top qualifications from the leading technical university in the world in a very much sought after subject. My guess is that they were on six figure salaries before too long.

Duplos: In the Western Federation all money is coin. The main unit of currency is the dollar, the smallest is the farthing. 4 farthings = 1 cent, 4 cents = 1 groat, 10 cents = 1 dime, 25 cents = 1 crown, 2 crowns = 1 doubloon, 2 doubloons = 1 dollar ($1).

Farthings, cents and groats are bronze, dimes, half-crowns, crowns and doubloons are silver. Dollars are silver or gold. $5 and $10 are gold.

There is no minimum wage. Pror to first contact, labourers received between a groat and a dime per horum. An educated woman might expect to earn around $2,000 per annum from her own work on which she will live quite comfortably. At first, Astra paid Arté $500 per selenth of which 50% was deducted for his keep.

On Isla the main unit of currency is the Mark and the smallest the denar, but much of the economy functions without actual money. 4 denari = 1 groat, 8 groats = 1 quarter (mark), 4 quarters = 1 mark. Where wages are paid, a male labourer might get up to 1 groat per ihor. An educated woman in a clerical or professional role might expect a salary of 20 marks per period. Of the coins, anything less than a quarter is bronze, quarters, half marks, mark, and 2 mark coins are silver. There are gold 5, 10, and 20 mark coins.

Acknowledgements

My thanks to Philip Bannister for the cover design, to Philip Bannister, John Ramsbotham, Joyce Ramsbotham and Helen Walton for reading the manuscript and offering constructive criticism and to my wife Mary for putting up with me throughout the writing of this book.

R. A.
Worcestershire, UK
Earth

Author's Note

Thank-you for reading my book. I hope you enjoyed it. If so, please leave a review on Amazon. It doesn't have to be long but is really important for independent author's such as myself. This is because it is through the review system that Amazon positions books in its search listing. Please also visit my web site where I shall give news of sequels and occasional blogs by some of the characters. I also welcome any feedback or other comments via email to author@richardarthur.uk.

Also by Richard Arthur

Twin Worlds - First Contact

About The Author

Richard Arthur was born in India just before he and his soldier parents were ejected following independence in 1947. His earliest years were spent as a camp follower of the British Army, until his father retired to spend more time with his family. After Prep School in Buckinghamshire and Grammar School in South London, Richard spent six years studying mathematics at university, emerging with a PhD. Richard then spent three years as a lecturer before joining GCHQ. Since retiring from the day job he has maintained some academic links and consulted in Information Security. He still enjoys mathematical problems, but spends most of his time helping his local pub to survive and growing fruit trees in rural Worcestershire. The Twin Worlds books are his first foray into writing science fiction. Richard is married and has a daughter and grand-daughter.

www.richardarthur.uk

Email: author@richardarthur.uk

Printed in Great Britain
by Amazon

73947268R00181